THE SINGER
Song of Life – Book 3

Tony Chandler

THE SINGER
Song of Life – Book 3

DOUBLE DRAGON

*For Bill and Katine Naile
and their daughters, Victoria, Isabella, and
Alexandra*

Prologue

"A great danger has come on the wind."

The largest and most distinguished-looking Barn Owl paused a moment to allow his words to sink in. Silence filled the air while he looked slowly around the gathering of birds. The silence grew more intense as every bird fixed their gaze on the Speaker.

"Many birds have reported death and sickness recently. Even animals and people are affected. This unseen danger threatens us all!"

"This poison is from man!" a single bird shouted from the crowd.

"Yes," another shouted. "It is man that kills us!"

"What can birds do?" a Robin shouted back from the ground.

"That's right -- what can we do?"

"We can find its source. Once we locate it, perhaps we can determine the next step," the Barn Owl said with confidence.

"Man must fix this problem!" the same Robin shouted again.

"Perhaps we can get some animals to assist us. After all, it is killing them too. Once we locate the source, we can analyze the situation and determine our options." The Barn Owl raised his white face and looked around at the gathering.

"Man must fix this problem that they created!" a Wren twittered angrily.

"Then we must help man to fix it. Somehow, we must try," the wise Owl replied.

Bluesky listened in respectful silence. As he pondered the Barn Owl's words along with the cries of those gathered in audience, he thought of KC. He remembered how KC had told him her dad's daughter had gotten sick with the poison the last time they'd experienced *Death on the wind*.

He remembered how KC had said that '*Dad would know what to do*', would know how to protect them -- and he was a man!

Bluesky wondered how KC communicated with her dad and the other humans in the house. KC was his friend, and if somehow he and the cat could get the man to help them ...

"Who shall go for us? I propose we pick a special flock to seek out the source of this poison, birds of many feathers who shall combine their unique skills and go forth to save us. But first, there must be a leader, a bird of great insight and courage who will lead this flock on this most dangerous mission." The Barn Owl narrowed his eyes and gazed at the crowds with a stern expression.

"Who shall lead this special mixed flock of birds and find the source of this poison?" The Barn Owl and every Owl on the limb looked slowly around at the great gathering, but as their eyes passed over the thousands of birds gathered, not a single bird raised a wing to volunteer.

The thick silence of the thousands gathered filled the air with a heaviness, a palpable tension, as if a terrible storm were about to burst forth. The eternal seconds dragged on, and the very air seemed to vibrate with uneasiness and indecision. In the minds of all present, it seemed the problem had grown insurmountable -- impossible. The fear of everyone present seemed to come alive with a sudden blast of wind. While the trees swayed and the leaves danced, many birds cried out as if the terrible and unseen poison were attacking them that very moment.

The same thought occurred to everyone at once -- was death on this wind too?

Now their fear turned to an urgent need to flee!

The sound of hundreds of birds fluttering their wings as they prepared to flee added to climax of fear.

"I will go!"

Everyone froze. The bold words of the volunteer had somehow evaporated the climate of fear in a single instant.

Surprised murmurs filled the air, and everyone looked around for the brave bird who had spoken.

"Who said that?" the Barn Owl cried out as the strong breeze continued to ruffle the feathers across his head.

Nightwind turned and looked directly at Bluesky perched with the Mourning Doves on the other side of the ancient oak. The other Owls followed his gaze.

"Here I am! Send me! I'll go for all the birds!" Bluesky cried out courageously.

"Fly over here, my good Mockingbird," the Barn Owl said in a calm and deep voice.

Bluesky flew over and sat next to the large Owl.

"What is your name?"

"Bluesky."

"My name is Moonlight," the Barn Owl replied.

"You are a brave bird to answer our dire call for help."

"I-I will do what I can," Bluesky said with a bow.

***

The cheering and chirping now rose to a new crescendo, and at that moment Moonlight leaned over and whispered in Nightwind's feathered ear, "This is the most bizarre mixed flock of birds I've ever heard of, Nightwind."

"It is true. Who would have ever dreamed it possible?"

"And yet, the skills and talents of each of these different species may be needed to face this terrible poison at its evil source," Moonlight acknowledged.

"I am sure of it." Nightwind nodded somberly.

"But as surprising as it is that a Hawk and a Sparrow, a Hummingbird and a Crow -- as unthinkable as all these wildly different birds joined together, it surprises me most that a cat and a man may also join!"

"Not really, if you knew Bluesky." Nightwind chuckled.

"Really?"

"Yes, but all the other birds are most surprised over the one thing that should not matter at all," Nightwind said.

"What is that?" Moonlight asked.

"The fact that ... *a one-legged Mockingbird will lead them all.*"

10

Chapter One

Bluesky sang with a golden voice while the first rays of the sun streamed through the trees.

He felt so happy inside! In fact, he was filled with such pure, unbridled gladness that it even made him feel a little giddy, like he had eaten one too many overripe berries. And yet he wasn't quite sure why he felt so wonderful. All he knew was that his heart was filled with joy and he just had to sing out for the entire world to hear.

The sky grew brighter as the golden orb of the sun rose steadily higher. The sky gradually, almost imperceptibly, transformed to a deeper shade of blue. In the distance, a line of large, mountain-like clouds became visible in the west. The eastern flanks of these sky mountains glowed pure white from the light of the morning sun, but underneath they were swollen and purple-black with the promise of heavy rain later that day.

The sky finished its transformation into its normal blue, but the distant storm clouds grew more ominous. The air quickly grew laden with humidity, soon becoming sticky with a pervasive wetness that blanketed every creature it touched. The air itself grew heavy, pressing against each living thing like an invisible vise from the pressure of the impending storm growing ever closer. A brisk morning breeze caressed the leaves and sent them wildly dancing as the world fully awakened.

Every creature knew these signs; this would be a

day of thunder and lightning, a day of storm and high winds fueled by the blazing heat of the summer sun.

As the sun rose above the tree tops, Bluesky flew up and perched on the highest branch in the tallest tree and then sang even louder. After an especially long and melodic trill, he looked down and noticed KC watching from the ground far below. He flew down to talk with his friend.

"Guess what? I'm part of a team that is going on an expedition! And a lot of my bird friends have joined me!"

"That sounds like fun," KC purred.

Bluesky's expression turned serious. "Well, actually it won't be that much fun."

"Oh, why not?"

"Our mission is to locate the source of the poison that is killing so many birds and animals."

KC stopped purring. Her green eyes narrowed as she leaned closer to Bluesky. "And it makes humans sick too. It might even kill them. You're right -- this could be very dangerous." KC paused a moment, obviously thinking things over. "Yes, very dangerous indeed! Why were you picked?"

"Well, I ... uh ... I volunteered."

"That was very brave thing to do," KC said with awe. "I am proud of you."

"Thank you... and, um, I have a favor to ask of you too ..."

"Oh really? Go right ahead."

"Um, didn't you say your dad would help you -- if you needed help? And protect you?"

KC purred a moment in contented thought

before she spoke. "Of course he would -- he's my dad."

"And didn't you say Katie got sick from the poison?"

"Yes, it made me very sad. It made everyone sad in our house. Buddy and I stayed near Mom and Dad all day to provide them comfort."

"Do you think you could get your dad to help us if we found the poison?"

KC froze in shock.

She raised her paw and carefully licked it for several, long seconds as she considered the matter. The silence continued for so long Bluesky began to wonder if she had heard him.

"I don't know. I mean, I'm not sure. What do you have in mind?" KC asked.

"Our mission is to find the source of the poison. That is the first step. We hope after we find it, a solution will present itself." Bluesky wagged his long tail as he gazed hopefully at KC.

"That is a good plan. Hmmmm." KC continued licking her paw, deep in thought.

Bluesky waited nervously, wagging his tail faster with his growing excitement.

Finally, KC spoke. "If the poison is not too far away, I think I could lead my dad to it. He will follow me, and when I show him the poison, I'm sure he'll know what to do."

"That's great!" Bluesky shouted.

"But what if it is far away?" KC asked.

"I'm not sure. We'll have to fly over that tree when we get to it." Bluesky shook his head slowly. "But you will help us no matter what, right?"

"You tell the other birds this exact message, okay?" KC purred louder. "Tell them, 'KC the kitty cat will help the birds!'"

"That's wonderful!"

"Do you want me to go on the expedition with you today?" KC asked.

"No, we're going to fly far and fast and try to cover a lot of territory, but when we find it, I'll take you to see it. Then we can decide how to get your dad to follow you to it."

"Sounds pretty easy," KC purred.

"We can only hope."

Bluesky felt even better. KC had agreed to help, and it seemed she could get the man she called her dad to follow her to the poison. Bluesky felt deep inside that KC was right -- if her dad saw the poison, he would fix it and everyone would be safe.

Bluesky flew off to find one bird in particular -- Dancingleaves.

He soon spotted a familiar flash of bright blue feathers against the green leaves. Bluesky was happy he had found his friend so easily, but Dancingleaves sat on the branch looking lonely and sad.

"Hi, Dancingleaves." Bluesky settled on the branch next to the Bluebird. "I kept looking for you at the Council of Birds. Were you there?"

"Yes." Dancingleaves averted his eyes.

"I was hoping you'd join us yesterday."

A pained expression filled Dancingleaves' face. He stared at the ground far below for a long moment. The Bluebird shook his head and spoke in a trembling voice. "I'm ... I'm too scared."

Bluesky put his wing around the shoulder of his friend. "I'm scared too. See, we're both scared."

"But you volunteered -- and I thought you were very brave for doing so." Dancingleaves looked straight into Bluesky's eyes. He smiled a brief moment before quickly turning away.

"Believe me, I was scared when I did it, but I kept thinking -- I want to help. I want to do something." Bluesky shrugged. "I thought about my sister, Songjoy, and her eggs that will hatch soon. And Treeflower has eggs. So, although I felt scared, I also felt determined to help them and their babies. I don't want any more birds to die!"

"You were scared?" Dancingleaves asked in disbelief.

"Yes, but I focused on my desire to help, and somehow, I wasn't quite so scared anymore."

"You're a brave bird, Bluesky." Dancingleaves smiled with a sparkle in his eyes.

"And today, we fly our first mission." Bluesky smiled hopefully at the Bluebird.

"But how will you find the poison?"

"We're going to search off toward the eastern fields and woods first. After that, well, we'll just have to wing it." Bluesky chuckled at his play on words.

Dancingleaves nodded absentmindedly, oblivious to Bluesky's pun.

"I'd like you to join us. KC said she'd help too." Bluesky squeezed Dancingleaves' shoulder reassuringly. We need another good bird, like you."

"I'm too nervous around birds I don't know. I'm too shy, and... I'd just get in the way."

"You flew with Tootight and Coolbreeze when we all went up inside the clouds! You weren't scared then," Bluesky said in a warm, encouraging tone.

"But there are lots of birds on your team. There's a huge Hawk, and a Crow, too! I-I just couldn't do it. I would be so scared the whole time. I wouldn't even know what to do ..."

"I'm not going to pressure you, but if you decide you'd like to join us, you can." Bluesky patted Dancingleaves on his back. "I would value your help."

Dancingleaves stared in puzzlement at Bluesky a moment. Then he smiled. "I'll think about it."

"Good! I'll come back and tell you what we find ... if you want." Bluesky looked at him with hope.

"Y-yes. Let me know what you find."

"I'll see you tomorrow then."

"And Bluesky ..." Dancingleaves' eyes grew wide as if some terrible thought suddenly frightened him.

"Yes." Bluesky replied.

"Please be careful.

Chapter Two

Bluesky flew off toward the tree at which they'd all agreed to meet. Deep inside, he felt bad for his friend, but in his heart he knew Dancingleaves could help. In fact, somehow he knew the team would not be complete without the shy Bluebird.

"Why don't you just fly away, you weird little bird!"

Bluesky felt his heart thump in panic on hearing the all too familiar words.

He recognized a Mockingbird's voice shouting in a demeaning tone. The happiness and joy that had filled his heart evaporated, and a haunting sadness enveloped him. Bluesky sighed as he looked around to see who was taunting him this time.

He didn't really want to face them, but he felt he must. After all, he was trying to help them too. Didn't they understand that? He was risking his life in trying to find the source of the poison. Didn't he deserve some measure of kindness even from the Mockingbirds now?

He gazed about a moment.

He finally noticed four Mockingbirds in a nearby tree and flew over. As he got closer, he realized they had no idea he was there, so they hadn't been shouting taunts at him. He also realized that all four were young females, but one of them was very small.

Actually, she was tiny, and the other three were taunting her.

17

Bluesky landed above them and decided to observe in silence a moment in order to discern this situation.

The petite female hung her head sadly as the other three continued to throw insults at her.

"You're not even big enough to be a sparrow!"

"She's too thin! She's all feathers and bone!"

"We don't want to play with you anymore. None of the other Mockingbirds like you either!"

The diminutive Mockingbird remained silent, not even raising her head. A moment later, she began to cry.

Bluesky had heard enough. He flew down and landed right beside the little Mockingbird.

"You three leave her alone -- don't you see you've hurt her feelings!" Bluesky said in a firm tone.

The three Mockingbirds gasped in surprise.

"Who are you?" the small Mockingbird asked as if in a daze. "I-I don't know you ..."

"He's that one-legged Mockingbird!" one of them suddenly shouted.

"Yeah, I guess it takes one weird bird to like another weird one! Ha!"

"Right! No self-respecting Mockingbird would be seen with him either. He's a loner -- he's weird, too!" shouted the third.

"They make quite a pair, a midget and a one-legged Mockingbird."

Bluesky flew right up in their faces and flapped his wings at them to make them leave. All three leapt into the air in shocked surprise.

The three flew off as Bluesky gave chase.

He turned around after he was sure they wouldn't return. He returned to the little Mockingbird to see if she was all right before he continued to the meeting.

"Are you okay?" Bluesky asked after he landed on the branch beside her. "I can take you to your parents if you like."

"I'm one season old already. I don't need you to take me to my parents like I'm a new hatchling!" she replied with a defensive tone.

Bluesky gulped. He hadn't meant to offend her.

Bluesky looked at her closely and quickly realized that although she was the size of a Mockingbird who had just left the nest, her eyes and her manner revealed she was his age at least. She was just very petite, and that made her seem younger at a glance.

"I'm sorry. I didn't mean to insult you. I only wanted to help. I'll just go then ..."

Bluesky turned to fly.

"No, wait!" she shouted.

Bluesky was so surprised he almost fell off the branch. He flapped his wings vigorously in order to regain his balance again. He started laughing at himself as he settled down, knowing how close he'd come to falling flat on his beak.

As he continued chuckling, the young female giggled right along with him.

"I guess I looked pretty silly, eh? Right in the middle of launching into the air and stopping all at once -- flapping my wings as fast as a Hummingbird!" Bluesky laughed harder.

"Yes," she said, with a twinkling in her eyes. "It

was hilarious!"

Their laughter gradually faded.

She looked down at his leg.

Bluesky steeled his heart, expecting rejection.

She looked up at him and peered deep into his eyes a moment before she spoke. "You're the Mockingbird who volunteered to find the poison, aren't you!"

"Um, yes," Bluesky said tentatively.

"I think you're very brave, and, well..." She looked away as if embarrassed but then quickly looked back at him. "I want to thank you for helping me just now. I don't know what to do any more. Those birds are always making fun of me, and nothing I do seems to stop them. So, I was just trying to ignore them, hoping they'd go away, but I started crying. And then, you arrived ..."

"Um, yes ..." Bluesky's thoughts became jumbled in confusion as he realized how pretty she was. And her eyes, they were so beautiful.

"Yes ... I did ... er, sort of ... um ..." Bluesky stopped speaking. He couldn't remember what they were talking about. All he could think about was how pretty this tiny bird was.

She giggled with the cutest expression on her face.

Bluesky smiled dumbfounded in silence as he continued to gaze into her eyes.

"You don't even know my name!" she exclaimed suddenly.

Bluesky hopped back in surprise. "Um, my name is Bluesky." He smiled at her distractedly, finding it difficult to focus.

"Yes, I know. I remember your name from the Council of Birds," she said with a twinkle in her eyes. "My name is Windwhisper."

"Windwhisper," Bluesky repeated her name almost in a whisper. "Windwhisper! What a beautiful name. It's such a nice name ... yes, nice ... very ... nice!"

Windwhisper giggled again.

Bluesky stared at her with his mind lost in thoughts of her cute face and her dreamy eyes.

"Have you found the poison yet?" she asked.

Bluesky shook himself. All at once he remembered the search. He looked up and realized the sun was at its highest point in the sky for the day.

"Oh, I've got to fly. I'm going to be late." He leapt into the air and flew toward the house where KC lived.

A moment later, he realized Windwhisper was flying beside him.

"Um ... I was wondering." She flapped her wings harder in order to keep up with him.

Bluesky reduced his speed to make it easier for her.

"Wondering what?" Bluesky asked. He was filled with amazement that she was flying beside him.

"I was hoping ... that we could be friends!"

Bluesky nearly fell out of the sky.

He flapped out of rhythm -- almost as if this were his first flight out of the nest. He fell a dozen feet, flapping his wings so hard he lost his breath and fell forward again toward the ground.

21

It took him several seconds to regain his normal flying motion and flight speed. After what seemed an eternity of struggling to remember how to fly, he simply took a deep breath and relaxed, and then he found himself flying again in a steady, normal motion.

He looked over at Windwhisper, dumbfounded, and saw an expression of profound sadness spread over her face.

"Well, you probably know that I don't have many friends because I'm so small. Birds don't like me, which makes me sad. If you don't want to be friends, well, I understand." Windwhisper turned to leave.

"Oh, no! I want to be friends. I'm just ... surprised ..."

They flew side by side a distance without speaking.

Finally, Windwhisper spoke. "Do you really want us to be friends?" she asked in a fearful tone.

"Yes, I do! Absolutely! I want us to be friends!" Bluesky shouted joyfully.

All the birds in the nearby trees turned in surprise at the loudness of his outburst.

"Ooops, I didn't mean to shout. Sorry."

"That's all right." Windwhisper laughed.

"It's just ... well ... I'm just not used to others asking to be my friend ... especially a girrr ... um ... a bird who's not a boy, I mean ..."

Windwhisper giggled -- a happy, trill-like chirp that made Bluesky's heart pound with joy.

Bluesky's face grew warm with embarrassment, but a wonderful feeling inside his heart built with each new stroke of his wings through the clear air. In fact, it wasn't just her pretty laughter that sent a thrill through his heart. He felt happy just flying alongside her!

"I saw you when you volunteered yesterday, and I think you're the bravest Mockingbird in the entire world."

Bluesky lost his flight rhythm and almost forgot how to fly again, except this time he didn't quite fall right out of the sky like before.

He came close though.

"I'm ... I'm glad you feel that way. I just want to help."

They talked a long time. They didn't talk about anything in particular, just different things, whatever came into their mind as they flew.

Bluesky discovered that Windwhisper loved to watch the clouds too, and she loved to sing, though most of the time she sang by herself because no other birds would sing with her, with the exception of her siblings and parents.

"At least you have your family!" Bluesky said after she mentioned again how lonely she was with no real friends.

He then explained how his family had scattered, though he had recently found his sister again, and he spoke sadly of his mother's death.

When he saw her eyes fill with tears for him, he quickly told her of how he met Ol' Gray Mama and that she was now his second mother. Then he told her how he met Dancingleaves and Tootight and Nightwind and the other birds he now called friends.

"Wow! You have lots of friends. I'm surprised you want another friend like me," Windwhisper whistled.

"A bird can never have too many friends!" Bluesky laughed out loud after he repeated the oft-spoken proverb.

They flew onward, sharing what was inside their hearts with each other.

All too soon, Bluesky reached the meeting tree.

"I've got to go now. When the other birds arrive, we've got to go find the source of the poison." Bluesky's voice was full of regret at their imminent parting.

"Can we sing together tomorrow? And you can tell me what you find!"

"Yes, I'll meet you in the dogwood tree that grows over there." Bluesky pointed to the nearby tree.

Windwhisper flew into the air, but as she started to go over the top of the house, she looked back and whistled a happy little tune back to Bluesky.

Bluesky closed his eyes and almost fell off the branch.

He opened his eyes as he regained his balance and looked up, hoping Windwhisper hadn't seen almost fall again. Thankfully, she was out of sight.

Bluesky whistled the tune Windwhisper had sung to him, a little melody filled with joy and happiness. He repeated it a second time with a little embellishment of his own.

The most exquisite feeling filled his heart -- something he'd never experienced before. As he breathed deeply, his heart quivered as this wonderful feeling of pure joy rushed through his entire being.

He was so happy!

Bluesky spread his wings and flew from branch to branch. All the while he sang the new tune -- Windwhisper's tune -- creating variations on the melody until he filled the air with his joyous trills and warbles.

In less than five minutes, he had flown to every branch in the tree. He started over again, singing non-stop. As soon as he landed on a branch, the feeling inside seemed to erupt like a volcano and he leapt into the air, flew to another branch, and sang Windwhisper's melody again.

He couldn't stop singing!

He couldn't stop flying!

He didn't want this amazing, wondrous feeling that filled his heart to ever go away! It was like he had dreamed the most beautiful dream and woken up and realized it wasn't a dream -- that it was real.

"What exactly are you doing?"

Daymoon's black face and scarlet form appeared next to him.

Bluesky stopped singing in mid-melody.

"You've got the silliest smile on your face, you know," Tootight said with a chuckle. "You look like the bird that ate the biggest bug ever!"

Bluesky laughed out loud.

"I think I know what happened," Bushhopper said with a wink at Daymoon and Tootight.

"You know what?" Coolbreeze squeaked happily after he zoomed up and hovered before them. The bright sunlight caught his red gorget and

25

caused it to sparkle like thousands of tiny rubies.

"I know why Bluesky has that silly smirk on his face," Bushhopper chirped. The Towhee's sleek black feathers glistened in the sun and contrasted with the white of his belly and the reddish feathers on his sides.

Coolbreeze hovered closer to Bluesky and stared at him a moment.

"You're right, and look; he's got a goofy look in his eyes too."

"Oh yeah, I see it now," Daymoon said with mock concern.

Bluesky looked from one bird to the other in total shock.

"What is it?" Bluesky asked with a hush.

"It's quite serious, you know. It happens to every bird sooner or later," Daymoon said in a very solemn tone.

"What? What?" Bluesky asked urgently.

"But the good news is -- it's not usually fatal," Bushhopper added with a sly smile.

"Fatal?" Bluesky gasped.

"But it will change your life forever!" Tootight chuckled. "Like it or not!"

Bluesky froze in anticipation of the dire calamity about to be revealed.

"What?" Bluesky asked.

"You met a girl," Bushhopper said with a smile.

"Yes, as obvious as the sky is blue," Coolbreeze squeaked.

"There'll be no living with him now!" Tootight laughed.

Coolbreeze, Bushhopper, and Daymoon laughed

along with Tootight.

Bluesky's beak dropped open in shock, but after a few moments, their mirth became contagious and he laughed right along with them.

"What's all this laughter about?" Thundercloud's deep, bass voice boomed. "We've got a job to do."

"It's time to focus, birds. This is not a laugh festival," Blackfeather added in a serious tone.

"Oh, boys will be boys," Highclouds twittered from a branch above all of them.

"Yes, unfortunately, we had to endure the entire spectacle," Treeflower added with a wink at Highclouds.

"It was quite educational." Highclouds laughed.

Treeflower joined her, and soon every bird was laughing again except for Thundercloud and Blackfeather, who simply looked at each other with exasperated expressions.

"Birds! Focus!" Thundercloud boomed again.

The songbirds instantly became silent.

Thundercloud nodded at Blackfeather.

Blackfeather hopped over to Bluesky and the other small birds. He opened his shiny, black beak and spoke in a deadly, earnest tone.

"We're all here, Bluesky. It's time to search out the source of the *Death on the Wind* ..."

Chapter Three

"But how will we know what direction to search?" Bluesky asked Blackfeather.

"Yes ... yessss, a good question, my young Mockingbird. It shows you are thinking." Blackfeather chuckled knowingly.

The other birds stared wide-eyed at the wily old Crow and waited for the answer. Thundercloud alone seemed unaffected while he stood stalwart and gazed around as if in total control.

"What do we know about it, yes?" Blackfeather smiled at each bird in turn. "This is what we know; it has gotten stronger. It no longer just kills eggs and hurts the unborn. It now kills adult birds."

"And even animals!" Daymoon exclaimed. "I heard that a squirrel was found dead yesterday."

"And the time before, KC said the little girl in his house got quite sick," Bluesky added.

"See, it gets stronger. What else have we just discovered from the last two occurrences?" Blackfeather nodded and proceeded to answer his own question. "The *Death on the Wind* was strongest when a rare east wind blew."

All the birds nodded in eager agreement.

"Then, we must search toward the east?" Bluesky asked.

"Yes, and remember, we search for the source of death ... what should we find along its deadly path?"

A tense silence filled the small flock of birds.

"D-d-death?" Tootight gulped nervously.

"Yes!" Blackfeather pointed his wing at the rotund Robin and smiled with approval.

"We'll follow a path of death?" Treeflower shuddered.

"Death emanates from it, so we will most likely follow a trail of the dead that will lead us to its terrible source." Blackfeather looked around at each bird to ensure they understood.

Every bird gazed back with solemn expressions, each with the full realization of what lay before them.

"It is time," Thundercloud said in a deep baritone. "Give us the word, Bluesky. You are the leader of this mission."

Bluesky cleared his throat and took a deep breath. He suddenly felt inadequate for this position. He looked at the muscular Hawk and realized that he should be the leader. After all, he was big and strong and exuded courage.

He glanced at Blackfeather. Everyone, including Bluesky, knew Blackfeather was a great and wily leader of the Crows. He had already displayed his thinking ability in revealing to them how they should go about seeking this foul poison. Bluesky knew the Crow would make a better leader than he would.

"Bluesky!" Thundercloud exclaimed.

"I don't think I can lead. You would make a better leader than me. And Blackfeather would --"

"No, brave Mockingbird," Thundercloud said in a booming voice. "You volunteered when no other bird stepped forward. You led the way, and you can and will lead us to victory now."

Bluesky looked deep into Thundercloud's huge, black eyes.

"How do you know?" Bluesky asked.

"Because I believe in you," Thundercloud said simply.

The words sent an electric surge of confidence throughout Bluesky. His burning doubts melted away in that instant. When he looked around at the others to find them all nodding in agreement, Bluesky felt greatly encouraged. In a flash of wings, he leapt into the air.

"Follow me!" He flew upward as the other birds took wing after him.

They flew up into the stormy sky in a loose formation and turned toward the east as one flock.

The birds flew farther apart as Thundercloud soared high above them all in order to see far off. The Red-shouldered Hawk caught a steady breeze, spread his wings wide apart, and glided effortlessly, his keen eyes carefully searching everything below.

Bluesky flew out front with Daymoon on his immediate right and Highclouds on his left about the same distance away. Farther out on the right wing of their formation was Bushhopper, and next came Tootight and Blackfeather at the end. Beyond Highclouds on the left, Coolbreeze hummed along with Treeflower farthest out.

Bluesky looked up and noticed Thundercloud had glided farther ahead.

"What did KC say? Is she going to help?" Daymoon called out.

"Yes, and she has a message."

"Tell us," Daymoon urged.

"KC the kitty cat is going to help the birds!"

All the birds whistled out in a happy cheer.

They continued their search in good spirits. Each bird concentrated on the world below while they searched diligently.

Of course, none of them knew exactly what it was they expected to find, but they all cringed inwardly when remembering Blackfeather's words that it would be a trail of the dead.

However, they each pushed their fear aside, knowing the success of their mission would bring an end to this terrible, unseen menace and help everyone.

In his heart, Bluesky secretly hoped Highclouds would be able to smell the faint scent of the poison and lead them to it. He knew that Chickadees were sensitive and had been the first to detect the poison the other day. If Highclouds couldn't detect the poison's scent, they would have to look for dead animals and follow the trail to the source, which sounded terribly grisly.

Highclouds, however, reported only the normal aroma of the world around them each time he asked her.

The mixed flock flew a series of giant zigzag patterns while their eyes scanned the ground beneath them. They flew as slowly as they could and still maintain altitude. Because they didn't want to miss anything below, their progress was much slower than if they were simply flying in one direction. Time passed slowly and steadily while they searched.

After the sun began its inexorable descent to the

31

western horizon, the air around them grew oppressive with the weight of the storm. Bluesky glanced behind and noted that the line of ominous storm clouds had grown closer.

Bluesky grew discouraged. They had flown for a long time and not found a single thing. It felt as though he were letting them all down After all, he didn't really know where to lead them or how to lead them. They were just flying around and searching aimlessly ...

The doubts rose inside his heart and began to cloud his thinking.

With a forlorn sigh, he glanced over at Blackfeather. At just that moment, Blackfeather's gaze fixed on him.

Bluesky's eyes pleaded for the wily Crow to help him, and somehow, it seemed Blackfeather answered him with only his eyes.

"Caw, caw!" Blackfeather cried out. "Bluesky, why don't we fly back to the edge of the houses where the trees that are our homes stand? I have a new idea that may help us."

The mixed flock turned. After a while they crossed the large man-road for the twelfth time that day in their zigzag searching, but this time they passed over at a place nearest their home territory, drawing their search inward for the first time since they'd started.

"Look down. We must begin our search from this point!" Blackfeather shouted.

All the birds glanced over and saw the two dead birds that they had discovered the other day.

Treeflower gasped. The others stared in somber

silence.

"The trail of death begins here. I should have thought of this earlier, Bluesky. Please, pleeeessse forgive this old Crow his lapse in memory. I am your counselor and should not have allowed us to fly in circles all this time," Blackfeather said with a repentant tone.

"It is fine, Blackfeather. I had forgotten about these poor birds myself. Which way should we fly now?" Bluesky asked.

"Fly farther apart and keep your eyes sharp. Look for more death. We fly due east from this starting point. And you, brave Mockingbird, lead us onward."

"I will do my best."

Blackfeather winked at Bluesky and shouted, "Caw, caw, caw!"

The others nodded in agreement.

Bluesky felt his self-confidence growing again inside his heart and pushing aside his doubts. He turned eastward and picked up the pace.

They soon passed the rows of houses in the subdivision on the other side of the road that made up their territory. Earlier in the day they had avoided this place, instead searching the forests and fields farther up the man-road. Now they flew due east from their new starting point.

Next, a huge field of tall brown grass waved gently in the breeze below them. Bordering the field on one side was a thin stretch of woods next to the large man-road, with dense stretches of forest on this side.

They crisscrossed the fields until all were

33

satisfied nothing suspicious lay hidden among the grass.

And nothing dead.

"We must fly lower among those trees in order to see any evidence on the ground." Blackfeather nodded ahead.

The smaller birds all folded their wings and dropped down, while Thundercloud alone continued to search from on high.

They flew among the trees next to the man-road, the flock now in closer formation as they flitted around the branches and through the shadows. From time to time, each bird would pause on a branch and take a good look around, but all they discovered were more birds and animals -- all alive.

When they reached the end of this stand of wood, they resumed flying eastward toward a larger stretch of woods. They began flying farther apart, sometimes losing sight of each other. Again, they kept to their pattern of perching every so often and looking the area over carefully. When each was done, they would call out to the others and fly again.

Suddenly, Highclouds screamed.

The others quickly flew to her.

Bluesky saw Highclouds perched on a branch, staring at the ground with an expression of shock.

He followed her gaze. At first, he didn't see anything. And then he saw it: a small, furry form lying unnaturally still on the ground.

"A dead chipmunk," Coolbreeze squeaked nervously.

"Is it ... the, you know?" Bushhopper asked.

Highclouds hopped to a lower branch and sniffed. She shook her head and hopped to a lower branch.

"Be careful," Bluesky whispered. "Don't get too close."

She hopped down until she was about ten feet above the dead creature. She carefully leaned over and sniffed the air.

"Yes, I can smell it. *Death on the Wind* killed this chipmunk."

The others felt a wave of horror on hearing Highclouds' confirmation.

"We're flying in the right direction," Blackfeather said with confidence. He nodded toward the east. "We've got to keep searching in that direction."

With one last look at the poor creature, they all took off.

They continued their search pattern as before -- flying a distance and then sitting on a branch to take a good look around. This pattern continued for a long time until they reached a larger section of the forest at the far boundary.

Bluesky felt tired from his exertions. but none of the other birds complained, so he kept up the pace.

The countless tree trunks seemed to stretch on forever.

They were in a forest of young pine trees. The ground was covered by a thick layer of brown pine needles that muffled all sound. Bluesky and the other birds flew among the middle branches and perched for brief respites on them while they searched the ground below for any sign.

35

They could hear a distant 'kee-har' from high above the canopy of upper branches as Thundercloud called to them asking if they had spotted something.

An hour passed as they searched among the shadows of the trees.

Bluesky had never been in a forest this large, and he wondered how many like it were left in these parts. He knew that around the subdivision where he lived, there were only small pockets of trees between the man-roads and rows of houses.

He liked this place and determined to come back and explore it when this was all over.

Without warning, they reached the end of the woods. Before them another field of tall grass stretched.

Just as Bluesky flew out from among the trees and over the grass, he was startled by an urgent twittering from Treeflower.

"I found a dead bird! I found a dead bird!"

Chapter Four

He saw the Song Sparrow on the ground hopping around and twittering louder with each passing second.

Bluesky, Daymoon, and Bushhopper landed beside her.

"See, see!" Treeflower nodded toward a bird lying on the ground.

Bluesky waited, expecting the bird to move or sit up because of Treeflower's constant cries. After a few seconds he realized she was right: this bird would never fly again.

"It's dead," Bushhopper said in a hushed whisper.

"Do you think it died from the poison?" Daymoon asked.

Bluesky hopped closer but stopped as Daymoon's words sank inside his mind.

"Highclouds! Come here," Treeflower shouted.

The Carolina Chickadee flew into the air from a distant tree and quickly landed next to them. She looked fearfully at the dead bird.

"What kind of bird is it?" Bushhopper hopped closer and gazed over at the lifeless form.

Highclouds hopped up beside Bushhopper and peered cautiously over at the dead bird.

"It's a Robin," she said.

"Oh no!" Tootight shouted with dismay as he landed.

"Do you know him?" Highclouds asked.

"No, I don't, but he was a Robin, like me," Tootight said with a forlorn expression.

Bluesky felt bad for him. This was the first time he'd ever seen Tootight without a smile. He watched as the portly Robin turned and walked away with his beak pointed at the ground.

Blackfeather swooped down and landed. He folded his large wings and walked slowly toward the dead bird. He twisted his head to one side and peered hard at it.

"Can you smell any poison?" Thundercloud asked as he landed behind them.

All the birds looked at Highclouds expectantly as she sniffed the air. She took three hops toward the dead bird and sniffed again. She took a deep breath and took another three hops until she was beside Blackfeather.

She sniffed deeply. "No, I don't smell any poison."

Blackfeather walked forward until he towered over the dead bird. He stretched his neck forward and looked the body over carefully.

"A death-stick killed this poor bird," he said simply.

Several gasps filled the air.

The sound of thunder rolled across the sky. Dark and ominous clouds were quickly blocking out the sky above the group of birds. A sudden, stiff breeze whipped through the tall grass, causing it to sway violently.

Blackfeather glanced up. "The storm will break soon."

Every bird remained frozen, staring at the dead

Robin as the breeze ruffled their feathers.

Bluesky hopped closer for a better look.

"See the blood on its feathers? There, on its side." Blackfeather pointed with his huge black beak.

Bluesky saw the discolored feathers.

"The round stone from the death-stick entered the heart there."

Bluesky's own heart pounded faster.

"See those prints in the soft dirt over there?" Blackfeather pointed off to the right of the dead bird.

Bluesky stared at the well-defined print of a large animal.

He caught his breath in surprise as he realized the huge imprint was as big as he was, and it was only a single paw-print.

"That was made by a very big dog," Blackfeather said with a knowing tone.

Bluesky felt a twinge of fear grip his heart at the stark realization. He looked up at Blackfeather.

Blackfeather wasn't looking down at the dead bird, though. The crow searched the fields with a careful eye in every direction for several long seconds. Finally, he spoke.

"This is the field of the crazy man." Blackfeather shook his head and ruffled his feathers. "We will have to keep a sharp eye out for him, in case he is out walking with his dogs and his death-stick."

"I can fly cover for all of you while you keep searching the ground for the source of the poison," Thundercloud said.

"Good idea -- nothing escapes the watchful eyes of the Hawk," Blackfeather cawed.

The birds left the trees of the forest behind to fly over a sea of tall grass. Each bird flew a few feet above the grass as it swayed with the breeze of the oncoming storm.

Coolbreeze hummed along in his familiar zigzag pattern. He seemed to be the only bird flying confidently now.

Bluesky felt vulnerable -- naked -- flying over the wide-open field.

It seemed he could almost feel the man pointing the death-stick at him -- pointing the death-stick directly at him ...

He wanted so badly to fly down into the grass and hide, but he didn't want the others to know he was so scared. So he flew along searching the grass like them, although he did glance around more often to make sure no man was nearby.

A distant flurry of whistling cries slowly became audible over the whispering of the grass in the breeze.

"Do you hear that?" Treeflower asked as she landed on the ground in the midst of the tall grass.

Bluesky landed beside her, relief filling his heart. He knew that in the grass they were hidden from any danger.

Coolbreeze zoomed up to them and hovered as he too listened. "I hear them," he squeaked.

"A group of birds whistling, and they sound so forlorn," Treeflower said with a hint of sadness in her voice.

They looked up as the sound of wings flapping

hard against the air came to their ears.

Tootight landed awkwardly, his legs collapsing underneath him. He sat on the ground with them a moment, chuckling at himself, but the others turned back toward the direction of the soft, distant cries.

"Cedar Waxwings," Bluesky said with confidence.

"How do you know?" Coolbreeze squeaked.

"I've flown with some before. I recognize their whistling."

"They sound like they're crying," Treeflower said.

"They are," Bluesky whispered in agreement.

The rest of the mixed flock descended around them, every bird except for Thundercloud. The Red-shouldered Hawk continued to soar high on the wind above them with his wings stretched wide and motionless and his tail feathers fanned out. He flew in large, lazy circles while he maintained his vigilance.

The Hawk's cry pierced the air.

Blackfeather flapped his wings and hopped high in the air. He stared a moment with his wings beating hard. Slowly, he lowered himself back down.

"Thundercloud sees the birds. He spotted a group of them in a small bush a short distance ahead of us."

"I'll go," Bluesky said in a matter-of-fact tone.

"Take Coolbreeze and Treeflower too. You small birds shouldn't startle them, even though they seem to be in a bad way," Blackfeather said.

The three flew off and left the others in the

cover of the tall grass.

As they neared the bush, the individual forms of the birds grew discernable. Bluesky recognized the sable brown feathers and the familiar black mask and crest on their heads.

"Bluesky!"

Bluesky felt a fresh jolt of fear at hearing his name called out in the midst of this strange place.

Two of the Cedar Waxwings took wing and flew toward the trio.

"They know you," Coolbreeze said with surprise.

Bluesky recognized Rainday and Sunday.

"It's the Day flock," he said absentmindedly. "I hope nothing's wrong with them."

They quickly found out that something was indeed terribly wrong.

Rainday and Sunday jumped right to the point as all of them landed on the ground together. They told of how they had been devouring berries on a nearby bush the day before when a strong wind kicked up. As they watched, a patch of white dust whipped into the air. Several of the flock flew over to investigate.

They found a small hill covered with short grass, except on one side the ground had washed away.

As the others watched from the bush, another gust of wind caused more of the white dust to swirl into the air.

Instantly, all the birds near the hill fell down dead!

Bluesky's beak dropped open in surprise.

42

"What was it?" Coolbreeze asked in a worried tone.

"Poison dust," Sunday said simply.

"That's what we're looking for! It's killed birds all around here," Treeflower said with hope.

"We are so sad. We've done nothing but cry and cry over our dead brothers and sisters," Rainday wailed.

"Did you hear about the 'Council of Birds?" Bluesky asked.

"Yes, but we couldn't go -- our friends died that same day!"

"The day the *Death on the Wind* struck!" Treeflower gasped.

"We wondered if that is what killed them," Sunday said. "But we actually saw something swirling on the wind, and no one has ever mentioned that before."

"Yes! It could be the source," Coolbreeze said with a hush.

"If only you had sent someone to the council," Treeflower said.

"We had to mourn. We were so sad. So many of our friends -- dead! And so suddenly, and simply from a gust of wind!" Sunday cried out in a voice full of sadness.

"Can you show us where this hill of short grass is located?" Bluesky asked, his voice surprisingly determined and calm.

"Yes, it is close to a garden and a metal house, but it's a dangerous place," Rainday added hurriedly.

"We will be careful of the poison, once you

43

point out the hill," Treeflower said, her voice clear and sure.

"No, there's more," Sunday whistled softly.

"More danger?" Coolbreeze asked. "How can that be?"

"There's a man there -- a strange man. He has a stick that kills birds." Rainday shuddered.

"And there are dogs. The man calls the Rottweiler Bear -- he's a fearsome dog. The German Shepherd is called King, and he loves to kill, just like the man. They'll kill you if they can catch you," Sunday added.

"But the biggest dog is the most dangerous. He's a monster! The man said he is a Mastiff/Pit Bull mix, and his name is Jack," Rainday said in rapid-fire staccato.

"And do you know the man's name?" Bluesky asked.

"Yes, we've heard others call him. His name is Marcion!"

"Marcion," Bluesky repeated under his breath. He felt an icy chill grip his pounding heart after he whispered the man's name. Bluesky realized that finding the poison might be the least of their problems ...

Sunday flew back to the Day flock to tell the others that help had arrived. Rainday flew with Bluesky's group back to the mixed flock to lead them to the source of the poison.

Bluesky and Rainday quickly told the others about the sudden death of the birds the other day. Everyone felt a terrible dread after the Cedar Waxwing mentioned the white dust swirling in the air right before the birds dropped dead.

The dread grew worse when Bluesky mentioned Marcion's name and explained he was the crazy man with the death stick the Crows all feared.

As they all took wing with Rainday in the lead, Blackfeather eased close to Bluesky.

"If what the Waxwing says is true, we'll have to approach carefully -- very carefully." Blackfeather flapped his wings in a steady motion.

Bluesky's heart pounded hard inside his breast, but he said nothing.

"That's Marcion's house over there." Blackfeather nodded to the right.

Bluesky looked over and spotted it. He felt a natural repulsion with his first glimpse of its chaotic and dirty appearance. As he continued to gaze, he noticed a large animal curled up on the ground near a solitary tree.

"One of the dogs," Blackfeather said in a whisper.

"Do you see Marcion?" Bluesky asked quickly.

"No, but Thundercloud will warn us if he's out. Just listen for his warning cry ..."

Without warning, Rainday's whistling voice pierced the air. They all flew closer to the Cedar Waxwing just as he shouted, "There it is! That's the small hill where the white dust swirled and killed our friends!"

45

Chapter Five

They landed immediately in order to formulate their next move.

"Where is it?" Daymoon asked, gazing intently in the same direction in which Rainday stared with sadness.

The birds sat huddled in a spot of low grass. The grass near Marcion's trailer was shorter than in the rest of the field. The grass was brown and lay flat against the ground, packed down from the dogs and man walking over it. In many places, the brown earth lay exposed from where the dogs had dug into it over the years.

A solitary tree stood near the rusted trailer; the next nearest were those in the forest that surrounded the far edges of the field. In every direction trash and debris lay strewn -- countless empty cans, plastic, paper, rotting food, and mess of every description. Trash littered the landscape like a mine field.

"What a nasty place," Treeflower said with obvious distaste.

"How can anyone live among such filth?" Highclouds twittered, rolling her eyes.

"Hush!" Blackfeather warned in a harsh whisper. He turned to Rainday. "Where is it?"

"See that small hill over there?" Rainday pointed with his beak at a small rise in the field. However, it was quite a distance away toward the line of pine trees that ringed the field.

Bluesky followed their gaze. He saw the small rise covered in grass like the rest of the field. In fact, the small knoll was the only distinguishing feature in that entire section of grassy field.

Looking around more, he noticed the straight rows of plants growing near the metal house. Bluesky guessed this was the garden that Blackfeather had mentioned raiding in the past, the garden where vegetables would grow in the summer sun.

Over to the right, he saw large bushes laden with red and black berries.

"Those are the berries we were eating when it happened," Rainday said with sadness in his voice.

"What do we do now?" Bushhopper whispered excitedly.

"Should we do a flyover to check it out?" Coolbreeze squeaked with eagerness.

Blackfeather remained silent as he glanced straight up into the sky.

Bluesky and the others looked up and saw the distant form of Thundercloud circling effortlessly far up in the cloud-filled sky. Even though they could not see his face, they knew the keen eyes of the Hawk were vigilantly keeping watch over them.

Blackfeather looked back over to the filthy trailer and the black Rottweiler sleeping on the bare dirt in the shade of the lone tree.

"The man must be asleep inside the house, but there are two more dogs. I don't see any signs of them." Blackfeather craned his neck and looked slowly around.

"Let's fly up in that tree -- we'll have a better

view from there," Daymoon suggested.

"What if the man comes out with his death-stick? We'll be sitting ducks," Blackfeather pointed out.

"Oh, I hadn't thought of that." Daymoon shrugged.

"We couldn't all go at any rate," Blackfeather added. "We'd get too loud chattering to each other. We need to split up."

Bluesky didn't like that idea, but he remained silent. Blackfeather was a bird of great experience and knowledge; he would listen to the Crow's suggestions and abide if they seemed reasonable.

"Bluesky, Rainday, Coolbreeze, Highclouds, and I will fly to that tree. You others, fly to the edge of the tall grass over there. We'll send word when we're ready," Blackfeather whispered.

In a flurry of feathers, the flock split up.

Bluesky and those assigned with him flew toward the leaf-laden tree standing over the sleeping dog, landing in the uppermost branches. As he sat, the wind caused the branch to sway. Bluesky gripped it tighter.

"Yes, Yeeesss ... I see it better now," Blackfeather crooned confidently from his high perch.

Bluesky also saw it in better detail. The small hill rose above the level ground that surrounded it. As he studied it, he realized that one side of the hill was missing.

"The hill has given way," Bluesky chirped. "See, the grass and dirt are gone."

"Yes, looks like the heavy rains last year eroded

it away on that side." Blackfeather turned his head from side to side as he peered at the hill. "Yes, I see something manmade exposed -- brown metal."

"What about the poison?" Coolbreeze asked. "Is it there?"

"I came up here for another important reason, not just to get a better view. Please, be silent a moment." Blackfeather stood tall and let the wind ruffle through his feathers a moment. Finally, he spoke.

"The wind is out of the west. We'll use it to protect us. Let's circle around and approach the hill with the wind. When we get close, we'll land. The wind will still be blowing toward the hill."

"Why is that important?" Bluesky asked.

"If the wind blew from the hill toward us, it would bring the poison," Highclouds explained.

"Ohhhh," Bluesky and Coolbreeze said together in simultaneous understanding.

"I am afraid," Rainday said.

"Stay close to me. I'll help you." Bluesky smiled at the Cedar Waxwing.

Rainday managed a brief smile in reply, nodding in silent agreement.

"Highclouds, as we near that hill, keep testing the air for any scent of the poison. If you smell anything ..."

"I'll chirp out a warning!" Highclouds twittered boldly.

Blackfeather leapt into the air.

Bluesky and the others followed.

The five birds soared into the sky toward the right of the hill. In just a few minutes, they reached

49

the line of trees that grew on either side of the long, gravel drive that led to the big man-road beyond. Then they turned and rode with the wind toward the hill.

As Bluesky finished his turn, he realized that the hill sat at the far end of this part of the field near the line of trees. He guessed that if one of the taller trees ever fell over, the top would land against the hill.

As they flew closer, he noticed a tree lying on the ground. It was almost invisible because the tall grass had again grown up all around it. It must have lain there quite some time; the few naked branches that rose in the air were dry and brittle. Most had snapped off and lay on the ground next to the dried-up trunk.

Bluesky realized it must have been the force of this tree's topmost branches hitting the small hill that had first started the erosion.

As they came even closer, he saw the spot where the tree struck the hill those untold months ago.

"Highclouds, you smell anything?" Blackfeather called out urgently.

"No, the air is clean."

"Good. Follow me." Blackfeather folded his wings and dropped toward the ground with the others right behind him.

The birds landed about twenty feet from the exposed side of the small hill.

Even here, rains had eroded away the ground after the force of the tree caused the initial damage. At the base of the hill, near some broken branches, clumps of dirt were piled up where the rains had washed it.

"Look, a man-thing!" Coolbreeze squeaked.

Now plain to see at this close distance, the man-thing's rusted metal side lay fully exposed.

The birds did not know what it was, only that it resembled an oversized trash can that had rusted badly. On both sides, outlines of other barrels buried inside the hill were barely discernable.

"Look -- it is leaking," Rainday whispered.

As they stared harder, they saw that the rusted side of the exposed barrel had a large hole that started at the top and extended a quarter of the way down. Out of the bottom of the rusted hole, a whitish stain extended down to the ground.

"That must be where the poison comes from," Highclouds said with conviction.

"Why hasn't the poison killed Marcion?" Bluesky asked.

"Look." Blackfeather pointed with his black beak.

Bluesky looked past the hill and saw Marcion's trailer in the distance. The exposed barrel lay on the opposite side of hill from the trailer and quite a ways from it. He turned around and saw the line of trees behind them.

"Which way is home?" Bluesky looked around, unsure of which direction it lay.

"Straight down this edge of the field." Blackfeather pointed with his wing in a line parallel to the trees. "That is due west. When an east wind blows, it will take this poison and blow it straight where we all live, across the first group of houses and over the man-road to our trees and nests."

"That's terrible!" Coolbreeze shouted.

"Yes, I agree. We must get a little closer. Follow me, but if I or Highclouds cry out, fly back to the tree."

Everyone nodded in silent agreement.

Before they got very high in the air, Highclouds shouted a warning, her voice full of fear.

Every bird instinctively dropped out of the sky and onto the ground in order to hide, totally forgetting their instructions in their panic.

Bluesky's heart pounded inside his chest as he looked over at Highclouds and Blackfeather.

The big Crow stared first in one direction and then another, his eyes wide and full of fear.

"What is it?" Coolbreeze landed beside Bluesky and walked closer until he stood right next to him. The tiny Hummingbird peered quickly first in one direction and then another.

"I don't know," Bluesky whispered.

"I see it." Rainday's voice, deeper than normal, caused all of them to turn, but the Waxwing stared as if in a trance.

Bluesky and the others turned to see what he stared at.

He saw it too.

"Another dead bird!" Bluesky gasped.

"Birds," Blackfeather said with somberness. "Look around."

Bluesky felt his heart freeze. As he started looking, he saw three more Waxwings lying dead on the ground. They were just lying there on the ground -- so still ...

But there was more.

As he looked harder and focused, he saw death everywhere. Yes, everywhere he looked, he either saw a dead bird or dead animal: chipmunks, squirrels, a Robin, and a Blue Jay. All of them were in varying states of decay -- some with feathers lying loose around sunken bodies and other dead animals and birds that were unrecognizable due to decomposition.

Then he noticed the bones.

In fact, quite a number of bleached bones lay scattered between the rotting bodies of all the dead animals.

"This is a place of death," Blackfeather whispered ominously.

Chapter Six

"S-s-should we go closer? Is it safe?" Coolbreeze stuttered.

"No." Blackfeather looked over at Highclouds and nodded at her.

The little Chickadee sniffed the air tentatively. "Yes, I smell the poison in the air here. The scent is strong!"

Every bird took several steps backwards.

"Look!" Coolbreeze whispered

Bluesky turned back and looked at the barrel with the ragged opening.

From the rusted edge near the bottom, a puff of white dust swirled into the air with the breeze.

All five birds gasped.

As he watched, Bluesky noticed a tiny stream of white powder falling out of the hole onto the ground. He followed the slow stream of powder until it landed on top of a small pile of the same white powder on the ground. He focused his eyes and realized that the brown dirt all around the exposed barrel was stained white where it had leaked over time.

He realized that nothing, not even a single blade of grass, grew anywhere near the white powder. In fact, for a wide area around the leaking barrel, the ground was bare except for the bleached bones of dead animals ...

Bluesky shivered with all of this death so near.

"This is the source of the poison," Blackfeather

said with a somber tone.

"What is that white dust falling to the ground?" Highclouds shuddered.

"The poison is leaking out ..." Bluesky whispered.

All the birds stared in tense silence.

Suddenly, a sharp sound like the crack of thunder split the air.

Bluesky jumped straight up, his taut nerves triggered into an instant reaction by the unexpected noise.

Flying just below the dark and threatening clouds above, Thundercloud cried out.

Bluesky and the other birds looked up.

A blinding flash of lightning lit the sky and illuminated the boiling clouds above. Almost immediately, the ground shook with thunder, but the sound of this thunder was deeper and echoed more than the sharp report seconds before.

The storm was upon them.

Suddenly, they saw several tail feathers floating away from the Hawk as he cried out again. Then Thundercloud folded his wings and dove away in a blur.

"A death-stick!" Blackfeather shouted.

The harsh report of the death-stick thundered again. Now the birds knew the difference between the real thunder and the report of the death-stick.

All five birds cried out together, leaping into the sky.

Bluesky flew away from the noise, which emanated from the forest behind them, as did as all the others.

He soared into the air out of pure instinct. He also had to fly around the poison. He kept himself away from the boundary where the grass stopped and the place of death began. He dared not go any closer.

After he passed around the knoll of poison, Bluesky flew straight toward the solitary tree beside the trailer. He knew the others were nearby hiding.

"Keep low!" Blackfeather shouted urgently. "The death-stick will kill us if we fly up too high."

Bluesky flew just over the top of the tall grass. They had left the area of death behind and now raced over the seemingly endless stretch of grass toward the tree and their waiting friends.

"I'll go to the top of the tree and find out where Marcion is. The rest of you, find the others and hide with them until I locate the man." Blackfeather flapped his wings harder and sailed up toward the top of the tree.

The sharp report of the death-stick thundered again.

Again and again the terrible sound shook the air in rapid succession.

A huge bolt of lightning ripped the sky followed almost instantaneously by the rumbling sound of thunder, which shook the very air with its terrible closeness.

Bluesky's heart pounded so hard he felt it would jump out of his chest.

"He's trying to kill us!" Coolbreeze cried out. "He's really trying to kill us!"

Bluesky dove into a gap in the grass, and the others followed.

Without warning, the grass ahead shuddered and the ground erupted. A cloud of dirt spewed up. Seconds later, the sound of the death-stick shook the air again.

He twisted away, realizing the death-stick was getting closer!

Somewhere above them, Blackfeather cawed three times.

Bluesky dove around another patch of grass and suddenly saw the others crouched low in hiding.

Seconds later, Coolbreeze and the others were on the ground with them.

"W-what's happening?" Bushhopper asked with a fearful expression.

"The man has found us. He's trying to kill us with his death-stick," Bluesky whispered.

Daymoon, Bushhopper, and Treeflower crouched lower.

Bluesky looked up at the tree.

Blackfeather perched on the topmost branch, his black head and beak protruding from a mass of leaves.

Bluesky waited, but his heart continued to pound, and the urge to fly away almost overwhelmed his senses.

"Shouldn't we fly away?" Daymoon asked. "If we wait here, the man will find us."

"We've got to wait on Blackfeather," Highclouds said.

"Where's Thundercloud?" Treeflower asked in a tense voice.

Bluesky and the other birds searched the sky just as another jagged bolt of lightning leapt from

57

the storm clouds, but there was no sign of the Red-shouldered Hawk.

"He's not dead, is he?" Highclouds whispered with a frightened look in her eyes.

"I don't know. I hope not." Bluesky lowered his head and stared at the ground.

"I see the man -- he's running towards us from the woods!" Blackfeather cried out. "Hold on. He's stopped."

Bluesky and the others waited tensely.

"He's got a death-stick. He's lifting it up again. When I cry out, all of you need to fly around this tree and head toward the forest on the other side of the trailer. Then, fly through the woods back --"

Blackfeather never finished the sentence.

As Bluesky stared up at the Crow, a cloud of leaves exploded into the air, and small pieces of wood flew in every direction.

Blackfeather let out a loud 'CAW!' and leapt into the air under the flash of lightning.

"Okay, let's --" Bluesky stopped in mid-sentence.

The tall grass parted right before his disbelieving eyes while the sound of thunder echoed.

The head of a huge dog shot out. The bloodshot eyes of the massive dog narrowed, and his powerful growl shook the ground.

All the birds froze in fear.

The dog was so close they felt its hot breath blow over them as it growled ominously a second time.

Suddenly, the grass parted on either side of the

growling dog.

Now, three huge dogs growled together at the small birds.

Bluesky couldn't move. He felt the eyes of the biggest dog staring right at him. Bluesky somehow knew that this horrific, huge dog was the one they called Jack.

Jack stopped growling and spoke in a low, terrible voice. "You shouldn't have come here today, birds."

"Why?" Bluesky asked automatically, as if in a trance.

The biggest dog bared his fangs before he spoke again. "Because I'm going to kill you."

Bluesky felt his heart miss a beat.

At just that moment, two more shots rang out.

The three dogs leapt at them under another flash of lightning.

Bluesky and all the birds flew into the air while the dogs snapped their jaws and twisted their heads from side to side, trying to snatch the birds out of the air with their fangs.

"Get'em, dawgs! Eat'em up!" Marcion shouted ruthlessly. "Eat'em up!"

Bluesky felt the hot breath of the biggest dog right on his back while thunder echoed in the air.

He twisted and changed direction just as he heard the dog snap his jaws shut right behind him.

Bluesky felt a sudden flash of pain as one of his tail feathers was snatched out.

He flapped his wings harder.

His friends cried out in fear from every direction as they flew away from the other two dogs chasing them.

The deadly snapping of jaws seemed to be everywhere.

Another shot pierced the air, and the ground erupted beside Bluesky.

He turned again -- and he came face to face with the huge Rottweiler.

Bear leapt forward.

Bluesky cried out, folded his wings, and dropped down immediately.

Bear snapped his jaws shut in the air where Bluesky had been only a moment before and quickly lowered his head and chased after Bluesky. Bear leapt forward in a mighty bound to catch the fleeing bird. The big dog's lower jaw hit Bluesky and knocked him onto the ground between his forelegs.

Gasping for air, Bluesky leapt up and flapped his wings in a flurry of motion as he tried to get off the ground. He felt the dog right above and knew if he didn't get airborne quickly, the dog would kill him.

Bear put his nose down to the ground in order to find the fallen bird.

At just that moment, Bluesky flew up and bounced off Bear's chest.

Bear jumped back, shocked at the unexpected thump, and Bluesky was flung a few feet away and back onto the ground. He fluttered his wings and cried out.

Bear quickly realized what had just happened and leapt for the helpless bird.

Bluesky's foot touched the ground, and he

pushed forward, flapping his wings furiously -- but instead of flying away, he flew straight at Bear! He flew between the dog's forelegs and under his belly.

Bear howled out in frustration and confusion. The bird's movements were a blur, and somehow the Mockingbird had disappeared right before his eyes.

Just as Bluesky was passing between Bear's hind legs, the dog jumped sideways as it tried to find him, and Bluesky flew into Bear's right rear leg.

The huge Rottweiler yelped with surprise and turned completely around, his fangs bared for the kill.

Bluesky ricocheted sideways and flew onto the ground in a cloud of dust, but his wings never stopped flapping. Instantly, he was in the air with Bear chasing inches behind.

Lightning again ripped across the sky followed by another blast of thunder.

Bluesky couldn't catch his breath. Every muscle in his body burned white -hot with his furious exertions. He flapped his wings harder, trying to gain altitude and get away, but he couldn't do it; he barely managed to fly just above the ground itself. It seemed his heart was in his throat, and he couldn't get his breath.

Worst of all, he couldn't gain the altitude he needed to escape.

He felt the dog right behind him -- and closing in for the kill!

Bear howled and made a mighty leap forward with his jaws agape.

Bluesky turned hard right.

Bear brought his head around and snapped at the fleeing Mockingbird, but his momentum carried his huge body onward. He lost his footing and rolled over onto his side in a massive cloud of dust.

Bluesky heard the crash behind him and knew the dog had gone down hard. Finally, he managed to catch his breath. More important, he got his wings flapping in rhythm. He flew higher into the air, safely beyond the reach of any dog. He headed toward the trailer and the trees beyond it.

"CAW! CAW! CAW!"

Bluesky couldn't see Blackfeather, but he recognized his warning call.

The death-stick thundered again.

Bluesky could tell the man was shooting at Blackfeather somewhere along the line of trees to his left. The Crow was drawing his fire and helping Bluesky and the others to escape.

"Let's go, birds! Fly like the wind!" Bluesky cried out as he turned toward the trailer and the forest beyond it.

Coolbreeze zoomed right by him as if he were standing still. In seconds, Coolbreeze was over the trailer and out of sight.

Bluesky looked around and saw all the others flying with him as fast as their wings would allow.

"Fly, birds!" Blackfeather called from the edge of the forest. "Fly! Fly! Fly!"

Bluesky reached the trailer and started to fly over when the death-stick split the air again.

Right before his eyes, holes appeared in the metal of the trailer as pellets whizzed all around him.

"Faster! Faster!" Daymoon cried as he surged past Bluesky and over the metal roof.

Bluesky flew faster than he had ever flown his entire life.

At just that moment, the rain fell from the sky.

Seconds later, all the birds were on the other side of the metal house.

"We're safe! The metal house is between us and the man now!" Tootight shouted with joy.

The thunder of the death-stick erupted in reply while the rain fell harder.

Bluesky and his friends sailed into the protective branches of the forest moments later and disappeared among the leafy foliage.

None of them slowed down until they reached the familiar trees of Willow Hollow.

Chapter Seven

"It's impossible." Bluesky shook his head emphatically.

"Nothing is impossible," Nightwind replied in a soft tone.

"I'm just glad Thundercloud only lost a few tail feathers," Blackfeather said with a sigh. "The death-stick almost got him."

"I'm certainly glad no birds were seriously hurt." Nightwind's large eyes settled back on Bluesky. "Now, why do you think this is impossible?"

"It's too far away to lead the man. I've already told KC where we found it, and she said she couldn't lead him that far. That means we've got to bring some of it to him."

"Nothing is impossible," Nightwind repeated softly.

"But what can we do? We're just birds!" Bluesky hopped frantically along the limb where he and Blackfeather perched in consultation with the wise Owl.

"It does seem like a sticky problem," Blackfeather added.

Nightwind smiled benevolently at the old Crow.

"I mean, we can't pick any of the white poison up in our beaks. We'd swallow some of it and die before we could carry any back," Bluesky said with an exasperated cry.

"Actually, breathing it would kill you first." Blackfeather shrugged his shoulders

"What else," Nightwind prompted.

"We can't pick it up with our feet -- it is too fine. We'd get too little, and as we flew the wind would blow away most of it." Bluesky settled down now, halting his nervous hopping. His exertions were only increasing his anxiety, and he didn't need any more of that.

"It also seems that simply touching the poison, either on the foot or on our feathers, should be avoided. I don't think any bird can touch it and not be affected -- perhaps even fatally ..." Blackfeather coughed, as if clearing his throat. He shook his head, causing his huge black beak to swing from side to side.

"What else?" Nightwind's tone was still positive and hopeful.

"There isn't anything else!" Bluesky cried out.

"You only see the problem; it clouds your thoughts. And your negative thoughts are too powerful." Nightwind smiled kindly as his large yellow eyes twinkled in the late afternoon sunlight. "You must focus on what is possible, no matter how farfetched it might seem. You must see the possibilities and see beyond the problem. Your answer will lie there!"

"I'm too tired to think positively right now. I mean, I thought finding the poison would be the hard part!" Bluesky sighed.

"I must agree with our young Mockingbird, Nightwind. I saw the stuff." Blackfeather closed his eyes and shuddered. "I saw the death surrounding it, those birds and animals who ventured too close. I have no idea how any bird can get close enough to

65

it, much less bring some back!"

"Neither can I."

Bluesky and Blackfeather stared at Nightwind in shock.

"But wisdom is a treasure of every bird. Our answer may lie with one of the other birds on the team," Nightwind said with a wry expression.

"Really?" Bluesky said with a hint of doubt.

"Just as there is good in every bird, each also possesses their own inner wealth of knowledge and wisdom. Each bird brings forth this wisdom out of his own treasure, and it is a wise bird that listens and learns and adds it to his own unique store of knowledge."

"What must I do?" Bluesky asked intently.

"Go to each bird and ask them for ideas -- ask them how we can solve this seemingly impossible dilemma."

"But you're the wisest bird I know." Bluesky hopped and turned to Blackfeather. "And you're the greatest trickster I know. If you two can't come up with a way ..."

"Seek out the others. Ask them ..." Nightwind smiled again. "You will know when the right idea is spoken. Bring the idea to us, and we will help you bring it to fruition."

Bluesky looked from the Owl back to the Crow with a questioning look on his feathered face. Finally, he sighed and leapt off the branch. He shouted over his shoulder as he flew, "I'll return this time tomorrow."

"We shall be waiting for you!" Blackfeather cried back.

Bluesky flew first to KC. They had mentioned talking to each bird, but he wanted to get a cat's perspective on the problem first.

"It's too far away," KC repeated a second time. "My dad would never follow me that far. He'd pick me up and carry me back home before we made it to the big road."

"Yes, you told me that earlier. Could we somehow bring it back to him? Or should we even try it?" Bluesky shrugged his wings in despair.

"Dad will know what to do, if we bring it to him."

Bluesky stared at KC.

KC purred contentedly. She had spoken those words with such powerful trust, such implicit trust. Bluesky was convinced not by KC's simple statement, but by her strong belief in her dad.

"Then, we've got to bring some of the poison back -- but how?"

"I have no idea. All I know is -- bring it here, and Dad will know how to solve the problem." KC licked her shoulder a few times and purred louder.

Bluesky and KC talked a few minutes more, and then he flew off to talk to the others. First, he found Tootight, the plump and happy American Robin.

"Tootight, how can we bring some of the poison here?" Bluesky watched him carefully.

Tootight's beak fell open in surprise.

"That's the silliest idea I've ever heard." He smiled at Bluesky. "Are you making a joke?"

"No, no. We've got to bring some of it back to the man. KC says once he sees it, he'll know what to do -- he'll get rid of it all."

Tootight broke out in laughter.

Bluesky was taken aback. He looked at the Robin in total disbelief.

"This is not a laughing matter!" Bluesky said with indignation.

Tootight gradually stopped laughing, and with a deep breath, he shook his head side to side.

"I can't help you, Bluesky. I really thought that since we found it, we'd just tell the other birds to stay away. I can't imagine going back and trying to carry some of it. What if the man shoots at us again with his death-stick?"

"It's leaking, and it looks like the leak is getting bigger. If the east wind blows again, more birds will die! More animals will die! Even humans will die!"

"I'm no good at plans. I'll help, of course. I'll help out with a joke and a laugh to keep our spirits up. But ..." Tootight raised his wings and sighed.

Bluesky left him and flew off to search for Daymoon and Bushhopper. In his heart, he knew he should have sought them out first. After all, they were well-traveled birds, and they were open-minded and broad in their thinking. Surely, they'd have an idea.

"You're kidding, right?" Bushhopper laughed out loud, though it was a sound more of disbelief than humor. "I mean, if a bird breathes the stuff, or even touches it -- it'll kill him dead!"

Daymoon stood up straighter, his black face serious. His jaunty crest rose as his eyes narrowed in a thoughtful manner.

Bluesky could tell that Daymoon was carefully pondering the problem.

"What about you, Daymoon? A smart bird like you might have an idea." Bluesky paused with hope.

"You mean you're not kidding?" Bushhopper cried out.

"No, I'm not kidding," Bluesky replied, not wanting to get into an argument with the Towhee. "We've got to bring some back to show the man."

While the two waited silently as Daymoon pondered the problem, a familiar humming sound grew discernable on the wind.

"What are you birds doing?" Coolbreeze squeaked excitedly.

"Trying to figure out how to carry some of the poison back here." Bushhopper rolled his eyes and laughed. "Perhaps you can help?"

Coolbreeze hovered motionless in the air, his wings a blur of motion. Slowly, he rose higher, flicking his long tongue. Next, he hovered lower, the loud humming of his wings increasing and decreasing with each maneuver as he thought on the fly.

"Hmmm, I can't think of a thing," Coolbreeze said at last.

"I've got it!" Daymoon shouted in triumphant.

Bushhopper, Coolbreeze, and Bluesky stared at him, full of hope. As they watched, Daymoon proudly lifted his crest feathers erect.

"Okay, then, tell us!" Bluesky exclaimed.

"One of us will carry some on our tail feathers!" Daymoon smiled proudly. "See, the poison will be farthest from our noses, and any that blows off will blow away from us as we fly!"

"Wow, that's a great idea, Daymoon. That sure

69

is brave of you," Bushhopper said, obviously impressed.

"But how much can you put on your tail?" Bluesky asked. "And most of it would blow off flying back."

"That's why ..." Daymoon smiled from one bird to the other. "That's why we'll all put a little on our tail feathers, and together, we'll bring enough back!"

Bushhopper's smile of approval quickly disappeared.

"Are you crazy? That's the stupidest idea I've ever heard!" Bushhopper looked from Bluesky to Coolbreeze for their agreement, but they seemed lost in thought. The Towhee faced Daymoon and now shouted, "I mean, that stuff is poison -- we'll all die doing it your way!"

Coolbreeze looked back at his tail. "I think Bushhopper is right. I'd lose all of it long before we made it back here -- and what stuck to our tail feathers might make us sick!"

Daymoon looked hurt.

"My Cardinal friend, I think that it is the best idea I've heard so far." Bluesky noticed the shocked expressions from Bushhopper and Coolbreeze. "However, it is much too dangerous. We might all die and none of us make it back. No, there has to be some other way ..."

Daymoon looked down sadly.

"Well, I'm glad to see you've got some sense, Bluesky," Bushhopper sang out.

"Yes, Bluesky is a smart bird," Coolbreeze agreed.

"I'll just have to think some more." Bluesky

turned to fly.

"I'll think some more too. There has to be a way," Daymoon said eagerly. "One of us will hit on a good idea if we think hard enough."

"I hope it's not you, Daymoon," Bushhopper said with a mischievous wink.

"If you weren't my friend, I think I'd peck you on the head." Daymoon laughed.

Bluesky left his friends and flew to the tree where Ol' Gray Mama and the other Doves liked to roost for the evening. He soon found them perched in the limbs of a wild cherry tree.

Bluesky settled down close to Ol' Gray Mama.

"Is something bothering you, Bluesky?" Ol' Gray Mama smiled warmly at him.

"Yes, there is. We found the poison, but now we don't know what to do. I thought once we found it, the rest would be easy." Bluesky let out a long, forlorn sigh.

"What did our wise friend Nightwind suggest?"

"He told me to talk to all the birds and ask them for ideas, and ... and he said to be positive and look for the solution -- not just look at the problem." Bluesky snuggled closer to Ol' Gray Mama.

She cooed comfortingly and put her wing around the young Mockingbird. "Sounds like good advice. Have you talked to all the birds yet?"

"No, not with Thundercloud. Nor Highclouds or Treeflower." He looked up at Ol' Gray Mama. "I'm not sure if I should bother the girls or not with this. What do you think?"

"Well now, I think the girls might have the best ideas of all." Ol' Gray Mama chuckled.

71

Bluesky laughed along with her a moment. "Yes, I guess you're right. I just figured Treeflower is busy with her eggs and mate. I just felt it might be a burden to ask her. It might make her worry, you know."

"Well, I declare, I don't think that at all. She has eggs, she's a mama ... she wants to protect them. The parental instinct is perhaps the strongest instinct, the strongest emotion, in the entire world. Perhaps you should have asked her first!"

Bluesky shook his head in wonder. "Wow, I never thought of it like that at all, but it makes sense!"

"I tell you what, go to Thundercloud first thing tomorrow. Then talk to Highclouds -- she's a Chickadee, and they're very keen birds who are quite smart in their own right. Last, go to Treeflower, and see if you two can't look at this problem with all the ideas of the others fresh in mind." Ol' Gray Mama smiled down at him.

"Yes, I like that idea."

Bluesky yawned and soon fell asleep next to Ol' Gray Mama.

The next morning, he ate breakfast as fast as possible. Then he flew off and soon found Thundercloud perched proudly in the highest branch of the tallest tree in the neighborhood. Bluesky remembered the Hawk's words and knew it was safe to approach.

But after he laid out Nightwind's words and went over the challenge before them, the Red-shouldered Hawk slowly shook his head. Just like the others, Thundercloud could think of no reasonable solution.

Soon afterward, he found the little Carolina Chickadee with several of her friends twittering in the trees. Highclouds listened intently and agreed about the nature of the dire predicament they faced, but she also had no idea how to approach a solution. She readily agreed it would be too dangerous to carry it in a beak or even in a claw.

She laughed at Daymoon's idea about everyone carrying a little on their tail feathers, although after she thought about it a minute, she did agree it was the only suggestion that had even a slight chance to succeed.

A small chance, but still a chance.

Bluesky bid her good day and flew off to find Treeflower.

In his heart, he knew that if she couldn't come up with a workable solution, then the task before them was indeed impossible.

Chapter Eight

Bluesky found Treeflower next to a small nest.

"Hello, Bluesky. Have you come to see my eggs?" The Song Sparrow smiled proudly and hopped onto the edge of her nest.

"Uh, yes, sure. I'd like to see them." Bluesky hopped beside her and peered inside.

Three whitish green eggs sat nestled in the shallow bowl of twigs, dried-up blades of grass, string, and other soft material.

Bluesky's eyes widened with surprise.

It was hard for him to fathom that baby birds were growing inside those tiny, little eggs. He shook his head, his mind not really able to grasp the idea.

"Wow, the babies must be tiny. Your eggs are so small," Bluesky said.

"Yes, but they're growing fast. Soon, they'll hatch, and we'll have three hungry babies to feed and nurture." Treeflower's smile grew wider as she looked lovingly back at her eggs.

She stepped gingerly into the nest. She gently positioned one egg with her beak and then another and then finally settled over all three. She fluffed her brown feathers out until the eggs disappeared completely from Bluesky's sight.

"Have you and Nightwind figured out how we're going to get rid of the poison yet?" she asked with concern.

Bluesky felt the impossibility of the situation

overwhelm him again. Treeflower had asked him the question with a tone of total confidence that they had an answer, but in reality he had no answer. In fact, he had come to ask for her help in answering this very question.

He stood silent, once again feeling inadequate for this great task.

She smiled at him, and Bluesky felt her trust. She expected him to save her babies from this dreadful poison, and yet, he had no idea how he could do it. He felt like such a failure.

Bluesky sighed.

"Oh, you look like you're worried about something," Treeflower said with concern in her voice.

"Well, we're still not exactly sure what we're going to do next. I'm sorry. I know you expected me to have an answer to this problem." Bluesky looked down with shame.

"That's all right, I'm sure you and the wise Owl will come up with something."

Bluesky continued to stare down at his foot.

"Have you asked the trickster Crow? I bet he'll have a good idea." Treeflower giggled.

"No, he doesn't. I asked him, and I'm not sure we can come up with an answer." Bluesky closed his eyes and hurriedly continued. "I mean, we're only birds. This is man's poison, and the stuff is guarded by those three dogs and a man with a death-stick. It just seems impossible!"

Bluesky opened his eyes and looked at Treeflower, hoping against hope that she wouldn't be disappointed in him.

She sat silently on her eggs, still gazing back at him with an expression of quiet confidence and trust.

His heart sank; he felt like he was letting her down, betraying her trust as well as all the others who'd believed in him. He didn't want to let her down. He didn't want any more birds to die. He didn't want the poison to come again on the wind and hurt anyone!

But he didn't know what to do.

"I don't know what to do, Treeflower. I'm sorry. Maybe ... maybe you can help ..."

"I'll try. What can I do?" She smiled at him, but her smile faded when Bluesky didn't smile back.

"Somehow, we've got to bring some of the poison here. We've got to bring it to the cat's dad -- er, the man KC calls Dad. Once he sees it, KC is positive he will know what to do." Bluesky shook his head forlornly.

"We can't carry it with our beaks -- that would kill us," Treeflower said, thinking out loud, "and we can't carry it with our feet. It looked too soft, like dust."

"Right. We've discussed that. Daymoon suggest we all put some on our tails and carry it that way."

Treeflower laughed with a merry warble. "I don't think that will work. Besides, even touching the poison might kill us -- or at least make us sick."

"I agree."

"So, it seems impossible." Treeflower sat in the nest deep in thought.

Suddenly, she froze.

"Are you okay?" Bluesky asked.

"One of the eggs moved! It startled me," she said with excitement.

Treeflower and Bluesky stared at each other intensely.

"I wish we could ..." she began.

Treeflower suddenly rose and stepped out of the nest. She stared at it with a strange and amazing expression in her eyes.

"What are doing?" Bluesky asked.

"See the eggs."

"Yes, I think they're beautiful."

"No, look at them."

"Yes, I see them."

"What keeps them from falling out?"

Bluesky looked all around. He bent closer and inspected them.

"Why, the nest. It holds them so they don't roll out."

"We need something like that to hold the poison."

Bluesky stared at the nest again, but this time, while he gazed intently his mind whirled with different thoughts and ideas.

"It would take several birds to carry a nest. It would be awkward to carry in flight."

"No, silly. Not a real nest." Treeflower chuckled.

"What then?"

"We need a seed-nest."

Bluesky remembered the seed-nest full of seed hanging from the window.

"That's even bigger than --"

'No! Wait." She closed her eyes tight in thought.

"You called it something else that day ... a food-nest?"

Bluesky remembered their visit to the place where people ate food. He remembered how the little boy threw out the small food-nest filled with salty crumbs of yellow sticks.

He also remembered it was very light -- Treeflower had easily carried it by herself.

"Yes! That's a fantastic idea, Treeflower!"

"We would have to set it down so the poison would spill into it first," she quickly added.

Bluesky's mind suddenly filled with ideas. "Yes, we'll have to let it sit there a long time."

"It leaks slowly -- you might have to leave it there for a day and a night even," Treeflower said.

Bluesky remembered how the wind blew the food-nest after it was empty.

"How will we keep the wind from blowing it away? It was so light, almost like a white leaf."

"You're right -- when it was empty, it was as light as a leaf." Treeflower paused, and then her eyes took on a trusting glow once again. "You'll have to ask Nightwind and Blackfeather for help on that."

"I will ask them." Bluesky turned to leave but stopped. "You know, Ol' Gray Mama told me you'd have a great idea, and she was right."

"I'm glad I could help." Treeflower smiled proudly.

Bluesky flew as fast as his wings would carry him.

He found Nightwind and Blackfeather perched near each other in the Owl's favorite tree. They both

78

flapped their wings in surprise as he zoomed up and landed beside them in a rush of sound.

"Well, well, What do we have here?" Nightwind asked with a gleam in his eye.

"I think we have a Mockingbird with an idea!" Blackfeather chuckled with delight. "Come on, then. Tell us!"

"It's Treeflower's idea actually! Here it is!" Bluesky quickly ran through Treeflower's idea, describing the paper French fry bag they had taken after the boy threw it out the car window.

When he finished, the Crow jumped up with excitement. "I've seen those things. In fact, I've eaten those tasty yellow sticks myself. They're very salty, right?"

"Yes!"

"You know, that might work. If we leave it a day or two, enough of the poison will leak into it, and then we can fly away with it. The bird carrying it will only have to touch the food-nest, not the poison inside." Blackfeather laughed confidently.

"That little Sparrow is brilliant!" Nightwind exclaimed in agreement.

"But there's one problem." Bluesky looked from Nightwind to Blackfeather.

"What's that?" Nightwind asked with inner calmness.

"When the food-nest is empty, it's as light as a leaf. The wind will blow it away after we sit it under the poison."

"He's right! The smallest breeze will blow it away." Blackfeather started pacing up and down the branch, clicking his black beak deep in thought.

"If we could only --" Bluesky began.

"Shhhh. He's thinking." Nightwind nodded at the pacing Crow.

Blackfeather continued his restless pacing for several minutes. Suddenly, he came to a complete halt. "I have it!"

Before they could ask him anything, Blackfeather flew down to the ground.

Bluesky and Nightwind peered down at him.

He poked his great beak on the ground searching for something. After a moment, Blackfeather cried out and picked up a small object. He flew back up to the branch.

Bluesky stared at Blackfeather as he placed the small object on the branch before them.

"It's a rock," Bluesky said in surprise.

"A small rock. If we put a few inside the bag, it will make it heavy enough so the wind won't move the food-nest when we set it down."

"That's brilliant!" Nightwind laughed.

"We Crows are quite the Tricksters, you know!" Blackfeather laughed proudly in return.

"And so you are!" Nightwind laughed even louder.

Bluesky grasped the idea and hopped up and down, laughing with them.

Suddenly, he remembered the dogs and Marcion.

"What about the dogs? And the death-stick?"

"Yes, let's think this through," Nightwind said. "We've got to do this with some careful forethought since we now understand the full extent of the danger we face."

"And another thing! Whoever carries the food-nest and sets it under the leaking poison needs to practice first. The bird doing it can't breathe near it! He must either hold his breath or somehow drop it while flying," Blackfeather said with great urgency.

"That is true, he'll have to fly up near it and kind of toss it -- just so!" Nightwind agreed.

"I'll carry it," Bluesky said, full of confidence. "I'll practice with it. There's something like the metal barrel in the backyard where KC lives."

"Good. Well, let's discuss the dogs and the death-stick," Nightwind said.

As the Owl and Crow went over details on how they would get the food-nest in position, Bluesky's thoughts meandered. He heard them discuss how they would need lookouts so neither Marcion nor the dogs would surprise them next time. He knew this was a great idea. They needed the most observant birds on the team to be the lookouts. They began adding more details to the plan when something clicked inside Bluesky's mind.

All at once, he realized he had completely forgotten about Dancingleaves. He'd told his Bluebird friend he would share what they discovered.

And ...

His heart began pounding like a jackhammer. He realized there was another bird he'd entirely forgotten about -- Windwhisper!

"Hey, I've got to go."

Bluesky leapt into the air.

"Where are you going?" Blackfeather called out in surprise. "We're not done planning yet."

"Let him go, old friend. You and I can put the finishing touches on this ourselves." Nightwind chuckled.

"But where are you going in such a hurry?" Blackfeather shouted again.

"I've got to go tell Dancingleaves what we found, and then, I'm going to sing with a new friend!"

Chapter Nine

"Were you scared?" Dancingleaves asked.

Bluesky admired how the bright sunshine made Dancingleaves' feathers glow a deeper shade of blue. The red feathers on his breast and sides contrasted gorgeously against his glowing blue feathers and the pure, white feathers of his belly.

Bluesky also enjoyed the comforting warmth of the sun on his own back right at this moment. As he took a deep breath, he suddenly realized Dancingleaves was waiting for him to answer.

"Oh, yes. Sorry about that. I was just admiring how blue your feathers look today."

Dancingleaves looked at him as if he were crazy.

"But, yes, I was scared at times. Especially when I tried to fly between the dog's legs and got knocked down on the ground. I was terrified at that point!" Bluesky whistled for emphasis. "I thought he had me for sure, but somehow I got away."

"You are so brave." Dancingleaves stared at Bluesky with awe.

"I don't know about all that." Bluesky shrugged and smiled with modesty.

"But you are!" Dancingleaves said with conviction. "You were confronted by three killer dogs and a crazed man with a death-stick -- that's true bravery!"

"We all faced them, not just me, and someone has to do it. Someone has to find a way to rid

83

ourselves of this terrible poison. I'm just trying to help." Bluesky nodded to himself.

Dancingleaves' words made him feel uncomfortable. Deep inside, he didn't feel brave at all. He was simply doing what had to be done.

"I couldn't do it -- no way." Dancingleaves smiled sheepishly. "I don't think most birds could do what you've done either."

"Yes, they could, if they really wanted to protect their family and friends."

"I think you're being far too modest," Dancingleaves insisted.

Bluesky stared at Dancingleaves a moment in silence as he thought about everything they had just discussed..

"We need you too, Dancingleaves. We need your help to finish this business." Bluesky's tone was earnest and sincere.

"I'd be too scared. I'd probably fall out of the sky the first time I saw one of those dogs."

"No, you wouldn't. You could do it."

"What could I do? I'm so shy, you're about the only bird I will sing or play with right now. How could I help?"

"Well now, you could ..." Bluesky paused in thought.

"See, you know I wouldn't be any help!" Dancingleaves said quickly.

"You're very observant. You love to watch the clouds, don't you?"

"Yes," Dancingleaves agreed.

"You'd make a good lookout. Before I left, Nightwind and Blackfeather decided we needed to assign certain birds to perch in strategic spots to keep a lookout and warn us of danger. You could do that!"

Dancingleaves fluttered his wings with interest. He preened the feathers on his left wing while he contemplated Bluesky's suggestion.

Bluesky waited patiently, knowing his shy friend needed more time to let his words sink into his heart. Deep inside, Bluesky knew Dancingleaves could do much more than he thought possible. He also knew the Bluebird would make an excellent lookout, maybe as good as the little Chickadee, Highclouds.

"I'll think about it, and ... and I might make a good lookout."

"I know you would." Bluesky smiled.

"Maybe ... maybe I could do that -- be a lookout."

"I'll let you know when we decide to return. The next time should be somewhat easier -- we're just going to drop the food-nest under the poison and let some fall into it for a day or two. It should be a fast mission -- in and out."

"Y-yes. That does sound easy," Dancingleaves replied hesitantly.

"I'm going to go sing with a new bird I've met." Bluesky's face grew warm with embarrassment. "Actually, I'm going to go sing with a female Mockingbird I met."

"Oh, that sounds fun."

"Um, why don't you join us?"

"I don't know. I mean, I don't know this bird and ..."

"She's a tiny Mockingbird. Really, she's smaller than you, and she's really polite and nice." Bluesky's face grew even warmer.

"She must be about as big as a large Sparrow then?" Dancingleaves asked, his interest piqued.

"Yes, about that big."

"And you say she's nice?"

"Yes, and friendly. She's kind of shy like you too, actually."

"Oh, really?"

Bluesky added this last bit more to encourage the shy bluebird come along, although Windwhisper did strike him as being somewhat shy.

"Yes, really."

"Okay, I'll come sing with you two."

Chapter Ten

The Eastern Bluebird and the Northern Mockingbird sailed through the open sky just above the islands of treetops that dotted the landscape. Above them, ragged wisps of clouds etched the sky under the power of the jet stream. Everywhere they went, birds sang and whistled, warmed by the bright sunshine.

They found Windwhisper sitting in a Dogwood tree at the end of Willow Hollow.

"I thought you'd forgotten about me," Windwhisper said, smiling happily. She stood straight up and quickly preened herself.

Bluesky admired her prettiness as he landed on the branch next to her.

She smiled even more when their eyes met. Bluesky felt his heart thumping like a jackhammer.

He noticed how beautiful her face seemed in the sunlight. She was so pretty, and her eyes sparkled like jewels.

Bluesky fluttered his wing violently as he felt himself losing his balance.

"Oh my!" Windwhisper exclaimed.

Bluesky hopped forward so he wouldn't fall over, but he completely lost his balance doing that. He fluttered his wings so fast they became a blur, almost like a hummingbird.

"Are you all right?" Windwhisper shouted with concern.

"Y-y-yes ..."

He lifted off the branch, his wings were fluttering so rapidly. He slowed them down and tried to grip the branch with his toes to keep himself still.

All at once, he fell forward and bumped into Windwhisper.

"Ohhhhh!" Bluesky groaned as he felt himself falling against her.

She cried out and landed flat on her rump.

Somehow, Bluesky managed not to fall on top of her. He finally regained his balance and hopped back a step.

"I'm so sorry!" Bluesky felt his face burning with embarrassment. He stared down at her while she hopped back on her feet. She quickly brushed her wings with her beak and checked herself out to make sure no feathers were out of place. Satisfied, she glanced up at him.

Bluesky steeled himself in case she was mad. After all, he had just bumped into her and almost knocked her off the branch.

Windwhisper started laughing.

Bluesky was shocked for a moment, and then he started chuckling. Seconds later, they were both laughing hysterically.

"I thought you were doing some kind of new dance!" Windwhisper laughed.

"I felt like I was doing a dance! A crazy dance!"

They both howled with laughter. Finally, the humor passed and they looked at each other.

"Let's see, where were we?" she asked. "Oh yes, I almost thought you'd forgotten me."

"Um, well, um, I'm sorry, but I was so busy with

Nightwind and Blackfeather." Inside, he was afraid to tell her he really had forgotten about her -- for a little while -- while they answered the perplexing questions of what to do next.

"We had to figure out our next move. I mean, it's getting a little dangerous."

Windwhisper's expression immediately changed from cheerfulness to one of apprehension.

"Yes, Bluesky is so brave!" Dancingleaves said with awe.

"Who's your friend?" Windwhisper asked.

"This is Dancingleaves." He nodded at the Bluebird. "And this is my new friend, Windwhisper."

The two birds smiled at each other.

"So, what do you mean -- dangerous?" she asked with quiet concern.

Bluesky quickly related their adventures in locating the poison. He tried to gloss over the encounter with the man and his death-stick, trying to make it sound less dangerous so as not to frighten her. He also tried to skip over the scariest parts with the dogs, but Dancingleaves kept interjecting and making him add the details until it sounded more dangerous than it actually had been. Dancingleaves also kept making it sound like he was some sort of hero.

He wound up telling her every detail of his narrow escape.

"Oh my, you must have been frightened?" Windwhisper exclaimed as he finished. "That dog almost killed you!"

"Yes, it was a bit scary, but we all got away

safely, and that's the important part," Bluesky said.

Windwhisper smiled proudly at him.

"I think you're the bravest bird I've ever met!" Her eyes sparkled with admiration as she gazed at him.

Bluesky felt more uncomfortable than ever. After all, he knew he wasn't all that brave, and he certainly wasn't any kind of hero. Deep inside, he knew he didn't deserve all these accolades that first Dancingleaves and now Windwhisper tried to shower on him.

But hearing Windwhisper say them made him feel so good inside. It made him feel ... happy ... knowing she thought him so brave -- knowing she was so proud of him.

And ...

All at once, a feeling blossomed inside his heart. *He wanted Windwhisper to like him.*

"I said the same thing!" Dancingleaves added enthusiastically.

"Yes, you're a brave bird." Windwhisper sighed. Her eyes twinkled with delight, and her smile grew wider.

Bluesky felt like he was going to melt.

"Oh, I don't know. Really, I was as scared as the next bird." His face grew so warm he thought his feathers would surely start to smoke any second.

Dancingleaves whistled out a short song, and Windwhisper sang out right after his last note and mimicked his song perfectly.

Dancingleaves laughed happily. "That was perfect, Windwhisper. You sang it better than I did!"

She laughed in return and then said, "Singing is one of the great joys of life, and singing with others only adds to that joy. I just wanted to imitate your pretty song to make you happy." She smiled at the shy Bluebird.

Bluesky then sang Dancingleaves' little ditty and added some happy trills of his own at the end.

In a few moments, all three birds filled the air with joyous sounds. Each bird sang out with their own unique talent, their own unique voice. And both Windwhisper and Bluesky, in way of all true Mockingbirds, copied each other and Dancingleaves too and embellished the songs until the melodies grew more complex and fascinating.

Bluesky couldn't contain his joy any longer.

He launched himself up into the air, all the while singing out with his entire heart and soul because he felt so happy. After flying in a great circle he came back and landed on the branch, singing all the way.

The three birds sang and sang until it seemed their entire world was filled with song and joy.

All too soon, however, their happy concert came to an end.

"Bluesky!"

Bluesky stopped in mid-note. He turned to find Blackfeather perched on a limb above all three of them. He'd never even heard the Crow fly up, much less land.

"Hi, Blackfeather. I didn't know you were there."

"Of course you didn't, not when you were singing up such a storm."

Bluesky noticed that both Dancingleaves and Windwhisper took a few steps away as they realized the large Crow was so near.

"Don't be afraid. Blackfeather is my friend."

Dancingleaves stared at Blackfeather with a mixture of puzzlement and fear. Windwhisper simply watched the Crow carefully.

"Yes, don't mind me. I'm just an old Crow." Blackfeather turned to Bluesky. "I need you to practice."

"Practice what?"

"For the mission. Daymoon and Bushhopper were given the task to find another food-nest, and they should be at KC's house soon. You've got to practice before we fly out tomorrow."

Bluesky sighed at the thought of leaving so soon, but he leapt into the air after Blackfeather took wing. He shouted back over his shoulder, "I sure had a great time. When I get back tomorrow, maybe we can sing together again!"

"Watch out for those mean dogs!" Windwhisper shouted with concern in her voice.

"Yes, take c-c-care, Bluesky," Dancingleaves called out.

"We will. Nightwind and Blackfeather and I have a plan. Things will go better this time! I just know they will!"

He caught up to Blackfeather, who flew along with slow, steady strokes of his larger wings. Bluesky settled beside him. They flew toward the house where KC lived on Willow Hollow.

"Things are going to be better this time, right?"

"We're going to try," Blackfeather replied.

Blackfeather flew on a moment in silence. Finally, he spoke again. "But I guess any time poison, dogs, and death-sticks are involved, nothing is guaranteed."

Chapter Eleven

Daymoon and Bushhopper were indeed waiting Bluesky in KC's yard. The two birds had flown to the place where they knew people went to eat food; they'd soon found one of the empty food-nests and brought it back with them. They stayed to watch while Bluesky made his practice runs and were joined by other members of the mixed flock, who stopped by to offer Bluesky encouragement.

Bluesky practiced very hard carrying the food-nest. The weight of the paper French fry bag with three pebbles inside made him feel strange as he flew through the air. He felt awkward and had trouble flying at a steady pace. He kept finding himself flying lower and lower to the ground from the weight of the pebbles. He had to struggle to regain altitude.

That was why Blackfeather and Nightwind wanted him to practice.

"You're doing better!" Daymoon encouraged him with a positive tone.

"Yes, you're flying almost normally now," Bushhopper said cheerfully.

"It's difficult. The food-nest drags me down if I rest my wings for even a second. I almost feel like I'm falling," Bluesky said, panting.

"You have to keep flying at a steady pace and not rest your wings as you would in your normal, undulating flight," Daymoon said.

"I realize that now."

Bluesky practiced and practiced. When he flew over KC's house, he saw her curled up in her usual chair watching him attentively.

Two hours passed quickly.

"Okay, it looks like you've got that part down," Blackfeather called out from a tree where he had been quietly observing.

"Whew, I'm glad that's over. I'm tired from carrying that thing." Bluesky settled down near the chair where KC rested.

"Now it's time for the hard part." Blackfeather flew down and stood next to Bluesky, his jet-black form towering over the Mockingbird.

"The hard part?"

"Remember, we can't breathe the poison, or it will kill us." Blackfeather eyed him carefully.

"I remember."

"And we don't want to touch it either."

"I know."

"So, you've got to practice flying in low and fast and then dropping the bag at the bottom of the barrel with the open end facing up in order to catch the poison."

"Oh, is that all?" Bluesky asked sarcastically.

"You also need to hold your breath the entire time while you make the drop."

Bluesky's beak dropped open.

"Whoa, that does sound hard," Tootight said as he dropped down beside them. "And I bet you thought you just learned the hard part, eh?" The rotund Robin winked.

Bluesky sighed and shook his head. "I don't know ..."

"That's why you've got to practice," Blackfeather said with a fatherly tone.

"But dropping it from a dive and making sure the open end is facing up? And holding my breath the entire time!"

"See the trash can over there?" Blackfeather nodded at it.

"Yes, that's why you're practicing at my house," KC purred. "Dad leaves the trash can here in the back yard every day except for one day each week. You can practice dropping the food-nest at the bottom of it."

"See the stain at the bottom?" Blackfeather asked.

Yes," Bluesky replied.

"Pretend that stain is poison leaking out. Your goal is to drop the food-nest right there."

Bluesky looked closely at green trash can. It did resemble the rusting metal barrel in shape, though it was a bit smaller and instead of being made out of metal was made of plastic.

He focused on the stain near the bottom. The dark stain was only about twice the size of the bag; he would have to aim carefully.

"Okay, I'll do my best."

Bluesky waited a few moments to catch his breath and rest up from his exertions. After a few minutes, he was ready.

He hopped over to where he had dropped the bag after his last practice flight. He grasped the edge of the bag with his claws and leapt into the air. He flew around and around the back yard as the other birds cheered him on.

Once he finally got up enough speed, he turned and flew as fast as he could toward the trash can.

"When you get close enough, drop it!" Blackfeather shouted.

"Remember, the bag will drop fast with those pebbles in it," Daymoon called out.

Bluesky kept his eyes focused on the stain as he picked up even more speed.

As he approached the trash can, he dove lower and accelerated even more. When the trash can and the stain filled his vision, he suddenly flew straight up.

Right at that moment, he released the food-nest.

Bluesky flew on, over the top of the trash can. As he passed it, he heard a loud noise.

He turned in time to see the food-nest bounce off the side of the trash can and land a few feet away.

Bluesky slowed down and came back to land next to Blackfeather, Daymoon, Bushhopper, and Tootight on the picnic table. He shook his head.

"You're just going to need more practice. You'll learn how to do it," Tootight said with encouragement.

Bluesky rested a few minutes and tried again.

This time, he dropped the bag too soon, and it landed on the ground even farther away than his first attempt.

He tried again.

And again.

Finally, after his fifth attempt, he began to understand how the food-nest acted when he dropped it, or, more accurately, he learned how to leverage the weight of the stones inside the bag as he dove and to use that to help aim it.

With each new attempt, he was dropping the bag closer to the target until at last he understood just how to let the bag go so the weight of the pebbles would help guide it to the target spot.

Soon, he could make it land right next to the stain almost every time, and as they'd hoped, the weight of the pebbles in the bottom kept the open end facing upward even after it landed.

"Hooray!" Coolbreeze squeaked. The Ruby-throated Hummingbird zoomed around the other birds who were watching from the table.

"Yes, you've got it!" Daymoon cheered.

"Good show!" Bushhopper shouted.

"Well then, I guess we're ready," Blackfeather said.

Bluesky landed next to all of them. "What's the plan?"

"Nightwind and I talked it over, and we felt the food-nest should sit at least two full days in order for enough of the poison to spill into it, but we don't want too much in it or it might hurt you." Blackfeather smiled benevolently at Bluesky.

"I'm glad you're looking out for me." Bluesky laughed.

"We realized you would need to practice since songbirds don't normally carry objects much bigger than a small stick, although this food-nest is fairly light in itself. You're a good bird to volunteer for this job."

"I'm used to carrying it now."

"And you can quickly drop it, but most

important, you can drop it with a fair degree of accuracy."

"Yes, I think so."

"But remember, hold your breath during the final run. You don't want to breathe the air when you are close to the poison."

"I know. I've been holding my breath as I neared the trash can every time." Bluesky smiled proudly.

"We're going to have Rainday and Highclouds sit in the tree near the trailer to keep a lookout for the dogs, and they can watch for the man as well. We're going to fly in early, so we hope he will still be asleep." Blackfeather nodded.

"What about us?" Daymoon asked.

"You and Bushhopper will watch in those bushes between the poison and the woods." Blackfeather nodded at Coolbreeze. "You and Treeflower will keep watch on the other side of the poison -- the way that leads back here."

"Got it!" Coolbreeze squeaked enthusiastically.

"Thundercloud will soar high above us and keep watch as he did before."

"Got it," Bluesky said.

"We meet at first light tomorrow."

"Why is that?" Bushhopper asked.

"All birds know that people migrate almost every day. Right?" Blackfeather cocked his head to one side and watched Bushhopper closely for his reactions.

"You're right -- we all know that. Every morning, people get in their cars and migrate. When the sun sets, they all migrate back home." Bushhopper nodded proudly.

"It's not as simple as that." Blackfeather chuckled knowingly. "They don't migrate every single day. There are two days they don't migrate."

Bushhopper thought a moment and then laughed out loud. "You're right!"

"So, we need to meet early before Marcion migrates. He should still be asleep or just rousing."

"That's good planning," Daymoon said.

"We'll meet at the pine trees next to the large road. We all need to be there before the sun rises above horizon." Blackfeather looked intently at Bluesky. "You will carry the food-nest."

Bluesky nodded with rising excitement.

They quickly went over their positions and responsibilities a second time until Blackfeather felt certain everyone knew their job. As the sun started to set, they all dispersed to their perches.

Bluesky found the flock of Doves in their usual tree. He settled next to Ol' Gray Mama and tried to go to sleep.

Sleep, however, would not come.

He sat there a long time, just thinking about the task before him and all the birds depending on him to save them from the poison. As tiredness gradually filled his mind, it suddenly seemed all too much. It was so overwhelming -- he could never do it, no matter how hard he tried. After all, he was just a one-legged Mockingbird.

In that quiet place somewhere between wakefulness and sleep, Bluesky cried out in fear. He cried out the same way he had the night his mother died.

"Now, now, Bluesky. What's bothering you?"

100

Ol' Gray Mama said softly from the darkness beside him.

"I can't do it," Bluesky whispered sadly.

"Pshaw! Yes, you can. You're just tired, little bird," she said in a comforting tone. "All our problems seem so much more daunting at night. We're tired, and we feel so much more vulnerable then."

"But it is a terribly difficult task before me! And everyone is depending on me! If I fail, more birds will die!" Bluesky closed his eyes, fighting back his tears.

"Listen to me, Bluesky. Try to push away your problems right now. Get some rest tonight, and tomorrow, when you're refreshed, they won't seem quite so bad."

Bluesky sighed deeply. He took a breath and spoke. "I will try not to think of my problems right now."

"Think pleasant thoughts -- think about your friends and the good times. It will help you to relax and fall asleep," she said.

"I have lots of friends now, don't I?" Bluesky smiled.

"Yes, you do, and they're all going to help you and support you."

"I need all the help I can get ..."

"We all do." Ol' Gray Mama put her wing around Bluesky.

Bluesky closed his eyes and leaned against her comforting feathers.

"And remember, little bird. Never think about your problems at night when you're tired and feeling vulnerable. They will always seem insurmountable then." Ol' Gray Mama hummed softly a moment. "Focus your mind on happy, pleasant things at night. Leave the problems for the day, when your mind and body can fully deal with them."

"I will."

She hummed again and soothed Bluesky while he focused his mind on happy things.

Soon, Ol' Gray Mama was asleep.

Each time he was about to fall asleep, though, he'd suddenly see the man aiming the death-stick right at him, and right as he turned to fly away, the three dogs would appear seemingly out of nowhere. Everywhere he turned, the death-stick was pointed at him or a dog's jaws snapped.

In the air around these surreal images, a strange and poisonous mist reached inexorably for him ...

He couldn't get away, no matter how hard he tried.

Bluesky kept waking up with a startled jump, but somehow he fell asleep, albeit it was a fitful slumber filled with those same nightmarish images chasing him ...

Chapter Twelve

He woke up and left his perch beside Ol' Gray Mama while the stars still glittered in the velvety sky. He flew over and grabbed the food-nest where he'd left it at KC's house. As he flew up into the air, the familiar humming of Coolbreeze's wings came to his ears.

"Let's go!" Coolbreeze squeaked eagerly.

Daymoon and Bushhopper joined them, and soon after so did Tootight and Treeflower. They quickly reached the row of pine trees next to the large road, where they heard Blackfeather call out.

"CAW! CAW! CAW!"

They found the branch on which he perched and quickly landed. The rest of the birds were already there in the same tree with the old Crow.

Treeflower and Highclouds sat together with Rainday and Blackfeather.

Up in the highest branch, Thundercloud stood tall and proud.

"We're going to fly right in and fly right out. We're going to do it fast and silently. That way, no one will ever know we were there. Does everyone understand?" Blackfeather looked to each bird in turn.

Bluesky and the others nodded as Blackfeather's gaze fell upon them.

"Good. Thundercloud is going to fly cover for us. As soon as he's at altitude, we fly like the wind."

Blackfeather looked up and cried out a single

103

time.

Thundercloud spread his great wings and leapt into the air.

Bluesky and the others watched as the magnificent Hawk flapped his wings with a strong and steady motion and flew higher and higher. Several minutes passed whiles they watched intently.

Far up in the sky, Thundercloud spread his wings wide and sailed on the morning breeze while the rim of the shining sun slipped above the eastern horizon.

"Let's fly!" Blackfeather shouted.

Even though Bluesky carried the weight of the food-nest and the pebbles inside it, it seemed they crossed the small forest in a very short time. He guessed it was because they had already flown this route and everything was somewhat familiar now.

The field of tall grass soon appeared, and he knew the trailer and the poison were on the far side.

The sun had just cleared the line of tree tops and risen into the sky when they reached their target.

Rainday and Highclouds flew quickly to the solitary tree near Marcion's trailer. Bluesky and Blackfeather landed on a patch of bare ground and watched until they saw them settle on two branches.

Highclouds twittered that she and Rainday were in place and keeping watch.

"Any sign of dogs?" Bluesky whistled back.

"None."

"Now, it's your turn." Blackfeather nodded at Daymoon and Bushhopper.

They leapt into the air and flew over to a group

104

of bushes between the poison hill and the woods beyond. Bluesky and the others felt that their post was especially important since it was at that spot where Marcion had surprised them before. They didn't want him surprising them again.

As Bluesky and Blackfeather watched, Daymoon settled among the green leaves of one bush while Bushhopper alighted on another.

They heard Daymoon's crystal-clear 'cheer' notifying them they were in place.

Bluesky and Blackfeather looked up into the sky. High above, Thundercloud sailed effortlessly in large circles with his keen eyes on the lookout while he flew cover.

Right at that moment, Thundercloud's piercing 'kee-har' echoed across the sky.

"He's got good eyes -- he knew we were looking up at him just now." Blackfeather chuckled.

They glanced out toward the middle of the vast field of brown grass.

"CAW!" Blackfeather shouted once.

A flute-like twinkling answered unseen from among the waves of grass.

Treeflower was in place, keeping watch for any danger from that side.

"CAW!" Blackfeather shouted again in the opposite direction

A high-pitched, squeaking answered; Coolbreeze was ready and watching.

"CAW!"

The cackling laugh of a Robin answered in reply. Tootight was in place among the grass and ready.

Blackfeather turned to Bluesky.

"It's your turn now, Mockingbird. You know what to do."

Bluesky swallowed uneasily and sat frozen in place. Some powerful, invisible force kept him from moving. In fact, he had trouble even breathing. He couldn't understand why he couldn't force himself to move. In the next instant, he understood.

He was scared.

He fought against it; he struggled against the paralyzing feeling that numbed his mind and pierced his heart with dread. He knew what had to be done. Bluesky took a deep breath and steeled his heart.

Finally, he nodded.

His heart pounded like a Woodpecker gone crazy on a rotten tree full of juicy bugs. He tried to act normally, but an intense nervous energy surged throughout his body.

"It's okay, just relax." Blackfeather smiled pleasantly and nodded. "Do it just like you practiced yesterday."

"Sure." Bluesky smiled weakly.

He took another deep breath and hoped his heart would slow down a bit. He took one last, deep breath, let it out slowly, and then hopped over to the food-nest lying on the ground. With another hop he stood on it. He clenched his toes until his nails dug into the paper.

With a determined expression, he leapt into the air with the food-nest firmly in his grasp.

He flew away from the target in order to make a long circle and come back around to start his dive.

106

He flapped his wings harder and harder as he gained altitude. He was soon flying as fast as his wings would allow.

Now that he was moving, he didn't feel the paralyzing fear as much. He concentrated on his task and turned around until the hill and the barrel with the poison came into sight.

Bluesky started into his dive.

He quickly picked up speed.

The closer he got, the lower he flew until he was soon only a few feet above the bare ground. He noticed with a blinding flash of panic that he had entered the 'dead zone.'

At just that moment, the rancid scent of rotting bodies came to his nostrils.

He remembered he was supposed to hold his breath.

Bluesky lost his balance and started to tumble to his right. He tried to hold his breath but instead sucked in a big breath.

He gagged and choked as he turned and flapped his wings harder.

He aborted his dive and turned away.

While he flew away from the poison, he realized the entire world was moving unsteadily all around him. He felt so dizzy, almost as if he were falling asleep ...

He beat his wings faster, trying to escape the strange feeling that gripped his senses, but the world grew even crazier around him.

Suddenly, he realized it was his senses that were somehow playing tricks inside his mind.

He flew away from the poison hill, flying faster

with each beat of his heart, but he couldn't fly exactly ... All at once, he dove straight down into a bunch of grass. Although he flew into the grass at full speed, the softness of the grass softened his crash.

He lay on the crushed grass a moment, too dizzy even to lift his head. Finally, the world seemed to slow down. Bluesky pushed his leg under his body and tried to stand.

"Hold on -- wait until the dizziness subsides."

He looked up and saw Blackfeather standing next to him.

"Forgot to hold your breath, eh?" He chuckled in a low tone.

"Y-yes."

"That's okay. Take your time. You'll remember the next time. The dizziness should pass soon."

Bluesky nodded.

Blackfeather was right: with each passing moment, the dizziness slowly faded away.

"Dog! Dog!"

The dizziness evaporated instantly with the warning cry from Highclouds.

"Where, where?" Bluesky asked frantically.

"Must be from over near the trailer. Get yourself ready -- you've got to put the food-nest in place on this next flight," Blackfeather whispered with great urgency. "We've only got time for one more run!"

Bluesky hopped up. The dizziness suddenly returned, and he swayed unsteadily a moment.

"Get your bearings, Bluesky," Blackfeather whispered.

"Dog! Dog!" Highclouds twittered with a

worried tone.

In the distance, a large dog barked angrily.

"Time to go!" Blackfeather commanded.

Bluesky hopped over and grabbed the food-nest.

In a flurry of movement, he leapt into the air.

As he flew over the grass, he heard a burst of movement behind him.

"CAW! CAW! CAW!"

Bluesky looked over his shoulder.

Blackfeather flew into the air just as King leapt at him from behind a bush.

Over to Bluesky's right, another dog barked. To his left, he heard a third growl ominously.

Bluesky flew higher and faster.

He had to take a big turn in order to get up to speed and make his final run. He had to be flying low and fast in order to drop the bag at the exact spot at the base of the barrel.

He only had one chance.

All around him, he heard his friends whistle out more warnings. In a flash of understanding, he realized the three dogs had encircled all of them and were attacking together.

Angry growls and frightened bird calls filled the morning air.

Highclouds and Rainday were calling out warnings nonstop now. They were safe, high up in the tree, but they cried out to all the others warnings about first one dog and then another as it attacked.

Bluesky made his turn and went into his dive.

He focused on his target, the small hill.

Seconds later, the outline of the rusted barrel grew visible. He focused on the whitish stain at the bottom of the rusting barrel. On the ground, he saw a small mound of white poison.

On top of that small pile of poison was where he needed to drop the food-nest -- with the open end facing up to catch more as it fell.

Bluesky increased his speed.

This time, he took in a deep breath and held it.

He again flew over the 'dead zone,' but his eyes didn't take note of any of the bones or carcasses that littered the ground. He held his breath, keeping out the stench of death and the wisps of poison that had clouded his senses the first time.

He focused solely on his target as he dove lower and lower.

His heart pounded harder with each second that he closed on his target.

Almost there ...

He gripped the food-nest tighter and prepared to drop it.

Almost ...

He dropped lower until his eyes were level with the stains near the middle of the barrel.

Now!

He pulled up and let go of the food-nest at the same time.

At just that moment, the heartrending sound of a death-stick split the air like a bolt of lightning.

"CAW! CAW! CAW!"

Bluesky started to tumble but somehow got his wings back in rhythm.

The death-stick thundered again.

Bluesky flew over the top of the hill and beyond at top speed. He continued holding his breath, but the world began to spin again.

He turned toward the sound of the death-stick and watched in horror as the man aimed the death-stick and fired again.

A bird fell out of the tree.

"No!" Bluesky shouted frantically. He sucked in a big breath and flapped his wings harder. He turned toward the falling bird.

"Keep flying!" Blackfeather shouted. "You can't help her now!"

Marcion quickly reloaded the shotgun.

"It's a different death-stick," Blackfeather shouted. "Its power cannot reach as far into the sky, but it spreads death in a wider area."

Bluesky didn't care. He only knew he wanted to help Highclouds.

He turned toward her.

As he flew lower, he saw her limp form lying on the ground at the base of the tree.

Suddenly, the death-stick thundered a fourth time.

Bluesky watched in horror-struck with total disbelief as the branches splintered and leaves erupted all around Rainday. A second later, the lifeless form of the Cedar Waxwing fell to the ground.

"No!" Bluesky shouted.

Bluesky couldn't think. He couldn't feel anything but disbelief and a mind-numbing shock, and yet, right before his eyes, two of his friends lay dead on the ground ...

They were so still.

"Don't do it!"

Bluesky heard Blackfeather's voice somewhere behind him, but he flew on. He flew just above the grass and headed straight for his fallen friends.

As he neared them, he looked up and saw Marcion pointing the death-stick right at him.

Suddenly, he was knocked to the ground.

"Stupid dog! I could'a shot yew!"

Everything went dark a moment for Bluesky. He couldn't breathe. He couldn't move. He couldn't ...

"I'm going to kill you this time, bird."

Bluesky opened his eyes.

The black dog named Bear stood over him. Bluesky felt the dog's hot breath wash over his face.

"Jack told us you'd come back," he growled.

"We're trying to get rid of the poison. Why do you want to hurt us?" Bluesky pleaded.

"This is our land. We don't allow anyone here."

"Don't you want the poison gone?"

"Just don't go near it. We all know that."

Bear's fangs came closer.

Bluesky closed his eyes.

"CAW! CAW! CAW!"

He opened his eyes.

Blackfeather was almost stationary in the air, flapping his great wings right in the face of the snarling Rottweiler.

Bear snapped at the Crow.

"Fly, Bluesky! Fly!"

Blackfeather flapped his wings and lifted himself up just above Bear's fangs.

Bluesky rolled over and hopped up.

Blackfeather flapped harder and rose higher.

"Git out of the way, dawg! I can shoot that crow

dead if yew jest git!"

Bluesky leapt into the air.

"Stay low and fly fast!" Blackfeather shouted

"What about the death-stick?"

Thundercloud's cry pierced the air.

Bluesky looked up and saw the mighty Hawk diving. The Red-shouldered Hawk swooped right over Marcion's head. Marcion dropped to his knees as he dropped the shotgun and covered his head.

Bluesky flew straight for the line of trees. It was only when he entered the protective shadows that he looked around.

Blackfeather flew alongside him, matching him wing stroke for wing stroke.

"What about Highclouds? And Rainday?" Bluesky asked breathlessly.

"Keep flying. Just keep flying."

Chapter Thirteen

"It's all my fault."

Bluesky stared at the ground, his heart burning with pain and regret. He knew it was his fault that Highclouds and Rainday were dead. If only he had remembered to hold his breath, then he could have dropped the food-nest on his first attempt and everyone would have made it home safely.

But, no, he had failed.

His mind flooded with memories of the past -- heart-struck pictures of his painful past.

After all, it was his fault that his family had broken up. If he had been born with two legs like a normal bird, his father would have loved him and kept the family together. Even worse, he knew his mother's death was a direct result of his family's breakup.

It seemed that in everyone's life he touched, he only caused pain and sorrow.

Now, Highclouds and Rainday were dead because of him ...

Bluesky cried bitterly.

"No, it's not your fault, my young Mockingbird," Thundercloud said, his deep voice full of sympathy and comfort. "You did not aim the death-stick and kill our two friends."

"I should have placed the food-nest on my first try!" Bluesky's tears fell down his feathered cheeks like rain.

"You did your best. That's all anyone can do,"

Treeflower said, her voice choked with emotion.

"The dogs were expecting us," Blackfeather said, his eyes far off. "I had not considered their lust for killing so powerful that they actually hoped and expected us to return."

"Well, I guess there's no way we can go back now," Bushhopper said with a sigh. "They'll kill all of us for certain, if we do."

Everyone fixed their eyes on Bushhopper.

"We have to go back and finish our mission," Thundercloud said firmly. "We don't want Highclouds and Rainday to have died in vain, do we?"

"And the poison is still there. The next east wind will bring death to our friends and family once more. We've got to finish this," Blackfeather added.

"They're right," Coolbreeze said sadly. "We've got to go back."

"Are you crazy?" Bushhopper cried out in shock. "We'll be killed! How can we get away from a death-stick? And the dogs! They'll be waiting again!"

"We'll have to plan this last mission carefully, very carefully," Blackfeather said in a hushed tone.

"You'll have to do it without me then! I'm not going back!" Bushhopper leapt into the air and flew away before anyone could reply.

Bluesky watched tiredly while the Towhee fly off into the trees.

Daymoon looked at the others. "I'm sorry. I'm sure Bushhopper doesn't really mean it. He's just ... scared." Daymoon sighed with a forlorn expression. "I'm scared too, to tell the truth."

"We're all scared," Thundercloud said.

"I can't imagine you being scared," Daymoon said as he looked up at the mighty Hawk. "You're so strong and powerful."

"I was scared too, but we had a mission to complete."

"I want to thank you," Bluesky said as he shook his tears away. "You saved my life. You dove right on top of the man and made him drop his death-stick."

"He saved both our lives," Blackfeather said with a smile. "I thank you as well, brave Hawk!"

"I saw you take on the dog for Bluesky, and I saw the man aim his death-stick at both of you. I dove on the man, hoping to surprise him. My bold attack did just that, and he dropped the death-stick." Thundercloud's baleful eyes narrowed. "But that won't work a second time."

"You're the bravest bird I've ever met," Bluesky said with sincerity.

"You were brave too, although a bit foolish, trying to help Highclouds and Rainday," Thundercloud said.

"I-I just wish I'd finished the drop the first time ..."

Treeflower gasped.

Everyone turned to her.

"Did you put the food-nest in place the second time?" she asked, her voice edged with fear.

"I don't know," Bluesky said. "The dogs attacked right when I let it go. Everything happened so fast after that ..."

"I only saw it falling toward the barrel,"

Blackfeather said. "I didn't see where it landed."

"I saw it."

Everyone turned to Thundercloud.

"I saw it land."

Thundercloud's hooked beak opened in a smile. "It fell right next to the barrel, in the middle of the spill, and its open end was upright, exactly in place to catch the poison when more of it falls."

"You did it!" Coolbreeze squeaked proudly. "You did it, Bluesky!"

Bluesky closed his eyes tight, fighting his tears. He spoke, his voice full of sadness. "I'm glad ..."

"What do we do now?" Tootight asked.

"We've got to wait at least two days to let enough fall into the food-nest." Blackfeather paused in thought. "But the dogs and Marcion are more dangerous than we imagined. We must meet with Nightwind and consider our next move carefully."

"You and Bluesky should meet with the wise Owl," Thundercloud said. "He is our counselor."

"I think you should meet with us too." Blackfeather nodded. "You were able to observe everything from on high. We will need you there as we consult together. We'll have questions about the layout of every tree and bush near that poison hill. We're going to have to use everything to our advantage."

"I'll meet you tonight after the sun sets into the western sky. I'll meet you at Nightwind's tree!" Thundercloud took wing and soared into the wind.

"Bluesky, we need you there too." Blackfeather watched him attentively.

Bluesky sighed. "Yes, I'll meet you there."

117

Blackfeather spread his wings, leapt into the air, and flew away.

"I'm going after Bushhopper. I'll talk with him and ... try to calm him down." Daymoon spread his scarlet wings and flew after his best friend.

Bluesky looked around at Treeflower, Tootight, and Coolbreeze. They watched him silently in return.

Finally, he spoke. "I'll go alone. Nobody else has to go."

"No way!" Tootight said with a cackling laugh. "We're a team now. We'll go together."

"That's very noble of you," Treeflower said with a twinkle in her eyes, "but Tootight's right. It's going to take all of us. We'll help you, We'll all see this through."

"She's right!" Coolbreeze squeaked earnestly. He zipped through the air and circled all of them three times. "Nightwind and Blackfeather will come up with a plan, and we'll all go and bring back the food-nest, and this whole thing will be done!"

"I wish it was as easy as that ..." Bluesky said sadly. "I wonder now which is more dangerous -- the *Death on the Wind* or the man and his death-stick?"

"His dogs are pretty bad too!" Tootight added quickly. "I think we need to get rid of them all!"

They all laughed briefly.

"You laugh at everything, don't you?" Coolbreeze asked.

"Well, yeah. They say you live longer if you laugh a lot. Maybe that's why Robins live so long!" Tootight smiled broadly.

Everyone chuckled.

"See, we're all in this together," Treeflower said in her sweet voice. "We're going to finish this, and everything will be all right."

Bluesky paused in thought. "I didn't think anyone would ... would actually die ..."

A terrible silence filled the air. They all looked at Bluesky, but the one-legged Mockingbird only stared down at the ground.

A short time later, Bluesky bid them all good-bye and flew off to find Dancingleaves and Windwhisper.

He wondered again why everything had to start turning so bad just when he had started making friends -- especially now that he had met Windwhisper.

Every time he thought about her, his heart sang out with joy. It was almost too much to hope that she would like him in return, and yet every time they met, she seemed to enjoy his company as much as he enjoyed hers.

It was like they were made for each other!

He found Windwhisper sitting with her parents. He didn't tell her of the tragic outcome of their mission. He only asked if she would come with him so he could tell her and Dancingleaves at the same time what had happened.

It seemed to Bluesky that she sensed something was wrong, but she didn't press him with questions. Instead, she followed him quietly to Dancingleaves' usual perch.

Dancingleaves sat on top of a telephone pole overlooking the street. He sang out with a happy song as Bluesky and Windwhisper landed nearby.

"Hello!" Dancingleaves said cheerfully.

Bluesky smiled back at the Bluebird in a sad kind of way.

"What's wrong?" Dancingleaves asked with concern. He turned to Windwhisper, but she simply shrugged and looked at Bluesky with a worried expression.

"I'm afraid I have bad news."

Dancingleaves and Windwhisper froze, each holding their breath.

"W-what happened?" Windwhisper finally asked when Bluesky remained ominously silent.

"Two birds died today."

"Oh, no!" Windwhisper said with a hush.

Bluesky told them the entire sad story.

Windwhisper stood perfectly still, hanging on his every word. Dancingleaves also listened with rapt attention.

As Bluesky spoke, he watched their faces. He expected to see expressions of sadness and shock, and both birds expressed those emotions silently while they listened with unblinking intensity. When he reached the part where Highclouds and Rainday were killed, their expressions changed to fear.

Bluesky waited.

After a few moments of silent contemplation, Dancingleaves' eyes narrowed and his expression turned hard.

It was the same with Windwhisper. Her expression of sadness changed to fear and then to determination, perhaps even tinged with anger.

Bluesky finished with how Blackfeather and

120

Thundercloud saved his life and how they all escaped.

"It must have been terrible," Dancingleaves said with a steady voice.

As Bluesky looked from Dancingleaves back to Windwhisper, he noticed how she stared so hard at him. Her eyes burned into him, full of emotion. It was almost like ...

"What happens now?" Dancingleaves asked.

"We're going to consult with Nightwind. We're going to plan our last mission as carefully as we can."

"Then, you are going back, right?" Dancingleaves' tone was matter-of-fact, unhurried.

"Yes. We can't let their death be in vain. Besides, the poison is still there, a danger to all birds. We've got finish this." Bluesky sighed.

"I want to help."

Bluesky was shocked at Dancingleaves' words. He stared at the Bluebird wordlessly. Something burned inside Bluesky's heart, and seconds later he knew what it was -- admiration.

"I'm glad you want to help us," Bluesky said with a smile. It was the first time he'd smiled since they had returned.

"I want to help too." Windwhisper smiled tentatively at him.

Bluesky felt panic.

In his mind's eye, he saw Marcion pointing the death-stick at Windwhisper. He heard the sharp report, and he saw her fall to the ground dead ... just like Highclouds.

"I-I don't know w-what you could do," he

stammered.

"I can help. I want to help!" she said emphatically. "Please, let me."

"We both want to help," Dancingleaves said with a great calmness.

"I just don't want either of you to get hurt," Bluesky's eyes pleaded with them. "I couldn't bear to see either of you hurt ..."

"But you've put your life in danger twice now, and you've come back," Windwhisper said.

Bluesky thought quickly.

She was right, of course. They weren't going to go back until they had planned out their every move and the safest way to retrieve the food-nest. Perhaps there was something each could do that wouldn't put them at the front lines of danger?

"When I meet with Nightwind and the others, I'll tell them you both want to help. We'll need more lookouts, I'm sure. I'll let you know tomorrow."

Windwhisper smiled at him with a twinkle in her eyes. "I'm glad you're going to let me go with you."

Bluesky felt a burning in his heart, and quickly a feeling of panic erupted inside again. He couldn't bear the thought of her getting hurt in any way, and yet he was proud that she wanted to help.

He wanted her help.

"I am too," Dancingleaves said. "I'm kind of surprised at myself, but something happened inside me when you told me how those birds died. I-I want to do something now. I feel like I need to do something."

"You will," Bluesky said with a smile. "I'm sure

you can help -- both of you."

"And with those terrible dogs and the man with the death-stick ..." Dancingleaves paused a moment and added, "You're going to need all the birds you can get ..."

Chapter Fourteen

"This is not going to be easy," Blackfeather said in a low hush.

In the midst of the small patch of woods off Willow Hollow, Blackfeather, Thundercloud, and Bluesky perched on the ground next to the trunk of the great poplar tree. On the lowest branch, Nightwind peered from among the lengthening shadows caused by the setting sun.

"Life is never easy," Nightwind said.

"Don't talk in circles to me right now! This is serious business -- deadly serious." Blackfeather shook his great beak.

"How can any bird talk circles and confuse the great trickster, Blackfeather?" Nightwind chuckled knowingly.

"We're going to need every bird in this endeavor, Nightwind. This is a dangerous business! We're going to need you there."

"I will do my part." Nightwind nodded.

"I'm afraid more birds are going to die before this is over."

"We've got to do everything in our power to prevent that," Nightwind replied quickly.

"Death flies all around that crazy man's land ... I just don't know." Blackfeather shook his head.

"Be crafty, be swift. Trust your eye, trust your wing -- and most of all, trust your heart. Remember, you're not there to kill -- although your enemies will try to kill you. They fight you with their terrible

124

weapons. Your weapons are more powerful, though you do not yet realize it," Nightwind said mysteriously.

"What weapons do we have? Our claws? Our beaks? They are no match for a death-stick and monster dogs!" Thundercloud replied harshly.

"You fight with your heart and your soul and your spirit."

Thundercloud's eyes narrowed in thought. Slowly, he nodded agreement, but then his expression turned hard. "But you're not going to come with us -- you're not going to be there to help Bluesky!" Blackfeather said angrily.

"I have already helped him. Actually, I've helped him more than you may ever know."

"This will take trickery, it will take strength, and it will take courage! And the only way to display courage is to go along with us!" Blackfeather shouted. "I will be there; some of my Crows will be there! The Hawk will be there! The Cardinal and the Towhee and the Bluebird and the Robin, and, yes, even the tiny Hummingbird will face this danger. We will go, and this one-legged Mockingbird will lead us!"

Nightwind blinked his eyes slowly, but he did not say a word.

"Even a stupid cat, the enemy of birds, is willing to go with us and face the unseen death as well as these monster dogs and their crazed leader!"

"I will do my part, when it is time."

"A coward watches from afar!" Blackfeather shouted.

"A coward runs away ..." Nightwind smiled.

Blackfeather walked angrily around the base of the large poplar tree. He paced around for several minutes in silent agitation.

Bluesky sat quietly, listening intently, but he was afraid to say a word while these two old and wise birds argued back and forth.

Finally, Blackfeather cried out, "Listen, this man has a death-stick. He can shoot birds clear out of the sky. These dogs are killers; they kill simply for the thrill of it. On top of that, somehow this one-legged Mockingbird has got to get some of this man-poison and carry it back to a man with the help of a cat, so that man, who caused the problem anyway, can remove the poison. Even the act of carrying the poison may kill him -- and us! It's a huge problem!"

"You see the challenges clearly, trickster. You see the strengths of the enemy, you understand them. Now, use that knowledge and understanding -- it is more powerful than all the weapons they possess."

"You must come with us and fight them this time."

"I will act, but only at the precise time. I must remain in the shadows until then." Nightwind's eyes narrowed.

Blackfeather stared at the Owl a long time in stunned silence.

"I am afraid to die."

Nightwind, Blackfeather, and Thundercloud turned to Bluesky after he spoke.

Bluesky felt his heart quiver with fear. Icy fear gripped him; his heart grew cold and seemed to skip beats although somehow it beat even faster. He felt an overpowering urge to fly away -- far away from everything.

"Everyone is afraid to die," Nightwind answered softly.

"But I don't know if I can do this... and I may die simply by carrying the poison -- Blackfeather said it." Bluesky looked down in shame. "I want to live."

"Do you love your friends?" Nightwind smiled with a glowing kindness in his large eyes.

"I do, and I don't want any more birds to die," Bluesky said quickly and firmly as he looked into Nightwind's eyes. He looked back down in shame. "I want to finish this mission, but I don't want to die either ..."

"There is no greater expression of love than giving your life on behalf of your friends." Nightwind smiled with softness in his eyes. "Every bird living in this area is depending upon you and your flock, Bluesky. All of your friends are depending on you. Even if you die, your love will live on."

Bluesky swayed, nervously standing on his leg. He looked over at Thundercloud.

"One should die as one has have lived."

Thundercloud spread his mighty wings wide and held them out in a show of strength. He peered from Nightwind to Blackfeather and over to Bluesky with his large, piercing eyes.

"One should die as one has lived," he repeated in his deep, bass voice.

Bluesky thought the words over in his mind. He

127

breathed deeply and then flapped his wings vigorously, as if he were fighting off some unseen enemy.

"I am willing to give my life so others will live. I do love them -- as the Hawk loves his own and defends them at all costs. I will do the same!" He flapped his wings even harder.

Nightwind walked over, put his wing around Bluesky's shoulders, and hugged him tightly.

"Of course, Nightwind is right. Giving your life is the greatest sacrifice," Blackfeather said matter-of-factly from where he stood. He coughed, clearing his throat with a great show. "However, there are also certain advantages to getting this done with every one of us living to a ripe, old age -- including Bluesky."

Bluesky looked from Blackfeather to Nightwind a moment.

"I like Blackfeather's idea better," Bluesky said.

Nightwind broke out in hearty laughter. "And so do I!"

"Blackfeather makes a good point, and I hope none of us loses our life in this dangerous endeavor, but we must be willing to sacrifice everything. We must be willing to give our life -- if necessary." Thundercloud paused. "In the end, if we succeed and live, even better."

Thundercloud looked from one bird to the other.

"How will we finish this dreadful deed?" Nightwind thought out loud.

"Why didn't we ask all the birds in this flock to join in the planning?" Bluesky asked.

"Two Owls are wiser than one, but one Owl is

wiser than a hundred." Nightwind smiled with a twinkling of his large, yellow eyes. "There are enough here to consult and see this matter from all perspectives. If there were too many, it would only add confusion and delay."

"As I said, they have death-sticks, and worse, the dogs are powerful and have learned to enjoy killing birds. They'll be waiting for us again," Blackfeather said.

"Although I am the most powerful bird in this mixed flock, even I am no match for even one dog in a straight fight." Thundercloud folded his mighty wings.

"We recognize their power. We see it. We understand it," Nightwind said with an urgent tone. "We must outsmart them. We must discern their strengths and their weaknesses and use that knowledge to gain an advantage, and most important, we must anticipate their actions, their tendencies, and use that against them!"

Thundercloud's eyes widened with eagerness at the wise Owl's words.

Bluesky felt amazement as he slowly considered Nightwind's words.

"We know they will be waiting to ambush us, and so we will use that knowledge and counterattack!" Thundercloud said confidently.

"We won't simply counterattack; we'll hit them at their weakest points and turn the tables on them!" Nightwind added.

Blackfeather cackled at first, a low chuckling sound. Slowly his chuckles turned to outright laughter. He spread his black wings, flew up, and landed on the limb beside Nightwind. "Ah, I now perceive that wisdom is the greatest form of trickery!"

Nightwind laughed with him.

Even Thundercloud's stern expression changed to merriment as he joined in their laughter.

"Thundercloud, you must watch the dogs and Marcion by day. Observe them from afar -- learn their habits, seek their weaknesses ..." Nightwind paused. "And I will observe them by night. Each night, I will watch their every movement. I will observe their habits and see if we can use them to our advantage. You must do the same by day!"

"Yes! Yeeeessssss," Blackfeather whispered excitedly. "I too will observe them, both at day and at night, and we will meet and discuss what we observe each day. Yes! We will learn the weaknesses of the man and the dogs and use them when we fight back!"

"Bluesky, the four of us will meet and consult each day at dawn. After each consultation, you must go and meet with the rest of the birds. Each morning, you must inform them of our plan as we add to it, and each day, our plan will grow until we are ready!" Nightwind shouted triumphantly.

"This may take more than two days," Blackfeather said.

"The poison leaks slowly, but we should not wait too long. We don't want the food-nest to fill up." Thundercloud nodded.

"I don't understand," Bluesky said.

"We will enlighten you as we formulate the plan. You will then teach the plan to the others. You

130

must explain it carefully -- each bird must know his part and act exactly on cue," Blackfeather said, his voice now full of confidence.

Thundercloud spread his wings, leapt into the air, and landed on the same branch with the two wise birds.

"Let us begin our great plan tonight," Nightwind said with laughing eyes.

Bluesky nodded in silent agreement. Then, he spoke with firmness and conviction. "But this part must be mine -- I must be the one to carry the food-nest with the poison. I don't want any other bird to risk their life in that way, and I alone will take it along with KC to the man." Bluesky took a deep breath and slowly let it out.

"And so you shall." Nightwind smiled at him.

"Now, how will we use their strengths and tendencies against them?" Thundercloud asked in a serious tone.

"We must understand our strengths first, the strength of each bird in our mixed flock. We must evaluate each bird on our team and use them effectively," Nightwind said.

"Yes ... yeeeesss," Blackfeather replied with a mysterious tone. The old black Crow flapped his wings enthusiastically as the others watched.

"And right here among us -- Hawk and Owl and Crow and Mockingbird -- we will scheme up a plan! Yes! The plan of plans! We will combine all the trickery of the Crow and the power and courage of the Hawk with the deep wisdom of the Owl. And ... and ..."

Blackfeather and Thundercloud stared down at

Bluesky with a questioning glance.

"And what will I add?" Bluesky asked, full of curiosity.

"Mock them to death?" Blackfeather chuckled.

"No, Bluesky will add the most essential and the most necessary quality of all," Nightwind said with confidence.

"What?" Bluesky asked.

Thundercloud laughed under his breath a moment, and then he answered for Nightwind, correctly following Nightwind's train of thought.

"You will add heart ... strength of heart!"

Chapter Fifteen

The next day, just after the sun rose above the eastern horizon, the four met again in counsel. Bluesky was quite surprised at their first question.

"How far will KC's dad follow her?"

Bluesky quickly flew off and asked the kitty cat. He returned right away.

"That's not far enough. Ask her if the other cat, Buddy, will help and if the 'yappy' little dog next door will help. What's his name?" Blackfeather asked.

"Bounce."

"Yes, that's the one."

"How can Bounce help?" Bluesky asked, his curiosity piqued.

Nightwind and Blackfeather explained.

Bluesky sat amazed and still a little confused after they told him, but he flew off a second time and talked to both KC and Buddy. Once they both heard what the birds wanted them to do, they all walked over to the fence, much to the delight of the Jack Russell Terrier.

Bounce began bouncing up and down three feet in the air as they approached.

Once KC got her to calm down, she explained what they were doing and asked Bounce if she could play a part.

"Yes! Yes! Yes!" Bounce barked excitedly.

"Okay, here's what we want you to do." KC paused and then explained.

133

"Of course, yes, absolutely! It's what I do best!" Bounce jumped up and down like a yo-yo.

Buddy turned to KC. "I don't like this plan," he groaned.

"Hush, Buddy," KC said. "Just do your part."

"Easy for you to say," Buddy replied.

Bounce's expression turned to one of supreme disappointment. "Oh, please, please, please, please, pleeeeeeease, Buddy! It will be soooo much fun!"

Buddy shook his head and sighed. "Oh, okay. I guess I'll do it."

Bluesky flew back to the council and reported that both cats and the little dog were willing to do their part.

As he thought about it, he suddenly realized Windwhisper could also help -- assisting Buddy and Bounce -- and she would be relatively safe as well while still taking a role in this part of the plan. He felt better inside.

A firm outline of the plan took shape that first meeting, and the roles of each bird on the team grew clearer. Bluesky also suggested a part for Dancingleaves, one not quite as dangerous as most of the others, as well as the idea of Windwhisper working with Buddy and Bounce. All agreed with Bluesky's two suggestions.

The morning meeting ended. Thundercloud soared into the sky on his way to observe the enemy. Blackfeather flew above the trees to observe from a hiding spot near Marcion's trailer. Nightwind went to sleep to prepare for his watch, and Bluesky took off to find Ol' Gray Mama and eat.

Later that morning, Bluesky met with Daymoon,

Bushhopper, Coolbreeze, Tootight, Windwhisper, Dancingleaves, and Treeflower. He explained the plan as it existed so far.

Seven beaks fell open in utter astonishment.

"You're kidding, right?" Tootight asked with incredulity.

"No, that's the plan so far," Bluesky said.

"I sure hope it gets better," Bushhopper replied with a hint of sarcasm.

"Keep positive," Daymoon reminded his friend, "and stay focused."

"You know, parent birds will sometimes use that to trick predators," Treeflower reminded them all. "It does work!"

"Yeah, but has any bird tried it with a rampaging dog?"

Nobody answered.

The following morning as the sun rose, Bluesky met in council again. Thundercloud, Blackfeather, and Nightwind compared their observations. All the habits of each dog were discussed in great detail.

Thundercloud described how the three dogs hunted down a rabbit that had inadvertently traveled into the field. He described how they closed in from three directions for the final kill.

They talked especially about the behavior of the dogs after the kill in case it helped them understand the bizarre blood lust of these dogs. But it did not, and in a way the birds were glad they could not understand.

They went over everything and finally determined there were two things they could use against the dogs. In fact, they knew without a doubt the first trick would work to perfection if they could somehow 'motivate' the biggest dog.

Blackfeather suggested an effective tactic Crows used against dogs who attacked them. It would require at least three Crows that were fearless and had excellent aim.

"Yes, that just might work!" Thundercloud laughed and then added his own idea to make doubly sure they 'motivated' Jack adequately.

"Yes, yeeeesssss," Blackfeather said in agreement. "Our two ideas combined should really do the trick!"

Bluesky remained silent and more than a little scared. He felt deep inside that the ideas were getting more and more dangerous, but he didn't have any better suggestion and so he kept his fears to himself.

They next discussed the habits of Marcion.

Thundercloud and Blackfeather had especially watched him during the day, but there didn't seem to be anything in particular they could use to their advantage.

Everyone felt a touch of discouragement, but Nightwind quickly spoke up. He shared all he had observed, especially one odd habit in which Marcion indulged for almost the entire evening.

They all discussed the strange behavior in great detail. At first, none of the birds could quite comprehend what Marcion was doing. They focused on the facts.

He scattered more trash after drinking an amber liquid, and it made him act crazier as he staggered around in the darkness shouting and gesticulating wildly. He even kicked the dogs if they came too close, and late into the night, he would stumble to his bed and sleep. Even then, Nightwind heard him make loud and strange noises.

None of the birds could fathom what Marcion was doing, but finally, they likened it to what they had observed in certain birds and animals when they ate berries that had become over-ripe.

They realized it was something they could use to their advantage, and it might neutralize the effect of the death-stick at the same time!

But they needed Nightwind to confirm that Marcion repeated this habit each night.

They all agreed that this would affect the day they began the final mission -- if they could use it to their advantage. Yes, Nightwind would carefully observe Marcion each night to see if he repeated this habit. When he did drink this amber liquid again all night, they all felt they should move the very next morning.

However, there would be no way to know in advance which day it would be. The mixed flock would need to be on alert, ready to move each morning. They only hoped it would be soon, since the food-nest had been capturing poison for two days now.

"Our plan is set. We only need Nightwind to let us know the exact morning we attack," Blackfeather said confidently.

"Attack?" Bluesky asked with a hint of fear.

Nightwind, Blackfeather, and Thundercloud looked at each other a moment.

"Yes, this mission is more of an attack on our

part this time. We have to create a diversion for the real purpose of our mission. It's the only way we can attempt to maneuver matters in our favor," Nightwind said.

"Agreed. We've got to take matters into our own talons this time," Thundercloud said with a twinkle in his eyes.

"But no matter how good our plan, or how well we execute it, things will happen that we could never foresee," Blackfeather added. "It will be at those critical times that courage and loyalty must save the day."

"Hear, hear," Thundercloud said.

"Then, we're agreed?" Blackfeather asked.

"Agreed!" Bluesky, Thundercloud, and Nightwind replied as one.

"We must strike with the rising of the sun, the earlier the better," Blackfeather said.

"Right, but what if Nightwind observes it tonight?" Bluesky asked.

"Bluesky, the sun has not quite set. Before you go to sleep tonight, you must seek out each bird and fill them in on the final details, just in case Nightwind gives us the word to go tomorrow at first light," Blackfeather said.

"I will, even if it takes me all night." Bluesky hopped with excitement.

"Tell all the birds that we meet before the first light at the tallest pine tree on the big man-road -- the place we first met. Tell them to be ready to fly! But if Nightwind does not give the word, we must meet again the next morning at the same place and same time."

138

"I will!"

"Good, then until we meet in the morning."

Bluesky flew off. He searched until he had found and updated each bird with the latest updates. Each bird nodded solemnly after he finished. All agreed to meet the next morning and to be ready to do their part.

Bluesky found the Doves and quickly fell asleep from all his exertions.

Sometime later, Bluesky awoke and stared up at the stars twinkling in the night sky above. He yawned and stretched a moment. Finally, he spread his wings and flapped several times to warm himself up.

He looked to the east and noticed that the lowest stars were already fading in the lightening sky.

It was time to fly.

Chapter Sixteen

Bluesky landed on a limb with Tootight and Treeflower. He looked around and quickly spotted his other friends perched on nearby branches.

Tension permeated the air around the birds.

"Where's the cat?" Bushhopper asked.

Bluesky looked at the ground frantically, but KC was nowhere to be seen. He flew down.

"KC!" Bluesky called.

The black and white cat did not reply.

"I wondered what happened to her." Coolbreeze zoomed into the air and flew around the tree searching for the cat.

"Maybe she decided she doesn't want to risk her life for birds after all," Bushhopper said with a touch of sarcasm.

"She will help!" Bluesky said in almost a shout. "She gave her word."

"Now, now, no need to get yourself all worked up about it," Bushhopper replied.

But deep inside, Bluesky was concerned. He'd told her about the meeting right before she went inside her house last night, and he had stressed that she needed to be here early. Bluesky sighed with frustration.

"W-w-when do we leave?" Dancingleaves stuttered.

"We wait on Nightwind. He will give us the word if we fly today." Thundercloud's voice boomed from somewhere higher in the tree, but in the darkness, he could not be seen.

They didn't have long to wait.

Blackfeather and Nightwind flew up together from the direction of Marcion's land. Two younger Crows accompanied them.

Bluesky felt his heart pounding inside his chest as the Owl and Crow landed.

"What's the word?" Thundercloud asked from on high.

"We don't go today."

The tension around the birds evaporated immediately.

Nightwind looked at each bird in the tree before he spoke again. "We will not fly until everything is ready. The man, Marcion, did not repeat his habit of the previous night. Instead, he went to sleep early and slept the entire night."

"What else is he going to do?" Daymoon asked in disbelief.

Nightwind opened his beak to reply, but Dancingleaves spoke first. "It doesn't matter, does it? I mean, the Owl says we don't go, and so we don't go." The Bluebird shifted nervously.

"Yes, he's right. Let's just leave it at that," Treeflower added quickly.

"Right," Nightwind said at last. "But although we don't fly today, we need each and every one of you back here tomorrow morning just as you are now. Do you understand?"

All the birds nodded.

"Because if we go tomorrow, we must be at the target before the sun rises." Nightwind looked at Bluesky first.

He nodded.

The birds nodded to him as he looked at each one in turn.

"Good. Now, go and get some breakfast and get to sleep early tonight. We want you bright-eyed and ready at this same early hour tomorrow."

The birds began to disperse.

"Bluesky."

He turned to Windwhisper.

"Could we talk?" she asked politely

"Of course," Bluesky said.

"Could I come with you too?" Dancingleaves asked.

Windwhisper looked away quickly, as if disappointed somehow.

"Sure, let's fly together and grab some breakfast. Then we can talk." Bluesky spread his wings and took off with Dancingleaves and Windwhisper right behind him.

They landed in the backyard of the house where KC lived.

"Keep an eye out for KC," Bluesky said to the other two. "I need to find out why she didn't show up."

"It's a good thing we didn't fly today,' Windwhisper said. "Or else we would have had to cancel because of her."

"I guess it was a good thing," Dancingleaves said with a tone of disappointment.

"Are you okay?" Bluesky asked him.

"Well, my heart is still thumping inside my chest. I mean, I was revved up and ready to go before it was cancelled." Dancingleaves shook his head. "I kind of wish we had gone on and finished it, while we were all ready."

"We have to wait until everything is set," Bluesky said. "We've got to stick with the plan. And maybe no one will get hurt this time."

"Exactly," Windwhisper said.

Dancingleaves sighed.

"Cheer up," Bluesky said. "We'll fly the mission soon."

"I think I'll fly back to my parents and eat breakfast with them. I just don't want to think about it right now." The Bluebird took flight and left.

"I hope he'll be all right," Windwhisper said with concern.

"He will. We're all disappointed we didn't go today. Everyone was focused and prepared, and then ..."

Windwhisper nodded with agreement.

They separated and began hunting. Soon, they had each snagged a few, good bugs and felt better. Bluesky was just about to fly up to a branch and clean his beak when Windwhisper approached.

"Bluesky, can I ask you something?"

"Sure."

The diminutive Mockingbird looked around nervously a moment. Windwhisper's expression grew serious, and a moment later it changed and became almost fearful.

Bluesky began to worry. He couldn't imagine what was making her act this way.

She seemed to come to a decision and hopped closer.

Bluesky held his breath, not sure what to expect.

"I was wondering," she began.

"Yes ..." Bluesky said questioningly.

"Do you like me?"

Bluesky felt a surge of relief. He had almost thought she was going to tell him that she no longer wanted to be his friend -- or something like that. She had gotten herself so worked up he had felt she was going to say something bad to him, but now ...

"Of course I like you." Bluesky smiled innocently.

"I mean -- *do you like me*?"

Bluesky paused, once again in a quandary. She had asked the same question again, but her tone indicated something more ... something more important than just liking her.

Could it be true?

His heart began pounding harder than it had when they had waited on Nightwind this morning. He felt a rush of emotions as he looked at the tiny Mockingbird, who looked back at him expectantly.

Windwhisper's eyes twinkled, and her smile grew wider the more his own nervousness increased.

"Uh, do you mean ..." Bluesky suddenly found himself out of breath. He'd forgotten to take a breath in the last minute or so! He began gasping.

"I mean, well, you know how a boy bird will meet a girl bird and they begin to like each other." Windwhisper came closer.

Bluesky felt his heart almost leap out of his chest. It seemed what he had wished for -- no, what he had earnestly yearned for -- was coming true!

He nodded in agreement in a dazed, albeit a

keenly happy, way.

"Good," she continued. "What I'm getting at ... I mean, before two birds can fall in love, they have to like each other. Right?"

"Yes! Absolutely!" Bluesky shouted.

Windwhisper jumped back a step, startled at his unexpected volume, but then she smiled even more.

Bluesky stared deep into her eyes. Her eyes were so lovely, and she was so very pretty.

"Do you like me, Bluesky?" she asked again, point blank.

"Yes, I like you."

She hopped up next to him and rubbed her wing against his wing.

Bluesky's entire body shuddered with the sheer delight of her gentle touch.

Now a new feeling filled his being, an electric feeling of joy and happiness.

After all, he liked a girl -- and she liked him back.

The world suddenly seemed to make sense. Everything fell into place. He knew what he wanted to do with his entire life -- or rather, with whom he wanted to spend it!

"Have you ever thought about taking a mate?"

"Yes. I have thought about it a lot lately." Bluesky smiled. "I've thought about it even more since I met you."

"I ... I have too." Windwhisper blushed.

Bluesky smiled wider.

"Why do you seem so surprised that I like you?"

"It's just, well, I never thought a girl would ever like me. I mean ..." He looked down at his one leg.

"I'm deformed."

He felt a wave of sadness shoot through his body and chase away his joy in a single heartbeat.

"I don't see your missing leg."

"Huh?"

"I only see you."

Bluesky felt confused. "Uh, but if you look at me, you have to see that my leg is missing."

"No, I see ... *you*."

She had that tone in her voice again. He knew she meant something more than what she'd said.

Then he remembered Nightwind's words from long ago.

"You mean you can see my heart?"

"Yes, I guess so. I see your goodness and your courage. I see how you treat your friends in such a kind way. Bluesky, you are one of the nicest birds I've ever met. I feel so comfortable, and so at ease, when I'm with you."

Bluesky felt a little overwhelmed.

"And I think you're cute too," Windwhisper said breathlessly while her eyes twinkled like diamonds.

His leg almost collapsed under him as the world spun out of control, but somehow he stayed upright.

Finally, he spoke about what he felt inside his heart.

"I think you're the prettiest bird I've ever met. I feel wonderful when I'm with you too... and if I were to take a mate, I'd want her to be just like you."

"Or ... could it just be me!" She laughed.

"Yes!" Bluesky shouted with emotion.

"I would be so happy to have you as my mate,"

Windwhisper whispered.

A flood of adrenaline flowed throughout every fiber of his being. Bluesky leapt into the air and burst forth in song. He flew in a great circle, singing so loudly that all the birds sitting nearby stopped in surprise and listened to his joyous birdsong.

After a few minutes of this song-filled outburst, Bluesky landed right next to Windwhisper.

"It's almost unbelievable that such a nice and pretty bird like you would like me."

"But I do." Her eyes twinkled brightly.

"And I like you."

The rest of the morning passed in a blur of emotions. They stayed close together wherever they went. Bluesky even shared the fattest and tastiest bugs he found with Windwhisper, and whenever she brushed her feathers against him, a wave of sheer, delightful ecstasy filled him.

Soon, however, she had to return to her parents.

They bid each other a fond farewell, and she flew away.

Bluesky thought of Thundercloud in that moment. He remembered how the mighty Hawk had said that loyalty was the Hawk's greatest attribute -- and not courage or strength.

In that moment, Bluesky vowed to protect Windwhisper no matter what transpired.

He would protect her with his very life ...

Chapter Seventeen

"I met a girl."

KC purred at Bluesky's words. The black and white kitty sat up and placed her nose almost against the end of Bluesky's beak.

"Well, that's an interesting development in your journey!"

"Wow! I'd forgotten about that with all that's going on." Bluesky took a deep breath. Suddenly, he remembered why he had searched for KC.

"What happened to you this morning?"

KC shook her head. "My dad doesn't get up until just before the sun rises. I tried to wake him up early, but he threw a pillow at me and told me it was too early to go outside."

"Oh, what are we going to do tomorrow? We need you! I mean, your part is essential," Bluesky said with emphasis.

"I know." KC licked her forepaw and gently cleaned the fur on her cheek while she thought.

Bluesky remained silent, realizing KC was thinking it all through.

Finally, she spoke. "I don't know. Dad never lets me out too early -- he says he doesn't want me to go and 'dance with the coyotes', whatever that means."

"KC! You have to be there! And you need to be there long before the sun rises, while it's still dark," Bluesky pleaded.

"I'll have to figure some way to get Dad to let me out early, but don't worry -- I'll be there tomorrow, one way or another." KC purred contentedly.

A flash of red heralded the approach of Daymoon. The red bird and his faithful companion, Bushhopper, landed near the two.

"What happened to you?" Bushhopper asked KC with a subtle, yet accusatory tone.

Bluesky quickly explained.

"Oh well, guess that's one advantage about not being domesticated -- we don't have to wait for someone to let us out. I mean, we're always outside!" Bushhopper chuckled.

"We can't live in the past," Daymoon said quickly, trying to help. "You'll be there for us tomorrow, right?"

"Absolutely," KC said without hesitation.

Daymoon smiled and flapped his wings vigorously. "I will be glad when this thing is over."

"I agree with that," Bushhopper said with emotion.

"Nightwind, Blackfeather, and Thundercloud are keeping watch to make sure things are right. We have a workable plan -- we're going to fly in, do our business, and fly right out," Bluesky said with conviction.

"Well, most of us will fly right in and out." KC smiled at the birds.

Treeflower flew up and landed next to Bluesky.

"It was Treeflower's idea to use a food-nest. Without it, we'd be nowhere right now," Bluesky said.

"It's a team effort. We all play our part. We need each other in order to succeed," Treeflower said cheerfully.

"Yes, and most important, we do it for everyone," KC added. "We do it for the birds, the animals, and the people. We do it to save them from the deadly effects of the poison."

"We put our lives on the line -- to help others." Bushhopper nodded.

"Ours is a noble cause," Daymoon added.

"To rid our world of the *Death on the Wind*," Bushhopper said with a courageous tone.

"We do it to help all," KC repeated.

"Especially the babies ... and the soon-to-be-born, so they won't be hurt by it in any way." Bluesky glanced down at his missing leg with a twinge of sorrow.

They parted.

Bluesky spent the rest of the day trying to relax, but all too often, the mission and the dangers surrounding it would crowd out happy thoughts. He would try to busy himself with hunting bugs or singing at those times. Finally, the sun set below the distant horizon.

But even as he grew sleepy, fearful thoughts and images crept into his mind. He remembered Ol' Gray Mama's advice and forced his fears away and focused on happy things. Of course, the smiling face of Windwhisper was what he thought upon most.

Bluesky slowly fell asleep with a smile on his face.

Best of all, he dreamed of her.

Chapter Eighteen

He awoke with a buzzing in his ears. Bluesky opened his eyes and smiled when he saw his friend hovering before him.

"Good morning, Coolbreeze. I see you're ready to go." Bluesky yawned.

"I was born ready!" Coolbreeze squeaked enthusiastically.

Bluesky stood up. He turned his head right and then left and stretched his wings as he came alive. He looked around at the darkened tree and saw the Doves all sleeping peacefully, not even aware of the dangerous mission that was about to transpire.

Bluesky spread his wings and then leapt into the air. The refreshing coolness of the predawn air bathed his body as he flew through the darkness toward the meeting place.

Coolbreeze passed him easily. Several more times he zoomed back around and passed him again and again. Once, he even circled him five times, just to make sure Bluesky realized that Hummingbirds were still the fastest birds around these parts.

They soon reached the tall pine tree next to the main road.

Daymoon and Bushhopper sat together about mid-tree, watching in silence as he and Coolbreeze landed on a lower branch. Looking around, he saw Treeflower and Dancingleaves on another branch. Moments later, Windwhisper flew up and landed next to him.

Bluesky felt his heart flutter a little as she brushed her wing against his.

"Good morning," she said with a bright smile.

The others murmured greetings back to her.

Higher up, he saw Tootight sitting half asleep, his head nodding forward and backward. Higher still, he saw Blackfeather.

He suddenly realized it wasn't Blackfeather.

"Who are you?" Bluesky asked the strange Crow.

"I am Swiftwing. I fly with Blackfeather. I was with him yesterday morning when we aborted. Me and a few more of my buddies are here to join your little enterprise."

"Yes, we will add our 'special skills' to this mission!" another Crow added from darkness. He and Swiftwing began laughing.

Several other Crows joined their laughter, but only Swiftwing and the Crow who had spoken were visible in the darkness.

"Are we going today then?" Daymoon asked. "I thought we needed to hear from Nightwind first?"

"We do." The unseen, deep voice startled everyone.

Bluesky realized that Thundercloud and a second, larger Hawk sat perched at the highest branch of the tree.

"I didn't see you up there," Bluesky said. "You startled me."

"Didn't Nightwind teach you to always be observant?" Thundercloud chuckled. "We've been here all night waiting for the rest of you."

"Oh, my," Treeflower said with a nervous laugh.

"I thought I was the first one here. I never noticed either of you! I never heard the first sound from you until you spoke!"

"That's why we're the predators ..." Thundercloud said ominously. "My mate, Morningsun, is here too. We'll need her."

"I'm glad we're on the same team today," Tootight said. He let out a few cackling chuckles.

"Have you heard from Nightwind?" Coolbreeze asked.

"No, not yet." Thundercloud looked around with a careful glance.

"How many Crows are with you, Swiftwing?"

"Four others -- we figured the more the merrier."

A distant sound of flapping wings came from the darkness beyond the road.

All the birds turned toward the sound.

Blackfeather appeared out of the blackness, his shiny beak glistening under the starlight. The old Crow landed on the other side of Bluesky and glanced around at every bird gathered in the tree. "Good, we are all here except for Nightwind. He should be here soon," Blackfeather said.

"Everyone except the cat," Bushhopper replied with an I-told-you-so tone.

"I'm here too."

Everyone looked down and saw the outline of KC at the base of the tree. She swished her tail excitedly as her green eyes sparkled up at them.

"I've been here even before the Hawks. I had to stay out all night, much to Mom and Dad's displeasure. Or else I could have never gotten out of the house early enough." KC licked her forepaw.

"Good for you!" Bushhopper said, obviously impressed. "You lived like a wild cat last night!"

"Yes. Thankfully, I didn't dance with any coyotes, which is what Dad seems to fear the most if I stay out at night." KC smiled.

Bluesky nodded at her proudly. He had known she would come through for them.

"Then, we're all here, except for Nightwind," Bluesky said.

"He's still sitting in a tree within sight of our target. I left him there in order to fly here and give you the word from what he observed last night." Blackfeather looked from one bird to the other. "Nightwind says this is the morning. We go, now!"

"W-wait a minute," Bushhopper said hesitantly. "What makes this the morning we go?"

"Marcion has been drinking crazy-water most of the night. He fell asleep a short while back."

"What's crazy-water?" Daymoon asked.

"We think it's kind of like eating over-ripe berries. You know how that makes you dizzy and disoriented?"

"Not personally, but I've heard of it," Daymoon said.

"Crazy-water comes in small metal cans. Marcion drinks them by the dozen most every night, and he had even more last night. So, Nightwind feels that, with Marcion in a state of disorientation, he won't be able to use the death-stick as effectively."

"That makes sense." Bluesky nodded.

"What about the dogs?"

154

"We have a plan for them." Blackfeather looked up at Swiftwing and the Crows. "Are you and the others prepared?"

"Oh yeah!" Swiftwing shouted. "You bet. We've been feasting on two-day-old road kill -- and even better, it was a stinking possum at that!"

The five Crows laughed out loud.

The others stared in shocked silence, imagining the grisly feast the Crows had eaten the previous day.

"And to add a bit more spice, we found an open trash can yesterday. It was full of rotting fruit and other decaying food. We gorged ourselves good, right, boys?"

The Crows let out another round of hearty laughter.

Treeflower gagged and turned away. Windwhisper, too, looked away.

"Sounds like you're ready to me." Blackfeather laughed in return.

"Let me tell you, about thirty minutes ago I let one rip! I thought the Crow next to me was going to fall right out of the tree it stunk so badly!" They burst out laughing again.

"Yeah, that was a rank fart -- we all had to find another branch until the smell went away!" a third Crow shouted.

The raucous laughter renewed even louder.

Bluesky and a few of the others joined in the laughter now.

"Good. Sounds like we're ready for that part of the plan." Blackfeather looked up at the top of the tree. "I see you and your mate are ready for your

155

part."

"We're ready to finish this business," Thundercloud said with quiet confidence.

"Good, well." Blackfeather turned to Bluesky. "We're ready then. Everyone knows their part. Everyone's here. I'd say we're ready."

Bluesky took a deep breath. "Yes, it's time to finish it."

"What if something happens that's not in the plan?" Dancingleaves looked around with a frightened expression. "I mean, something unexpected could happen."

"No doubt, it will," Thundercloud said. "We will face it with courage and overcome it."

"We'll just have to deal with it as it happens," Blackfeather added.

"But we're not going to leave anyone behind this time," Bluesky said with a commanding tone.

All the birds turned to him.

He felt their gaze on him.

"If something unexpected happens, we stick together, we help each other. If someone gets hurt, we help them," Bluesky added.

"I agree," Thundercloud boomed out. "We don't leave any bird behind."

"Yes, yes," Blackfeather said. "Agreed."

"But what will we do when the unexpected happens?" Dancingleaves asked in a pleading tone.

"We do whatever it takes." Bluesky slowly looked at each bird, one at a time. He looked deep into their eyes and saw both their trust in him and their fear of what lay before them.

He didn't want any of them to die.

He determined in his heart then and there that he would die before anyone else. He would face any unexpected danger himself.

"Whatever it takes ..." Bluesky repeated.

Chapter Nineteen

"You stay here, Windwhisper. When you first see the sun rise above the horizon, return to the house where KC and Buddy live. Your task is to guide Buddy and Bounce to the appointed rendezvous with us." Bluesky smiled at her and then turned to leave with the others.

"Bluesky!" she called with the slightest nervousness in her voice.

"Yes."

"Please come back."

Bluesky opened his beak and smiled as his heart beat harder. "That's the plan!"

Bluesky was glad that her role kept her away from the worst of the dangers. He wouldn't need to worry about her safety.

Still, his other friends were about to put their lives on the line. Everyone knew that the dogs would be waiting for them. Blackfeather, Thundercloud, and even Nightwind had taken note of that fact. So even though things were better in facing Marcion and his death-sticks, the dogs were another matter.

While the birds flew in the air above, KC bounded along on the ground behind them trying her best to keep up. Most of the birds flew on ahead to get in position, but Bluesky, Dancingleaves, and Blackfeather hung back in order to guide KC.

They reached the back of the subdivision that was across the main road from the subdivision where KC's house was located. A stand of woods stood between the last houses and the field of Marcion beyond.

"You wait here," Bluesky whistled down to KC.

"I'll go a bit further into the woods until I can see the field and wait there," KC meowed back.

"Okay, but make sure you rub against the bushes and leave your scent. Windwhisper, Bounce, and Buddy need to be able to find you."

KC went to the first tree, reached up, and scratched vigorously on the bark. She scratched so hard several pieces of pine bark flew off.

"There, Buddy will notice that easy. I'll make sure I leave a trail he can follow too," KC said as she trotted between the first two trees.

The three birds flitted from tree to tree, perching often on a branch in order to allow KC to catch up as she walked below. When the morning light began to overwhelm the shadows, however, Bluesky felt an urgent need to move faster.

"We'll meet you at the edge of the field!" Bluesky called out. He and the other two birds flew on to the trees that lined the boundary between the field and small forest. Bluesky fidgeted among the branches as he saw the sky grow lighter with each passing minute.

"We need to hurry," Blackfeather said calmly. "The others will be in place already."

"I know. We can fly quickly from here once KC arrives. We'll give her a couple more minutes." Bluesky looked nervously back into the shadows between the trees.

He was almost ready to leave when he saw her

come out around a tree.

"KC, wait right here. It's too dangerous for you to go any closer. You're already beyond the fence line, and if you go into the fields and the dogs find you, they'll kill you. If you stay here near the trees, you can escape up one of them if necessary." Bluesky watched KC's response.

"Okay, I'll wait here for you." KC sat down on some pine straw and gazed vigilantly forward. She was in position.

"Let's go!" Bluesky shouted. Then he leapt into the air with Dancingleaves and Blackfeather close behind.

They had only gone a short distance when Bluesky heard a bird cry out in fear behind him. He swung around and saw Dancingleaves settle down on a solitary bush.

"What's wrong now?" Blackfeather said with a hint of exasperation.

He and Blackfeather landed on the ground near the bush.

"I-I can't go on. I'm sorry. I'm just too afraid." Dancingleaves shivered and looked down with the most forlorn expression. "I'm s-so s-sorry." The Bluebird was stuttering again, he was so frightened.

Dancingleaves hung his head and whimpered.

Bluesky hopped closer, his mind buzzing with hyperactivity. He knew they were late, but he didn't want to leave his friend like this.

"That's all right -- you don't have to fly any further." Bluesky smiled confidently at the Bluebird.

"W-w-what do you mean?" Dancingleaves

asked in surprise.

"This was the very spot we wanted you to be a lookout."

"What?" Blackfeather said with surprise, but he quickly discerned Bluesky's point. "Yes ... yesssss!" He looked around as if surveying the area. "This is the very spot. So, you're set to look out for us, right?"

Dancingleaves' eyes widened. "Are you sure? I mean, I can't see the man's trailer from here or the poison hill."

"We didn't tell you before, but we want you to keep a watch for our backs. We don't want anything sneaking up behind us," Bluesky said with great sincerity. He turned and winked at Blackfeather as Dancingleaves surveyed the area.

"You think you can handle this?" Blackfeather asked.

"Why, yes, I can."

"Good. We're going to go on now. We'll call you when we're done." Bluesky started to fly.

"But... but... what will I do if I see something?" Dancingleaves asked.

"Fly up high and sing out a warning to us!"

Bluesky and Blackfeather took off and flew on toward the poison hill. A few minutes later, the solitary tree next to the trailer came into view. Bluesky looked toward the east and saw the first beams of light shining brilliantly through the trees.

"We've got to hurry! The sun has risen!"

They flew faster.

Finally, they neared the group of bushes where they'd first heard the Waxwings crying.

"Over here!" Daymoon whistled.

They landed under the middle bush.

Coolbreeze, Treeflower, Daymoon, and Tootight all stood on the ground waiting for them. A sudden rustling from inside the shadows startled Bluesky momentarily. A second later, Bushhopper hopped out and landed among them.

"Okay, the Hawks are ready, and the other Crows are ready," Daymoon said quickly.

"Where are the dogs?" Blackfeather asked.

"Two of them are sleeping next to the trailer. We haven't seen the big one yet."

"That's not good," Blackfeather said.

"He'll come quick enough. We just need to know from which direction," Bluesky said with a positive tone. "We just need to stick to the plan."

"I guess we're ready, then," Treeflower said with a hint of hesitation.

"Let's do it!" Coolbreeze squeaked.

"Okay, Zoomer." Bluesky smiled. "Go! Go! Go!"

Coolbreeze zipped away in a flash of feathers and in seconds disappeared over the tall grass.

Bluesky looked over at Daymoon and Bushhopper.

"Are you ready?"

"As ready as we'll ever be." Bushhopper shook his head and sighed.

Daymoon gave the Towhee a nudge that almost knocked him down.

"Hey!" Bushhopper said.

Daymoon winked at him. "Come on, Towhee. I have the hard part, not you. I need your help, brave

162

friend. I can't do it without you."

Bushhopper smiled at his friend. "I'll be there for you," he said with a surge of confidence.

The angry barking of dogs pierced the air.

"Coolbreeze is flying around the dogs and irritating them." Blackfeather held his head up carefully, listening to the distant barks.

Suddenly, the barks grew louder.

"Okay, they're chasing him here," Blackfeather said. He hopped to the edge and cocked his head to listen again. "Yes, they're coming ... and fast!"

"This is it!" Bluesky said.

The others stared at him, waiting.

The barks grew louder and louder.

"They're almost here!" Blackfeather whispered urgently.

"Hold a bit ..." Bluesky's voice trailed off. He listened a moment longer. Finally, he heard the faint sound of humming.

"GO!"

Daymoon and Bushhopper flew out.

The duo flew rapidly just above the top of the grass. Around them, the morning light finally conquered the last of the night's shadows. Everything grew clear all at once.

"There they are!" Bushhopper shouted.

King and Bear ran at full speed through the grass after the tiny form of Coolbreeze. They leapt through the grass almost as if they too could fly!

"Kill it! Kill it!" King barked angrily as he closed on the tiny Hummingbird.

"Kill it! Kill it!" Bear barked back.

Coolbreeze looked over his shoulder and stuck

his tongue out at them.

The two dogs redoubled their efforts.

"Now!" Bushhopper sang out to Daymoon.

Daymoon fell from the sky and landed in a puff of dust on the ground. He started flapping and crying out as though terrified.

The two dogs came to an immediate halt.

"There's another bird!" King shouted.

"And he's hurt. He can't fly!" Bear lunged toward the apparently helpless Cardinal.

"Look out!" Bushhopper shouted in fear, playing his part in the tense drama that was quickly playing out.

Daymoon timed it carefully. This was one of the oldest tricks in the books, but it was a dangerous trick.

Bear closed within a few feet. When he leapt for Daymoon, the Cardinal flew up into the air, just out of the reach of the massive fangs.

The lumbering Rottweiler's jaws snapped for the bird that was no longer there. Instead, his massive jaws dug into the ground.

"Arfff!" he cried out after he ate a mouthful of dirt. He shook his head and spat it out. "Ahhh! Stupid bird! I almost had you!"

Daymoon flew about twenty feet away and fell to the ground again in a heap of feathers, flapping his wings in a frenzy as if he could no longer fly.

"Help!" Daymoon cried out pitifully. "My wing's hurt! Help! Help!"

Bear spat out some more dirt, swung around, and lunged for the Cardinal again.

"Don't wait so long next time. He almost had

you!" Bushhopper cried out after he landed nearby. He looked around toward the sound of pounding footsteps. "Here he comes again!"

In the meantime, Treeflower and Tootight flew out toward King, who still chased vainly after Coolbreeze. As they came within sight, Treeflower folded her wings and fell hard to the ground while Tootight landed out of sight close by.

"He's seen you!" Tootight whispered.

King turned without missing a beat and headed straight for her. His barks grew more excited.

"Kill the bird! Kill the bird!" King shouted.

"Get ready!" Tootight whispered urgently.

Treeflower continued flapping her wings as she went around in circles raising a small cloud of dust. She kept one eye on the dog all the time.

He lunged for her, jaws wide open.

Treeflower leapt straight up into the air, catching the dog by total surprise.

First King tried to stop his forward momentum in order to leap upward, but as he put his four feet into the ground, he skidded on the soft dirt. Still, he leapt up for the escaping bird. He stretched his neck forward, his jaws almost around the Sparrow.

He snapped them shut -- on empty air when Treeflower surged forward just out of reach of his terrible teeth.

King's momentum kept him moving forward although he'd leapt upward. Then gravity pulled him down, and he tumbled several times until he came to halt flat on his side with a cloud of dust enveloping him He lay there, momentarily dazed and out of breath.

Treeflower cried out as if in terrible pain, folded her wings and fell back to the ground.

King immediately jumped up and ran toward the downed bird.

"Where is the big dog?" Bluesky asked. He and Blackfeather watched as both dogs chased after what they thought were injured birds.

"He'd better show up soon, or our plan will fall apart," Blackfeather said.

Chapter Twenty

Dancingleaves shuddered as the dogs' barking grew fiercer in the distance. He closed his eyes and huddled deeper inside the bush.

Suddenly, he froze.

The ground shook with the pounding of some huge animal. In a rush of movement, a monstrous dog burst between the tall grass and came into view. The huge dog swept right by him. The entire bush rustled violently when the dog brushed against it going past.

Dancingleaves almost cried out in fear, but he remained quiet.

When he opened his eyes, he saw the massive dog running toward the sound of the barking and his friends' frantic calls.

"It's the big dog!" Dancingleaves whispered in disbelief. "And ... he's coming up behind them!"

In a flash of panic, Dancingleaves leapt into the air and started back for home. Consumed with fear, the Bluebird could only think of the safety at his parents' side, but as he flew toward the woods, he heard Daymoon whistling for help in the distance.

Dancingleaves looked over his shoulder.

The monster dog jumped through some tall grass and disappeared.

"He'll take them by surprise ... and hurt my friends!" Dancingleaves said, his voice shaking. A determined expression filled his face as he remembered the two birds that had died.

He turned around and flew as fast as his wings would take him.

He heard the dog's ferocious growling when he passed over Jack, but he kept on flying. He forgot all about the man and his death-stick. He forgot about the poison and the other dogs. Dancingleaves' only thought was to warn his friends.

After all, that was his job.

But he didn't know where they were! Then remembered Bluesky's last words to him.

He flew up high into the sky and sang out, "The big dog is coming! The big dog is coming!"

Bluesky and Blackfeather looked up at the same time.

"It's Dancingleaves!" Bluesky shouted.

"He's spotted the big dog coming up behind us!" Blackfeather laughed. "So, Mockingbird, leaving the Bluebird back there was a stroke of genius."

"I'd have never guessed!" Bluesky replied with astonishment.

The ground began shaking under their feet.

"It's going to get interesting now!" Blackfeather whispered excitedly.

"Let's go!" Bluesky soared upward, with Blackfeather right behind. They both flew straight at Jack the Ripper.

Jack let out a bloodcurdling howl when he spotted them.

Bluesky turned and flew off to the side while Blackfeather flew higher.

Jack stopped when he heard King and Bear barking furiously as they each pursued their prey. The massive, mongrel Bulldog growled with indecision.

Bluesky looked back. Then he smiled, folded his wings, and fell to the ground like a rock.

"Oh, my wing!" Bluesky cried out.

Jack let out a howl of delight and raced after him.

Bluesky fluttered on the ground, pretending his wing was broken. He watched the huge dog grow closer and closer.

"Get ready!" Blackfeather warned.

Jack lunged for him.

Bluesky flew through the air just out of reach of the massive jaws.

"Okay, let's head for the big clearing and the next stage!" Blackfeather cried out.

Bluesky turned and headed for the clearing between the bushes and the poison hill. So far, the plan was working to perfection, but now came the most dangerous part.

Bluesky flew over the clearing, folded his wings again, and fell down like he had been injured. Just for good measure, he cried out as if in pain, "Owww! I'm hurt! I can't fly! Help! Help!"

Blackfeather soared in from the other side and landed about ten feet away. The two birds nodded at each other.

"CAW! CAW! CAW!"

Jack jumped through the grass and into the clearing with them. He growled so loud Bluesky felt his entire body shudder with the reverberations. His heart pounded harder than he thought possible as he faced the fearsome dog, who was only a few feet away.

Jack lowered his head, long lines of slobber streaming down both sides of his jaws.

"Ha! I have you, bird. You won't get away now." Jack laughed as his red eyes glazed with the thought of the kill.

"What about me?"

Jack stopped in mid-step and turned toward the Crow. "Well, what is this? An old Crow, eh? I guess Big Jack will be eating Crow again this day." Jack laughed maliciously.

"But I'll get away then," Bluesky whistled out.

"Yes, you'll only get one of us. The other will fly away easily," Blackfeather said with a chuckle.

Jack turned first to the Mockingbird and then to the Crow. He paused with indecision.

At just that moment, the sound of wings grew audible.

Jack looked up, a puzzled expression on his face.

"Take this!" Swiftwing shouted with a laugh.

Five Crows dove straight down toward Jack in a tight group. When they were almost upon him, they all arched their backs at the same time.

"Make it count, boys!" Swiftwing laughed.

Five streams of white liquid shot out from the birds.

"Huh?" Jack stared at the completely unexpected sight.

A second later, Crow poop splashed all over his face and muzzle.

Jack focused his eyes on his muzzle. He crossed his eyes, still not comprehending what had just happened.

Finally, the last squirt of white poop splashed directly across his nose.

"Bull's-eye!" Swiftwing cried victoriously.

The five Crows flapped their wings hard as they pulled out of their dive. They split up and flew in different directions as they retreated back into the sky.

Jack stood cross-eyed, staring at the white poop that slowly oozed over his entire muzzle. To make matters worse, as he panted from his exertions, some of the poop dripped into his mouth.

Jack froze instantly.

He spat continuously a few moments, fully realizing what had happened to him. He closed his mouth to prevent any more from dripping inside, at which time he took a deep breath through his nose.

He howled as white-hot pain seared through his nostrils.

Jack ran around in circles howling, all the time shaking his broad head in an effort to get the terrible stuff off.

"He's lost his sense of smell now. That's what we needed," Blackfeather said to Bluesky.

Bluesky nodded.

"Hey, big dog, did you forget about us?"

Jack stopped dead still. His eyes glowed red as he stared down at Bluesky. He lowered his head and growled so powerfully Bluesky felt the ground shake under him.

"Don't forget about me," Blackfeather added.

Jack's anger totally consumed him now. He remained focused on Bluesky.

"I'm going to chew you into little pieces, stupid

bird!" Jack growled menacingly.

"Kee-harrrrr!"

Jack's stare remained fixed on Bluesky a fraction of a second longer, despite the unexpected cry that split the air above.

Suddenly, Thundercloud swooped past Jack in a flash of feathers.

Bluesky blinked his eyes in surprise, and in the next instant, Thundercloud flew away.

Jack howled with pain. He jumped completely around after the Hawk's surprise attack.

Bluesky watched closely as Jack, blood streaming down his head, turned back around and faced him again..

"You've slashed me! You birds have actually hurt me! But you're going to pay for this outrage with your life!" Jack roared with burning anger.

Thundercloud's talons had indeed ripped two wounds across the dog's broad head. Several streams of bright, red blood fell around the dog's eyes.

"Keeee-harrrr!"

Jack froze instantly, and then in the next second he leapt away, trying to flee another attack, but Morningsun's talons ripped across his back in spite of his efforts to get away.

Jack bayed terribly while he lunged around in an entire circle, his jaws snapping in an effort to kill the Hawk. Jack reached forward, and his jaws snapped down on the fleeing Hawk.

Morningsun cried in pain when several of her tail feathers were ripped out. She lost her equilibrium and started to fall to the ground.

172

Jack roared with delight and raced after her.

"Keee-harrrr!"

Jack lunged around to face the new attacker with his fangs bared.

Thundercloud, though, expected this move. He realized the dog was getting wise to their attacks, and so his attack was only a feint to give his mate time to flee out of the reach of the dog.

"Do you feel the pain of our talons?" Thundercloud shouted. Instead of pressing his attack, he flapped his great wings and rose quickly into the sky.

Jack growled with hate and anger and pain. Streams of blood from Thundercloud's first attack flowed faster from the dog's exertions and mixed with Crow poop across his face while across his back blood streamed from the second attack. The pain and the hot stench of blood filled the dog's senses until something snapped inside his mind.

Jack screamed -- a blood-chilling roar that shook the very air.

Fear gripped Bluesky's heart as he realized the huge dog was mad with rage.

"We've done it," Blackfeather said. "That dog is now blinded by his lust to kill."

Bluesky froze a moment, afraid of what they had accomplished.

"It's time!" Blackfeather shouted.

Chapter Twenty-One

Bluesky flew up into the air and sang out to the others.

Daymoon leapt out of the reach of King for a fifth time, but he was out of breath and growing tired. This time, King managed to rip a tail feather out.

"It's time! Bluesky's calling!" Bushhopper shouted with relief.

"Good -- I'm getting tired." Daymoon flew straight for the clearing with King chasing right behind. He made sure to fly just over the top of the grass to keep tempting the dog.

King roared out in anger and leapt after him.

The Cardinal surged forward and flew out over the clearing. Directly ahead, he saw the monster dog. Daymoon gasped at the terrible sight.

Blood streamed all down Jack's face and around his eyes, which seemed to glow as red as the blood. His nose was covered by the most disgusting white stuff mixed with blood that Daymoon had ever seen.

While the Cardinal was distracted by the sight of Jack, King leapt for him. Daymoon had forgotten about the German Shepherd behind him.

King snapped his jaws shut, but instead of chomping down on the bird, his snout knocked Daymoon down. Even so, one of his bared teeth tore through the Cardinal's wing and slashed his side.

Daymoon fell dazed to the ground.

"No!" Bluesky shouted with desperation. He

dove straight for King as the dog reached down to crush Daymoon in his fearsome jaws.

"Leave him alone!" Bluesky cried.

King looked up. When he saw the Mockingbird diving at him, he barked and jumped forward.

At the same moment, Jack charged forward to grab Bluesky from behind.

The lust to kill overwhelmed the massive dog. The blood streaming down his face stung his eyes and partially blinded him while the pungent odors destroyed all sense of smell. Jack chased after any motion before his eyes now. He chased after any sound close by.

Bluesky landed next to his fallen friend -- right between the two charging dogs.

Both dogs leapt headlong at him from opposite directions.

"Get up!" Bluesky urged his friend, but Daymoon groaned and passed out.

King and Jack roared as they charged forward to make the kill.

Bluesky waited one fraction of a second longer, and then he flew to his right just above the ground, hoping to draw them away from the fallen bird.

Jack and King turned toward him at the same time. They both leapt at him simultaneously, but their forward momentum carried them into a massive collision with each other.

Jack the Ripper and King closed together with howls of rage and snapping fangs.

Jack, the huge half-Mastiff, half-Pit Bull, locked his jaws onto King's shoulder and shook him violently. King cried out in pain as his flesh ripped and blood streamed down his leg, but Jack didn't release his terrible hold.

In desperation, King locked his jaws across Jack's snout. Both dogs shook themselves violently, and King's fangs ripped more bleeding wounds across Jack's face.

Jack released his hold.

The stood facing each other, King's shoulder bleeding profusely while Jack's face was covered with blood.

Blinded by pain and blood, Jack prepared to attack again, but King struck first.

King's teeth sank into Jack's neck, and he growled and shook his head to drive his fangs deeper into the soft flesh.

Jack froze, the counterattack was so unexpected.

He growled menacingly and steeled his great muscles. Then, with a mighty shake of his body, Jack flung King off and attacked again, using his superior size and strength to overwhelm the German Shepherd.

Jaws snapped in the air as each dog lashed out and tried to avoid the others fangs, but more and more often each dog closed on flesh, which sent howls of pain mixed with their menacing growls into the air.

"What have we done?" Bluesky cried out. "They're hurting each other! We didn't want that to happen."

"Stay back!" Blackfeather shouted back. "It's too dangerous! They've both gone berserk!"

King finally locked his teeth on Jack's neck again and shook his head violently. He tore Jack's neck and caused a serious wound.

Jack shrieked.

Although King was still locked on his neck, Jack simply reached down and clamped his jaws across the back of King's neck. Jack's mighty jaws clenched tighter and tighter like a steel vise.

Yelping with fear and pain, King released his hold and fought to get away, but Jack continued to shake King like a rag doll. Finally, Jack threw him down hard onto the ground.

King lay panting a moment, stunned by his wounds and the intensity of the shaking. When he struggled to get up and escape, Jack easily blocked him. The huge dog lowered his head and growled ferociously.

The dogs locked their teeth into each other again, but the intensity of the fight now escalated. As they fought, both dogs now sought to kill the other.

"Oh, no!" Bluesky cried. "They're killing each other! They're really killing each other!"

"We knew this was dangerous," Blackfeather whispered in shock. "We're using their bloodlust against themselves, and it's more powerful than even I imagined. They're out of control ..."

"But our plan was just to have the dogs fight among themselves and maybe even chase each other away and leave us alone!" Bluesky shook his head.

"It's too late now -- the dogs are insane in their bloodlust," Blackfeather said.

Bushhopper flew in and dropped beside the wounded Cardinal.

"Get up, Daymoon. Those dogs are killing one

another, and when they're done, whichever dog survives will come for you!" Bushhopper nudged his friend with his beak, urging him to rise.

Daymoon grimaced and groaned with pain. "My side, it's bleeding." He groaned more as he tried to rise. "I'm hurt. I don't know if I can fly ..."

Bluesky flew up. He looked over at Bushhopper, whose face was full of fear and worry.

"Daymoon, you've got to hide in the grass."

Behind them, one of the dogs cried out in a high-pitched squeal. Then a sudden and terrible silence ensued.

They both turned and saw Jack holding the limp form of King in his jaws. Jack's massive jaws were clamped tight on the German Shepherd's throat. Jack growled intensely as he shook the limp form again and again.

Finally, he dropped the dead dog onto the ground.

"He's killed him! Come on, Daymoon, get up and fly! Fly!"

Daymoon rose unsteadily, groaning with each movement. Bluesky looked at his friend and saw the puncture and the mangled feathers mixed with blood.

Suddenly, the sound of running footsteps came to their ears.

"Fly!" Bluesky shouted.

Daymoon jumped into the air and flew about ten feet.

He folded his wings painfully and fell back into the grass. He groaned one more time before slipping into unconscious again.

178

Bushhopper screamed.

Bluesky leapt into the air just as Jack's bloody jaws snapped shut. He felt intense pain as two of his tail feathers were jerked out.

Even so, he flew higher.

He looked around, and to his horror the monster dog was sniffing the ground in his hunt to find the helpless Cardinal and kill him.

"Treeflower! It's time!" Bluesky shouted out in fear.

"Yes, bring the dog! Bring the dog now!" Blackfeather shouted in desperation.

Over to their left, Treeflower flew up out of the grass. The massive head of Bear appeared right behind her. She led the sturdy Rottweiler straight to the clearing.

Jack howled with bloodlust when he caught sight of the Cardinal and ran forward to take it with his jaws.

"Bluesky! It's time for you to fly and get the food-nest!" Blackfeather shouted.

A terrible panic gripped Bluesky's heart. It was time for him to retrieve the poison and for all of them to make their combined retreat after he had gotten it.

But how could he leave Daymoon at this moment?

He looked down at the still form of Daymoon and cried out in shock when he saw Jack heading straight for him!

Bluesky dove in attack at the charging dog, but Blackfeather reached Jack first.

"CAW! CAW! CAW!" Blackfeather dragged

his talons across the dog's back and then continued flying right over him.

Jack's roar shook the air. He immediately turned and chased after the Crow.

Blackfeather flapped his great wings slowly as he sailed just above the waves of tall grass, tempting the infuriated dog. After Jack gave chase, Blackfeather turned and headed back for the clearing.

"Go on, Bluesky! Fly! Do your part!" Blackfeather shouted.

Bluesky turned on his wing and headed for the poison hill.

At just that moment, the sharp thunder of a death-stick pierced the morning air.

"Kill it, big dawg! Kill it!"

Bluesky looked around and saw Marcion stumble out of his trailer with a death-stick in his hand and another, slightly smaller one strapped on his waist.

"I'll handle the man!" squeaked Coolbreeze, who had just arrived at the clearing. He zoomed straight for Marcion.

"What? What are you going to do?" Bluesky asked.

"I'll think of something!" And with a flash of ruby and emerald feathers, Coolbreeze flew toward the crazy man shooting his gun.

Bluesky shouted after Coolbreeze, "Don't get too close!"

"Look out!" Thundercloud roared out in warning.

Bluesky turned around just in time to see Jack

and Bear lock their jaws into each other in the middle of the clearing.

On the ground near them, Treeflower lay still, barely breathing.

Bluesky turned back to help.

"No! Go on!" Thundercloud shouted from on high. "I'll help the fallen Sparrow!"

The death-stick roared again.

Thundercloud folded his wings and dove away from the gun's blast while some of his feathers spiraled away.

The morning air shook with the terrible sounds that came from every direction. Cries of anger and fear and warning mixed with the growls of the dogs locked in deadly battle. All of these heartrending sounds suddenly overwhelmed Bluesky's senses.

He wanted to fly away and hide so badly! He just wanted to get away!

They had planned to have the dogs attack each other and for him to retrieve the poison in the confusion. After that, they'd all fly away home before the man awoke.

But everything was going wrong ...

The dogs weren't just fighting each other as they hoped; they were actually killing each other. Even worse, Daymoon and Treeflower were both down and wounded. Somewhere in the distance, tiny Coolbreeze was taking on Marcion all by himself.

And now, Marcion was shooting his death-stick wildly in every direction!

Bluesky wanted to cry out and stop everything, but it was too late.

The fighting was out of control; he could do

181

nothing to stop it now.

He turned and flew toward the poison hill. His only hope was that if he quickly grabbed the food-nest they could all fly away and leave this terrible scene behind.

Chapter Twenty-Two

Marcion stumbled down the steps of the trailer and fell forward toward the ground.

He squeezed the trigger and wildly fired the last round of his shotgun before falling right on his face. Groaning, he wrestled with his gun and the dizziness of his hangover until he eventually sat up.

He stared at his new truck in horror.

"I shot mah truck! I shot mah truck!"

He tried to stand but instead fell over several more times. Finally, he managed to get up on one knee. He pulled shells out of his shirt pocket and reloaded the shotgun. Then he stared open-mouthed at his truck.

Three rusting hulks, each truck bed filled with trash and countless empty beer cans, sat beside the lone truck that still had tires and fresh paint, but now its smooth body was peppered with tiny holes and its windshield shattered by the shotgun's blast.

The late-model truck had an especially large hole right in the middle of its windshield with a spider web of cracks extending outward. Dozens of pellet holes riddled the hood above the engine compartment. A hissing sound emanated from the damaged engine.

Marcion cursed vehemently while he finished reloading. "Yew stupid birds made me shoot mah truck!"

He screamed and shot toward an imagined movement directly above him. Marcion's mind was still clouded from another night of drinking cheap beer. The old man pumped his gun and ejected the empty shell. He finally managed to get up but immediately stumbled. He clenched his hand in reflex, and the gun fired.

Marcion screamed when he realized he had shot his truck again.

Suddenly, a loud humming sound zipped around his head.

Marcion froze as he listened intently to the strange sound.

"Whut is that?" He stumbled around in a circle searching vainly for the source of the buzzing sound. It was as though something were flying in circles around him deliberately trying to keep him off-balance.

"Whut's that squeaking sound? Whut's that buzzing? Is it inside my head?" Marcion screamed as he dropped the shotgun and put his hands up to his ears to block out the sound.

"I must be having those flashbacks they warned us about in the sixties!" Marcion stumbled around in circles with his eyes glazed over. Grasping his shotgun in one hand and reaching for the long pistol holstered at his waist with the other, the old man mumbled unintelligibly while he stared around in wide-eyed terror.

***

Coolbreeze flew up to Marcion and hovered right before his face. With a flash of inspiration, he repeatedly flicked his long tongue out at him.

The man's eyes grew wild as he stared at the apparition hovering right before him. "It's ... it's ...

it's a tiny bird!"

He swatted at Coolbreeze with his fist, but the Hummingbird easily dodged the clumsy blow.

"You're big, and you're ugly, and ... and you smell bad too!" Coolbreeze flicked his tongue out one more time for good measure.

"Whut is this, some kind of weird horror movie?" Marcion pulled the smaller death-stick out of his holster and aimed the long barrel right at Coolbreeze, but the zoomer simply flicked his tongue out again.

Marcion screamed, and then he fired the pistol.

Coolbreeze zipped away, but he felt a rush of air as the bullet sailed right by him.

The Hummingbird flew rapidly around Marcion's head again and again.

Marcion fired the pistol, shouted, and fired again while he stumbled around in a circle trying to follow the evasive movements of the Hummingbird.

None of his shots came close to the zooming Hummingbird, but Marcion managed to hit his truck twice more and his trailer three times. The rest of his shots went wildly into the air in every direction.

Finally, his pistol clicked empty.

He stood staring at the gun a moment. Appearing confused, he pointed the barrel directly at his face and pulled the trigger.

It clicked.

He pointed the pistol down at the ground and pulled the trigger again.

The gun fired, and dirt exploded next to his foot.

"Whut the!" Marcion shouted. He held the gun up in the air and fired off two more rounds before it clicked empty again.

Coolbreeze stopped right in front of Marcion's eyes again. He stuck his tongue out and laughed.

Marcion threw the pistol at the bird, but it sailed harmlessly into the grass. He then fell to his knees and closed his eyes, moaning as dizziness from all his rapid movements and the effects of last night's alcohol overwhelmed his senses.

Coolbreeze laughed and laughed in a long series of hysterical squeaks.

Chapter Twenty-Three

KC sat up straight after the first shot echoed through the morning air.

She had listened attentively to the angry barking of the three dogs and surmised the birds' plan was working, but she had heard none of the birds say anything about the man shooting his death-stick. In fact, the whole reason for this early morning mission was in the hopes he would sleep through it.

KC stood up and flicked her tail nervously from side to side. She hopped forward and trotted toward the sound of the dogs and the death-stick.

She knew she was leaving the safety of the trees and risking her life now, but she also knew the birds were facing death in their effort to get rid of the poison. She wanted to help them any way she could as long as it meant getting rid of the poison that had made Katie so sick and made Mom and Dad so sad.

KC's senses were on high alert when she entered the field. She kept a sharp eye and ear and nose out for dogs. She knew they were killers ... and they especially liked to kill cats.

KC's heart pounded as she walked up to a group of bushes. She paused and sniffed the ground near some tracks.

She smelled the powerful scent of Jack and realized he must be a huge dog. In fact, his scent was so strong she couldn't quite comprehend how big he really was.

Fear gripped her heart a moment, and she

paused.

The death-stick fired again.

She looked behind and realized the sun had cleared the tops of trees. She knew it was time for Buddy and Bounce to act. What would happen if they didn't find her?

The death-stick fired over and over again in rapid succession.

KC looked back at the safety of her post in the trees and then toward the sound of the fighting.

She hesitated, not sure what she should do, but from the continuous barking and the thundering report of the death-stick, she figured the birds might need help.

KC took a deep breath and ran toward the sounds of battle.

***

Buddy stood with his front paws at the bottom of the window sill. Sunlight was streaming through the leaves in full force.

It was time.

He heard Dad walking down the stairs for his morning cup of coffee. Buddy ran for the front door to meet him.

"Hello, Buddy. You want to go out already? I haven't put fresh food in your dish yet. Don't you want to eat first?" Mark rubbed the stubble on his face.

"Meeeowww." Buddy put his nose to the door, raised his right front paw, and stroked the door a few times to ensure his message came through loud and clear.

"Okay. Okay." Mark chuckled and opened the

door.

He leaned outside and called after Buddy. "If you see that sassy KC, tell her to come in, and tell her Daddy is mad. I don't like it that she stayed out all night."

Buddy ran a few steps and stopped to look back. "Meow. Mrrrrooooow!"

Once the door had closed, Buddy raced around the house to the backyard. He found Bounce waiting eagerly by the fence.

"Are you ready, Bounce?" Buddy asked.

"I'm ready! I'm ready! I'm ready!" Bounce leapt three times in a row for emphasis.

"Okay, go under the fence over there and run into your front yard, and I'll meet you there." Buddy turned but thought better of it. He turned back to Bounce. "Remember, you've got to bark loud. And bark a lot!"

"Oh, I will! I will! I will!" Bounce yapped excitedly. "I can't wait to chase you!"

Buddy squeezed through the gap in the gate and walked out into the front yard. He looked over and waited.

A few seconds later, Bounce squeezed under the chain link fence. She grunted and wriggled and grunted some more while she slowly pushed her pudgy little body through. She popped out on the other side with a happy bark.

"I'm free! I'm free." Bounce barked joyfully.

"Okay, act like you're chasing me," Buddy said.

Bounce lowered herself on her front paws and burst into a torrent of angry barks and yaps.

Buddy felt the hair rise on his back. He backed

189

up a few steps.

"Whoa, that's pretty scary," Buddy said.

Suddenly, Bounce leapt at Buddy.

"MEEEEOOOWWWW!" Buddy wailed. Then he shot away like a black streak, with Bounce running hot on his heels.

The duo circled the front yard twice before the front door opened.

"Hey! What's going on out there?" Mark shouted, holding a steaming cup of coffee.

Buddy slowed down, and Bounce immediately stopped.

"Are you ready?" Buddy meowed.

"Which way do we go?" Bounce yapped.

"This way. Follow me," Windwhisper whistled from the tree above them. She smiled down at them and then took off down the road.

Buddy raced after the diminutive Mockingbird.

Bounce barked a series of angry yaps and took off like a comet after the receding form of Buddy.

***

"Oh, no!" Mark shouted.

"What is it, honey?" Jane leaned against him and looked out. She was still wearing her robe.

"Bounce is chasing Buddy down the road. I've got to go get them." Mark ran upstairs to put his shoes on.

"Oh, I'd better phone Mrs. Williamson. She'll worry if she knows her little Bounce is out." Jane picked up the phone and dialed.

A few minutes later, Mark ran down the stairs. He met a frantic Mrs. Williamson talking with his wife at the front door.

"Oh, Mark. She's afraid Bounce will get run over by a car," Jane said with feeling.

"I'm going after them."

"Mrs. Williamson is going to stay with the kids. I'll go get the car and follow. When we find them, we'll put them in our car and bring them both back." Jane smiled comfortingly at the older woman.

"That's so nice of you. I worry so much about my little Bouncey girl," she said.

"Okay, they were running up to the end of Willow Hollow. Look for us there." Mark dashed out of the house.

He ran at a brisk pace down the street. His heart sank when he saw no sign of either animal. He made it to the end of Willow Hollow and looked first right and then left on the main street of the subdivision.

"Buddy!" Mark shouted when he suddenly caught sight of Bounce and Buddy still running far down the road.

He took off after them but kept looking behind until he saw Jane driving the car. He paused, out of breath, and waved to her. A few moments later, Jane drove up and he got in the passenger seat.

"They ... went ... that way!" He gasped breathlessly and pointed down the street.

Jane squealed tires as she mashed the accelerator.

"Whoa," Mark gasped.

"Sorry. I'm just a little anxious." Jane smiled apologetically.

She drove at a good speed down the road.

They soon caught up to Bounce, but when Jane

stopped the car and Mark jumped out, Buddy and Bounce both shot into the backyard of a nearby house and continued their trek toward the rear of the subdivision.

Mark started to follow them on foot but decided it would be better to cut the animals off. He jumped back inside the car. "Drive to the end of the road, to the rear entrance, and park."

Jane obeyed. She reached the rear entrance and quickly parked off to the side. Mark got out and positioned himself to intercept the pair. In the distance, he heard Buddy's frantic 'meows' and Bounce's nonstop yaps. The sounds grew steadily nearer with each passing moment.

"Here they come." Mark spread his arms apart and readied himself to catch the little animals like a goalie in a hockey game.

Suddenly, a small mockingbird landed on the roof of the car and started fussing away at him.

Mark turned in astonishment as the bird continued to chastise him with an endless stream of whistles and chirps.

"Well, I'll be ..." Mark scratched his head.

In the next instant, Buddy ran between his legs and zipped across Simpson Road and into the subdivision across the street.

Mark's mouth fell open in surprise. He glanced away from the mockingbird and watched with dismay and total puzzlement the fleeing form of Buddy. Then he jumped with surprise when Bounce appeared out of nowhere and shot like a bullet across the road.

"Oh, no!" Jane shouted while she stepped out of

the car. "It's a good thing there weren't any cars, or they'd have gotten run over for sure."

Mark started for the car but stopped short. The mockingbird continued fussing at him from the roof. When he reached for the car door handle, the mockingbird seemed to get more excited.

"Shoo ..." Mark waved his hands at the bird. "Shooo, bird!"

***

Windwhisper looked over and saw that Buddy and Bounce now had a good lead on the man KC called dad. She leapt up and flew over his head, forcing him to duck.

She laughed, and then she took off after the dog and cat.

***

"Did you see that crazy bird?" he asked Jane after he sat down in the car.

"Forget about the birds -- we're after a runaway cat and a dog!" Jane hit the gas and drove across Simpson Road in pursuit of the fleeing pair.

They drove slowly, hoping Bounce and Buddy would soon tire. They kept them in sight, driving about a block behind the two animals. Finally, they came to the back of the subdivision.

"Oh no, we don't want them to go into those trees. Stop the car!" Mark opened the door.

"Why not? Jane asked.

"Beyond those trees is where that crazy man lives, Charles Marcion. It's the back of his property, I found out one time while walking along the fence line." Mark started running toward the trees just as Buddy and Bounce disappeared into them.

Suddenly, a distant shot echoed in the morning air.

Mark stopped and listened. He looked back at Jane. "That sounds like it's coming from Marcion's trailer way back on the other side of his property. I'd better go and get Buddy and Bounce before they get beyond his fence and on his property." Mark ran forward.

Jane parked the car and hurried after him.

Mark reached the trees and ran on into the small forest. He stopped to listen, hoping to figure out in which direction the animals had run. After a moment, he clearly heard Bounce's constant yapping, but off in the far distance, he also heard the fierce barks of a large dog.

His stomach tightened when he recognized Jack's nightmarish howling.

Chapter Twenty-Four

Bluesky flew in a wide circle around the poison hill in order to make sure of the location of the food-nest and to check the wind direction. He spotted the small white bag at the foot of the exposed barrel. He did a quick survey to get his bearings and then turned to make his run.

"Hold your breath ... hold your breath ..." Bluesky kept repeating the words to himself all the time that he closed with his target.

He began his dive.

Bluesky picked up speed and dove straight for the food-nest. He took in a deep breath and held it as he passed the boundary above the dead zone.

The rusted side of the barrel grew closer and closer.

He clenched his toes together in anticipation and then immediately opened them wide.

The white edges of the food-nest contrasted sharply against the rusted side of the barrel. Bluesky focused only on it now. He held his wings straight out and sailed in for the grab.

He came directly at the barrel. He couldn't fly over it and grab the food-nest since it rested against it near the bottom.

Bluesky pulled up at the last moment and flapped his wings vigorously. Somehow, in a crude imitation of Coolbreeze, he hovered above the food-nest.

His toes slashed through the thin layer of the

white dust that coated the outside of the food-nest and into the paper. Bluesky cringed as he realized his toes were coated in the poison.

It couldn't be helped now.

Immediately, he flapped his wings to gain altitude.

Pressure built inside his lungs, and they began to burn. He felt an overpowering need to take a breath, but he was still too close.

He lifted higher and clenched his toes, holding the bag so tightly his claws ripped larger holes in the paper.

Bluesky's lungs burned like fire. He needed to take a breath of air.

He flapped his wings harder and rose above the top of the barrel and the hill beside it. He turned toward his right and took off.

The dead zone was still below him while he picked up speed.

His lungs ached now, and spots began appearing before his eyes. Without realizing it, he was dropping lower with each beat of his wings. Lower and lower he fell as the world danced and swirled inside his oxygen-starved brain. Somehow, he realized he was falling -- but he didn't really care.

He felt so tired. So very tired ...

A terrible, awful squeal echoed from somewhere close by.

The tragic sound of death startled Bluesky and made him gasp. Immediately, he took another breath.

He looked down and realized he was only inches from the ground. He took a deep breath, flapped his wings harder, and slowly rose.

A wave of gladness swept over him when he realized he was past the dead zone. He took in one breath of sweet air after another as he rose into the morning air.

"Get ready, Thundercloud!"

Bluesky changed direction instantly at Blackfeather's words.

He was near the clearing and the terrible scene that was still unfolding.

Jack stood like a bloody monster in the center, panting hard from his exertions. He carried the limp form of Bear by the throat while he trotted triumphantly around the clearing. When he came to the still body of King, he dropped Bear next to him.

Jack tensed his muscles and howled up toward the sky.

A shadow flashed over Jack, and he turned instantly toward it.

Thundercloud landed on the ground near Jack with his great wings still outstretched.

As Jack watched in disbelief, the Hawk gingerly picked up the unconscious Sparrow with the soft pads of his foot and leapt back into the air.

Jack charged

"Fly, Thundercloud! He's after you!" Blackfeather cried out urgently.

Thundercloud carefully held the limp form of Treeflower while he beat his mighty wings harder and harder. With each downstroke, he slowly rose into the air, but Jack was gaining quickly!

In a flash, Blackfeather sailed right across Jack's head in a blur of motion. With a quick jab of his big beak, he rapped the dog's thick skull.

Jack roared in anger and turned to give chase, but he quickly saw he had no chance to catch the fleeing Crow. When he turned to pursue Thundercloud again, the Hawk had gained enough altitude to elude him.

Jack howled with disappointment.

Bluesky whistled a cheer.

However, Jack now began searching furiously for other prey. Bluesky's heart sank when he saw Daymoon still lying just beyond the clearing in a clump of tall grass with faithful Bushhopper beside him.

Bluesky panicked. It was only a matter of time before Jack found them and ripped the two birds to pieces.

Indeed, while he watched in horror, Jack turned and began galloping directly at them ...

***

Marcion reached down and picked up his shotgun again. He quickly pulled out three more shells and reloaded, all the while keeping his eyes focused on the tiny hummingbird that darted all around him.

Marcion laughed crazily after he popped the last shell into place.

"I'm going to blow you to smithereens, you little turd!" He chuckled maliciously, slowly brought the gun to his shoulder, and aimed.

The hummingbird zoomed straight at Marcion.

Marcion looked down the barrel of the gun and aimed directly at the bird. He squeezed the trigger.

***

The shotgun blast erupted, but Coolbreeze had realized the big death-stick was pointed directly at him and went into a rapid dive. He zoomed in a blur and sailed right between Marcion's legs.

"Did I kill it?" Marcion staggered around searching the ground for a dead Hummingbird, but he couldn't find one!

Coolbreeze had already flown over the top of the trailer and far beyond to the other side. He turned back in the direction where Marcion stood in the distance and hovered a moment in the air. Coolbreeze squeaked and laughed boldly.

And then he stuck his tongue out at him.

***

"CAW! CAW! CAW!"

Blackfeather sailed right into the middle of the clearing and landed. He continued hopping and flapping his wings as if he could no longer fly.

Jack stopped in his tracks and howled. Then he turned and immediately gave chase.

Blackfeather hopped along a few more feet until he was sure Jack was after him. With a big, bouncing hop he leapt into the air right as Jack snapped at him with his fangs.

"CAW!" Blackfeather shouted back over his shoulder as he rose out of reach.

The big dog hadn't figured out their little trick yet!

"Keee-harrrr!"

Morningsun dove down and landed right next to Daymoon, who still lay motionless. Bushhopper hopped away in fright but then chirped happily when the Hawk picked up his friend and rose back

199

into the air cradling Daymoon within her mighty talons.

Bushhopper flew after them with a happy cry.

Morningsun was almost twice as big as Thundercloud, and her great wings lifted her quickly into the sky.

Suddenly, the death-stick roared again. Right underneath Morningsun, shotgun pellets ripped through the air and caused the tall grass to wave crazily

***

Marcion cursed his poor aim and last night's beer while he raised the barrel higher and prepared to kill the hawk with his final shot. He cursed again when he staggered and almost fell. He only had one cartridge left in the shotgun before he'd have to reload. Spreading his legs apart, he steadied himself and raised the barrel. He aimed at the fleeing hawk.

Marcion took a breath and smiled.

"I've got you now."

***

Coolbreeze zoomed back over the trailer like a rocket. He quickly reached Marcion and flew around his head several times, squeaking at the top of his voice to distract the man.

***

Marcion spun around first to his right and then back around to his left, trying to keep an eye on the tiny bird zooming around his head. He forgot about the hawk and readied himself to shoot his familiar nemesis.

"Come on, you pesky little bird. Circle me one more time!" Marcion muttered angrily, but the hummingbird had stopped his diversionary circling and was hovering behind him.

Marcion heard the humming of the bird at his back and slowly turned around with his gun ready, doing his best not to startle the creature and make it flee again. He noted with satisfaction that the humming noise continued to stay directly behind him.

**

Coolbreeze was matching Marcion's every move. As the man slowly turned, Coolbreeze kept himself in the same position behind him. The Hummingbird held still when Marcion paused. He wondered what Marcion would do next when the man suddenly jumped around in a single motion and fired. Even then, Coolbreeze had more than enough time to flick out his tongue and zoom straight up twenty feet before Marcion had pulled the trigger.

**

Marcion stared in disbelief and shouted in anger at what he saw. A huge spread of tiny pellet holes littered the entire side of his trailer.

"I shot mah trailer agin, you crazy bird!" He threw his gun down in disgust.

**

Coolbreeze squeaked in laughter from high above.

**

Thundercloud continued on toward the distant woods with Morningsun and Bushhopper not far behind.

"Come on, let's get out of here!" Tootight shouted.

"He's right -- let's go!" Blackfeather flew off with them.

Bluesky flapped his wings harder, the weight of the food-nest slowing him down. He looked back and saw Jack chasing after him, but he was easily out of reach, though he was only about ten feet up in the air.

"Come on, Coolbreeze!" Bluesky cried out.

***

Coolbreeze turned and saw the others leaving. He laughed again and then noticed that Marcion had grabbed his shotgun and was running after the fleeing birds too.

Coolbreeze zoomed to stop him.

He passed Marcion in a flash and once again circled the man's head several times.

***

Marcion stopped and cried out. Gripping the shotgun by the barrel, he swung it wildly like a baseball bat at the circling hummingbird. He turned around and around trying in vain to knock the tiny bird down, but the more he turned, the dizzier he became until he was swinging the butt of the gun in huge, crazy arcs.

***

Coolbreeze squeaked and laughed louder and louder. He realized the man was so dizzy that he was about to fall down. He zoomed around in a wider circle because Marcion was staggering so badly now.

Then the hummingbird made a terrible mistake.

***

Even though he was swinging blindly, Marcion

somehow smacked the hummingbird from behind as it flew around him and sent it flying into the nearby grass. He laughed with delight when he heard the hollow sound and realized he'd knocked the bird down at last.

He stopped turning and swinging and tried to focus on the spot where the hummingbird had fallen, but the world continued to spin.

Marcion staggered and twisted until he lost sight of the spot. He fell in a heap with the shotgun in his lap. He moaned painfully as last night's beers and this morning's exertions sent his mind reeling.

He leaned over and puked on the ground. He wiped his mouth, pulled another cartridge out of his pocket, and reloaded the shotgun. He sat a moment longer while the dizziness subsided.

***

Bluesky gasped. He saw Coolbreeze knocked out of the air and realized he was helpless.

"Blackfeather, help! Coolbreeze is down!"

Blackfeather swung around. "Where's he at?"

"He's behind Marcion. Over there!" Bluesky pointed with his beak.

At just that moment, Marcion jumped up with his shotgun pointed directly at them.

"Fly away, Bluesky, fly!" Blackfeather shouted. "We'll never make it in time!" The Crow shook his head and continued flying away

Bluesky's heart pounded with pain, but he turned away. But his heart burned with regret at the thought of leaving his friend behind.

***

Marcion aimed at the two birds, but the world

suddenly spun out of control again. His confused mind reeled. He stumbled and found himself once again pointing the gun at his trailer. He turned back to the fleeing birds.

"Ohhhh, forget about you!" Marcion realized the birds were out of range now. He quickly inserted a second cartridge and frantically searched the grass for the hummingbird. "I'm going to kill you, little bird, for all the trouble you've caused me today."

***

From the trees behind Marcion's trailer, Nightwind took to the air and flew on silent wings toward Marcion. He flew noiselessly until he closed with him.

The man was using the barrel of the gun to part the grass as he searched. Nightwind settled onto the ground a few feet behind him.

***

Marcion's mind finally cleared, and he now searched intently in order to finish his grisly business. A moment later, he parted the grass, and the unconscious form of the hummingbird lay right before him.

"I've got you now!" Marcion stood and pointed the barrel at the unmoving bird. He slowly squeezed the trigger and laughed under his breath.

Then the sound of wings came to his ears.

Marcion froze. Another bird was directly behind him!

"How'd you get behind me?" Marcion muttered. He readied himself to turn and fire in one motion.

***

Nightwind smiled. He opened his beak and cried

out in full throat with the terrible, haunting sound that gave name to his kind. The Owl's eerie and heart-chilling screech split the air.

***

Marcion felt the hair on the back of his neck stand up. He rose up on his toes in total fright at the unexpected, nightmarish sound right behind him.

***

Nightwind took a deep breath and flew forward until he was right behind Marcion's head.

He screeched again at full force.

***

Marcion screamed in sheer terror.

He lowered the gun and bent over, imagining that some terrible, ghostly entity was crying out right behind him. He clenched his eyes shut, not daring to look at what could make such a terrible sound, and without thinking tightened his grip on the gun. When the entity screeched a third time as it passed over him, he instinctively pulled the trigger.

Marcion screamed in pain, dropped the gun, and grasped his right foot with both hands.

"I shot mah foot! I shot mah foot!" he shouted again and again as he hopped around frantically. "I've shot mahself in the foot!"

***

Nightwind flew over and carefully picked up Coolbreeze. He looked over to see Marcion fall to the ground still holding his wounded foot and then took off, carrying the tiny bird in his gentle grasp.

***

Bluesky had turned when the death-stick roared and watched in amazement while Marcion danced

205

around on one foot. He cried out in relief when he saw Nightwind flying toward him carrying the still unconscious Coolbreeze.

"Hooray!" Bluesky shouted.

Suddenly, Jack roared again.

Bluesky looked down. Jack was still chasing him on the ground, though he was falling further and further behind.

Bluesky laughed. He knew in a few minutes it would be all over.

"Meow!"

Bluesky's heart froze. Down below was his friend KC standing in the path of the onrushing dog with nowhere to hide.

He saw KC stop after catching sight of the monster Bulldog crashing through the tall grass, heading straight for her.

In the same instant, Jack howled in delight when he saw the cat. He charged.

"Run, KC! RUN!"

But there was no way KC could escape. She was in the middle of the field with no trees to climb.

The monster dog ran faster. He was like a living nightmare with blood covering his face and open wounds all over his neck and body. He howled louder, a sickening sound that shook the air announcing his impending kill.

Bluesky cried out in fear for KC.

In the next second, he realized there was no way to stop Jack -- nothing stood between the dog and the helpless cat. He shuddered at the thought of KC being killed right before his eyes by the crazed dog.

Bluesky watched in horror.

KC arched her back and stood sideways to meet the charge of the monstrous dog. Every hair on her body stood straight up while she flattened her ears and hissed menacingly.

Jack roared with bloodlust and rushed in for the kill.

"No!" Bluesky shouted.

In that instant, he turned around.

Chapter Twenty-Five

Bluesky dove toward the monster dog.

He didn't know what he was going to do. He just knew he had to do something to help his friend. He wasn't going to let her face the dog alone!

"Don't do it, Bluesky. You can't stop that monster!" Blackfeather shouted.

"I've got to help her -- she's my friend. Or I'll die trying!"

Bluesky flew over KC in a blur of motion and shouted, "Run, KC! I'll divert him!"

He flew straight at the charging dog. Bluesky cried out and did everything he could to get the dog's attention.

Jack howled with delight when he spotted the Mockingbird coming at him. The dog changed direction in order to snatch the bird out of the air and crush it with his fangs.

"Run, KC! Now!" Bluesky whistled as he closed with Jack the Ripper, but KC remained frozen, appearing overwhelmed with fear at the sight of the terrible creature. She hissed furiously and seemed not to have even noticed Bluesky she was so frightened.

Jack lunged for Bluesky.

Bluesky turned on his right wing to avoid the massive, snapping jaws. He flew around the back of the dog and turned to attack. His heart sank when he realized KC was still frozen in place.

Like a parent Mockingbird fiercely protecting

his nest from any and all comers, Bluesky confronted the huge dog. He attacked to protect KC, because she was the first one ever to call him friend.

If he had to, he'd face this dog head-on to protect his friend, but just now he felt he had a better chance coming at him from behind ...

Bluesky flapped his wings harder and closed. He flew right for the back of Jack's head. When he reached it, he shoved his pointed beak forward, grabbed a tuft of fur, and yanked with all his might.

Jack howled from the sharp pain of his fur being pulled out.

Instantly, the huge dog twisted and leapt into the air. He caught sight of Bluesky right above his head. He leapt for the bird, but Bluesky surged just out of reach of his bloody fangs.

"Snap out of it, KC! Run, run, run!" Bluesky shouted. He turned for another pass at the dog.

Jack had stopped and was waiting for the bird this time.

Bluesky cried out and flew right at the dog's face.

Jack roared and jumped at him, snapping his fangs.

Bluesky rolled to his right and evaded the dog once more.

Jack lunged to the side after him.

Bluesky flew directly up, and the dog ran under him and beyond. Folding his wings, the Mockingbird dove at the dog and nipped another tuft of fur off the top of his head, but this time Jack realized the bird might attack from behind again. The dog's huge shoulders tensed for action. He

209

didn't even wince when the bird pulled his fur out this time. Instead, he lunged up a second after the pain with his massive jaws agape.

The dog's terrible fangs snapped shut, and Jack snatched Bluesky out of the air by latching his teeth onto the food-nest the bird held tightly with his claws.

Bluesky felt the gut-wrenching sensation of being stopped at full speed. With a sickening dread, he found himself dangling upside down. Bluesky closed his eyes and felt his toes tear the paper bag even more while he swung helplessly.

Jack shook the food-nest violently and then jerked his head back, trying to swing the bird into his mouth. The movement was so abrupt that Bluesky lost his grip on the food-nest and fell hard to the ground. The force knocked the breath out of his body. He couldn't move. He couldn't even breathe.

Knowing the dog was directly above him ready to make the final kill, Bluesky opened his eyes and looked up. Jack's snarling face was only inches away, the food-nest dangling from one of his fangs on his lower jaw, the paper pierced by that single tooth.

Bluesky clenched his eyes shut and waited to die. He held his breath and waited for the terrible, crushing pain that would signal his death ... but his heart continued to pound so hard he finally had to take a breath. He took it in quickly, knowing it must be his last.

A terrible growl shook the ground, and Jack's hot, putrid breath washed over him. Then Jack's wet nose pushed against him.

Bluesky couldn't move. He was so frightened, now that he knew death was so close.

He heard and felt Jack sniffing over his still form.

Suddenly, he heard the dog inhale deeply.

An eerie, surreal silence filled his mind ...

Bluesky waited pensively for the pain of the dog's teeth ripping into his body. His lungs burned for air, and he took another quick breath, his entire body tensed and waiting for Jack's final blow.

The seconds continued to pass -- and he was still alive!

He opened his eyes for a quick peek. Jack still hovered right above him in exactly the same position he'd been in the last time Bluesky looked.

Bluesky clenched his eyes shut again but then opened them immediately.

Jack was in *exactly* the same position. The massive dog wasn't moving a single muscle -- he stood frozen like a statue. In fact, he didn't seem to be breathing.

Bluesky looked the huge dog over carefully and realized Jack's eyes were glazed over.

"The poison ..." Blackfeather whispered, landing next to him.

Bluesky realized the food-nest still dangled from Jack's mouth and also under his nose. The dog's nose was coated with the poison where he had breathed it in while sniffing at Bluesky.

"He's breathed the poison," Blackfeather whispered again.

Jack's legs crumpled all at once, and the huge

dog collapsed in a heap onto the ground.

"Fly, Bluesky!" Blackfeather shouted fearfully.

Bluesky tried to move, but it was too late.

The food-nest fell on him after Jack's mouth opened fully. Fortunately, Jack's head fell at an angle and missed crushing him.

"He's ... dead." KC said in disbelief. She slowly walked up after coming out of her paralyzing trance. "The monster is dead." KC shook her head, and stared at the gargantuan dog lying dead on the ground.

She glanced over at the fallen Mockingbird. "Are you all right, Bluesky?"

"I-I think so."

"You saved my life!" KC purred.

Bluesky breathed deeply.

The stench of the poison filled his nostrils!

"Don't move, Bluesky! You're covered with poison dust!" Blackfeather shouted in fear.

Bluesky looked down at himself and saw a thin coating of white dust all over him.

"Help me!" Bluesky pleaded, his heart pounding with panic.

"Hold your breath!" Blackfeather shouted.

Bluesky took a breath and held it.

"What can we do?" KC asked fearfully.

Blackfeather stared at Bluesky. The Crow hopped over, picked up the food-nest with his claws, and hopped away with it. He dropped it and then turned back toward Bluesky and KC.

"You've got to get it off!"

Bluesky's eyes widened with fear.

"A dirt bath! I've seen Brown Thrashers and

212

Mockingbirds do it. Get up and give yourself a dirt bath and rub it off!" Blackfeather shouted with the greatest urgency.

Bluesky turned over and started rubbing himself against the ground. Spreading his wings and feathers, he lay down on the dirt and wriggled against the ground. He rolled over and fluttered his wings frantically while he wriggled his back against the dirt. Next, he lay on his right side and then his left and repeated his frantic efforts.

Now his lungs burned for air!

"Your back! Wash your back again!" KC urged with plaintive cries.

Bluesky rolled over and wriggled his back harder against the dirt, but he couldn't stand it any longer. He turned around, hopped up on his leg, and took in a long, wonderful breath of fresh air.

"Move away, first! Hop away from there -- you just brushed the poison off on the ground all around you!" Blackfeather shouted.

Bluesky leapt into the air and flew several feet away. When he glanced around, the world wavered and danced like in a dream. Dizziness caused his mind to reel, and he fell to the ground.

"What's the matter?" KC asked.

Bluesky lay on the ground a moment until the dizziness subsided a little.

"Yes, I'm okay ... I think." He slowly stood up.

Bluesky, KC, and Blackfeather all gazed at the food-nest lying on the ground where Blackfeather had laid it.

Bluesky wavered a moment, fighting the dizziness.

"Let's finish our mission," Bluesky said. He spread his wings and hopped over to the food-nest. He smelled the stench again and turned his head away, trying not to breathe any more of the poison. He grasped it with his claws and carried it aloft.

KC ran after him while Blackfeather took off into the air after him.

He flew higher and felt the dizziness grow stronger. He couldn't focus his mind, and then his vision blurred.

Suddenly, he found himself flying straight toward the ground.

"Look out!" Blackfeather yelled.

Bluesky righted himself right before he crashed. He was flying just above the grass now, but he was headed in the wrong direction. He looked around frantically, trying to figure out the right way. Finally, he recognized the line of trees and headed toward them.

He rose higher into the air, and once again the terrible dizziness and disorientation returned, this time stronger and more frightening. His heart grew cold.

Bluesky cried out, and then he fell from the sky.

He awoke to find Blackfeather and KC looking down at him.

"You passed out," KC said in a quiet voice.

"We've got to get the food-nest to KC's dad ... or it was all for nothing," Bluesky groaned. He looked down and realized he still clutched the food-nest with his claws.

He also realized he could smell the poison again. That meant he was breathing it again.

Bluesky coughed hard, hoping it would help expel any he had just inhaled.

Suddenly, he felt something tighten around him, and he was lifted upward.

He opened his eyes and discovered that KC was holding him gently in her mouth.

"D-d-d-on't ..." Bluesky pleaded, but KC padded along carrying him in her mouth while he still clutched the food-nest.

Blackfeather flew above them.

"P-p-put me down, KC. You'll breathe the poison too," Bluesky pleaded.

"Mmm-mm-mmm," KC mumbled.

"I-I can't understand a w-word you're saying," Bluesky said in a whisper, out of breath.

Bluesky tried to stretch his wings, but KC's mouth held him tight. He leaned his head over and looked up at KC. "Please, put me down. I can fly now."

KC stopped and gently placed him on the ground. Bluesky hopped up and spread his wings for balance even as the world started spinning around him again.

"I don't mind carrying you," KC meowed.

She suddenly sneezed, which startled Bluesky. He leapt into the air and flew toward the trees. KC ran right behind him.

Bluesky had flown only a few feet when dizziness overwhelmed his senses once more. He groaned, realizing he had lost his sense of direction.

"I ... I can't find my way ..." Bluesky moaned. Then everything went dark.

Once again, he plunged to the ground in a heap

of feathers. He smelled the poison and realized some more had spilled out. He heard KC walk up.

"Don't do it, KC. Please, leave me ..."

"I will carry you, my friend," KC meowed. "I will carry you all the way home, if I must."

"No ..."

"Yes. You came back for me, and I won't leave you now."

Bluesky opened his eyes and saw some of the white powder on the ground near the top of the food-nest. A small coating covered his toes as well. He let go and rubbed his toes in the dirt. Then he stood and grasped the food-nest again.

In the next second, he wobbled unsteadily and fell over.

KC gently picked him up in her mouth and carried him toward the trees.

"KC, I don't want anything bad to happen to you. Please, just leave me." Bluesky groaned, and his eyes fluttered.

KC walked even faster.

When he twisted his head and looked forward, he could see the line of trees slowly growing closer. Somewhere in the distance, he heard a small dog barking continuously, but he couldn't quite figure out where ... everything was so strangely out of place now ... so surreal and dream-like ...

He felt like he was falling ...

The stench of poison filled his nose, and he coughed and coughed until his body shook with convulsions.

KC stopped and put him down.

As Bluesky felt his head rest gently against the

216

warm ground, he slipped away into unconsciousness.

KC stood over Bluesky, and the muscles in her shoulders and neck quivered. She began to sway from side to side.

She sneezed several times, her body trying to throw off the poison she had breathed while carrying Bluesky.

"I'm not going to leave you." She reached down and gently took Bluesky back into her mouth.

***

KC tried to walk faster, but she suddenly leaned to one side and began heading in that direction. She blinked her eyes to clear her vision, but everything became even more blurry.

She stopped and looked around until she recognized the line of trees.

KC headed toward them but immediately stumbled. She flinched and walked more slowly, trying to step carefully, but her mind swirled and she grew more confused.

She was less than a hundred feet from the edge of the tree line when she fell.

Bluesky dropped out of her mouth and landed on the ground beside her. The food-nest slowly fell out of his grasp.

Blackfeather flew in a circle above the unconscious forms of KC and Bluesky, crying out over and over again.

"Help! Someone help my fallen friends! Please, somebody help us!"

Chapter Twenty-Six

"Buddy! Bounce! Come here!" Mark shouted with exasperation.

Bounce yapped excitedly somewhere ahead of them among the thick shadows of trees.

Mark peered ahead and saw the fields beyond.

"Uh-oh." He knew he had to get Bounce and Buddy before they drew the attention of Marcion's dogs.

"Honey!"

Mark turned at the sound of his wife's voice.

"I parked the car right at the edge of the woods," Jane said after she joined him.

Bounce began barking for what seemed like the hundredth time that morning.

Mark and Jane walked quickly through the trees until they came right to the fence that bordered Marcion's property. .Just a few feet away, Bounce stood with her stubby tail wagging furiously while she barked up a tree.

"Oh, Mark, that's Buddy up there." Jane pointed to a branch about fifteen feet above Bounce.

Mark reached down, picked up Bounce, and handed her to Jane.

"Take Bounce back to the car and put her inside. I'll be right there as soon as I figure out how to get Buddy down."

Jane took the Jack Russell Terrier from Mark and cradled her tight. She turned and headed back to the car.

Mark looked up.

Buddy's large green eyes pleaded to Mark for help.

"Okay, Buddy. I'm going to get you down ... somehow." He looked around for something, anything that might help. He was searching around the base of the tree for a way to step up and climb it partway to Buddy when the constant calling of a crow somewhere nearby caught his attention.

He looked over the field and saw the crow flying in a circle a short distance away.

"Must be something dead there." He turned back to Buddy, put his foot against the tree, and started climbing.

Without warning, that same, tiny mockingbird that had fussed at him earlier appeared and flew around his head, fussing at him once again.

Her sudden appearance startled Mark, and he fell down.

"What the?" He stood and brushed the dirt off his pants.

The small mockingbird continued to fly around him crying insistently at him.

"Why are you fussing at me?" Mark said to the mockingbird. "Have you got a nest up there or something?"

He looked up.

Buddy had climbed partway down and was right above him now. Mark reached up and carefully took Buddy into his arms.

"There, there. I hope you're okay, Buddy. That bad ol' dog didn't scare you, did it?"

Buddy purred contentedly while Mark cuddled

him.

"Well, you seem unhurt to me, handsome lad." Mark smiled and stroked Buddy's ears.

Buddy purred louder, and then he looked up with a startled expression at the fussing bird.

The mockingbird flew right up to Mark's face and twittered and fussed in a high-pitched voice.

"What in the world?"

The mockingbird flew off over the fence and into the field.

"What?" Mark stared in wonder at the bird. She was heading directly for the crow.

Buddy jumped out of his arms, ran under the fence, and took off after her.

"Buddy! Where are you going now?"

Mark felt his heart racing. He knew if one of Marcion's dogs was close by it would kill Buddy.

Without hesitation, Mark climbed the fence and ran after his cat.

He found Buddy about twenty feet beyond the fence, sitting calmly and licking his forepaw.

"Buddy, what are you doing?" Mark crouched down to pick him up.

The mockingbird and crow cried out simultaneously a short distance ahead.

Mark looked up and saw something black lying in the tall grass. As he looked harder, he realized it was some kind of small animal -- something with black fur. It had to be either a small dog or a ...

Mark jumped up and ran over. It was KC lying on the ground.

"What happened to you, KC?" Mark cried out with fear.

He hurriedly searched her fur for any wounds or blood, and he felt a rush of relief when he discovered neither. And yet, she was so still.

It scared him.

He noticed a tainted smell around KC's face, and when he looked more closely he saw a few specks of white dust on her neck and a couple on her nose. He took out his handkerchief and wiped her face and neck clean.

Although he wiped firmly, KC never moved. He brought the handkerchief close and sniffed. He immediately pushed it away, realizing it was some kind of poison.

Had Marcion poisoned his cat? Or had she gotten into some poison on his property accidentally?

Mark's heart pounded when he remembered the miscarriages and search for the unknown source...

A movement startled him, and he jumped to his feet. He feared it was one of Marcion's dogs about to attack!

"What is it, Mark?"

He turned and saw Jane with Buddy in her arms instead.

"Whew! You scared me. Oh, I found KC, and ... she's hurt ..."

He looked back down and suddenly realized a dead bird was nearby. As he looked closer, he realized the bird only had one leg.

"That's the one-legged mockingbird I've seen living around our house for about a year now!" Mark said in surprise.

"Is it ... dead?" Jane asked with a hint of fear.

221

As he peered closer, he saw the mockingbird's side move ever so slightly.

"It's alive -- I see it barely breathing. He's taking very shallow breaths."

Once more, he noticed specks of the dangerous white powder, this time on the bird's feathers. He gently wiped around the bird's beak and across his body. Then he saw an empty French fry bag near the bird's foot.

Except it wasn't empty; there was something inside it ... He leaned closer, sniffed... and jerked his head back.

He looked closer and saw some white powder inside it along with a few small rocks.

He quickly folded the top over and then wrapped his handkerchief around it several times before he put it in the back pocket of his pants. Somehow, he knew this was the answer!

But how did KC and this one-legged mockingbird come to be in possession of it? And where ...

"Let's get them to the vet fast," Jane said in a determined voice. "I'm afraid KC might die!"

Mark gently picked up KC in his arms. He leaned forward, still cradling her, and then picked up the mockingbird and laid him on KC.

They drove back home.

Bounce rode in Jane's embrace in the front seat while Buddy stared in silence at the unmoving forms of KC and the bird in the back seat.

Bounce looked over Jane's shoulder at the other animals in the back seat. The terrier began whimpering.

It seemed that both Bounce and Buddy were sad at seeing KC and the bird so sick, but he knew that had to be just his imagination.

Right?

He drove up into his driveway.

Mrs. Williamson immediately took Bounce back home while Jane took Buddy into the house to join the kids.

Mark rushed to the veterinarian's office with both KC and the mockingbird lying still and silent in the back seat.

Everything went by in a rush of movement. The next thing he knew, he was in the examination room with the veterinarian, who carefully checked the unconscious cat and then the bird.

The veterinarian first examined them externally. Then he took some blood from KC and took her temperature. Next, he checked inside her mouth.

He asked to see the powder in the bag after Mark explained how he'd found them. The veterinarian took a very small pinch of the substance and held it up to the light. He brought it to his nose and sniffed gingerly.

"This will have to be tested, but I think it's some kind of poison."

"I'm going to have that done right after we're done here," Mark said.

The veterinarian looked at Mark with a somber expression. "They must have ingested some of that poison. I'm afraid they may be suffering." He sighed, slowly removing his latex gloves.

Mark felt a wave of fear.

"I-I don't want her to suffer." Mark stared sadly

down at his beloved cat.

"The humane thing would be to put her down."

Mark's eyes filled with tears. He had not expected this outcome at all! Intense sadness filled his heart as he remembered KC as a tiny kitten following Jane home for the first time.

He'd expected the vet would give them some medicine and he'd take KC home. He had believed everything was going to be fine.

But now, KC was going to die.

He groaned and turned away, tears streaming down his face.

"You don't want her to suffer, right?"

Mark sighed deeply.

It felt like he was losing a member of his family. He remembered how she used to jump up in his lap each morning while he drank a cup of coffee and got ready for work. He remembered ...

"Mark, do you want me to put her down?"

He covered his face with his hands and quickly wiped away his tears. He stood there a long moment, just thinking. Finally, he spoke. "I ... I don't want her to suffer ..."

"I'll go prepare the injection." The veterinarian turned and left the room.

Mark felt his heart pounding inside his chest. He walked over to the unconscious forms of the cat and the bird.

KC lay there unmoving except for her shallow breathing. Her fur shone clean and neatly brushed after the veterinarian had carefully inspected and then brushed her.

KC and the bird just seemed to be sleeping ...

"I'm sorry," Mark whispered with regret to them. "I'm so, so sorry."

He stood over KC a moment and then, ever so gently, put his hand against her side as if to pet her.

He felt her side rise at his touch.

And just like he'd done thousands of times before, he lovingly stroked her.

He gently stroked her from the top of her head and all down her back. As he repeated the gesture, he took her ear between his thumb and forefinger and caressed it before continuing the motion.

KC remained unnaturally still.

A single tear streamed down Mark's cheek.

He petted her again in the same way. As he petted her, he started humming a familiar tune.

Mark leaned closer until his face was beside KC's ear. *"Who's Daddy's pretty kitty?"*

He started singing in a hushed whisper the familiar words of the song he always sang for KC. He sang it one last time.

"KayCee, the kitty cat ... the kitty cat ... the kitty cat. KayCee's the kitty, kitty cat ..." He quietly sang her little singsong ditty.

Suddenly, he froze. He leaned closer and listened.

KC was purring!

He stared down at her.

Yes, she was purring!

The door opened, and Mark turned. The veterinarian held a syringe in his hand.

"Um, hang on, Doc."

"What do you mean?"

"Well, let's wait overnight. I've had this cat for

225

seven years, and, well, she's been a good cat. She's part of our family. She deserves one more night to see if she'll come out of this. I'll look after her and check if she has improved in the morning."

"Okay, Mark, if that's what you want to do. You can bring her back here tomorrow if she doesn't wake up. Shall I go ahead and put the bird out of its suffering though?"

"Um ..." Mark stared at the one-legged mockingbird, unsure how to answer.

The vet held the needle just above the bird.

"No, no ... Somehow I imagine he's had a pretty tough life living with that handicap. Let's give him one more chance too. He deserves it."

The veterinarian arched his eyebrows in surprise. "You mean, you know this bird?"

"Yes, in a way."

Mark brought KC and Bluesky back home and placed each in a box lined with old towels to help make them comfortable. He put each box down in the basement where it would be quiet for them. He placed KC's food bowl and a small bowl of fresh water near her bed. He also put some water in a small bowl near the Mockingbird and spread out some birdseed on a paper towel. He looked one last time at each, but neither had stirred since he had put them in their new beds. He walked to the door and then turned out the light.

"I'll check on you in the morning. Try and get better." Mark looked at them a moment before he shut the door, hoping to see some small glimmer of hope from either of them.

Finally, he sighed and left.

Chapter Twenty-Seven

"Did you see what that man did? He carried Bluesky inside the house with KC!" Tootight said with a mixture of puzzlement and excitement.

Above the birds, the sun neared its zenith; soon it would be midday.

Dancingleaves flew up and joined Tootight, Thundercloud, Blackfeather, Windwhisper, and Nightwind on the branch in the dogwood tree that grew in the backyard.

"How is Daymoon?" Dancingleaves' expression showed his heartfelt concern.

"I laid him in an old, abandoned nest just above us," Thundercloud said. "He's resting with Bushhopper right beside him."

"What about Treeflower?" Tootight asked.

"I'm better!"

Everyone turned to the sound of her cheerful voice. She landed beside them.

The Song Sparrow smiled and flapped her wings vigorously a moment. "I got knocked a bit silly, but my head's clear now -- though I still have a terrible headache."

"I'm glad that's all you have after that horrible dog knocked you out of the air like that." Tootight shuddered at the memory of it.

"And Coolbreeze?" Blackfeather asked.

"I laid him in the fork of a nearby branch. He had awakened, but he was still a bit woozy." Nightwind chuckled. "He'll be fine."

227

Without saying a word, all the birds turned together and stared at the house below.

"Do you think Bluesky will l-l ..." Dancingleaves closed his eyes and turned away, afraid to say what everyone was thinking.

"Will live?" Nightwind finished for him. The wise Owl slowly shook his head. "It's too early to know. I'm afraid that both he and KC breathed a little of the poison. And ..."

"And that can't be good." Blackfeather sighed.

"Are they going to die?" Windwhisper gasped with tears in her eyes.

A terrible silence filled the air.

"We don't know," Nightwind said with a great sadness. "We just don't know ..."

"Can't we do something?" Dancingleaves blinked his eyes rapidly because they had filled with tears.

Out of nowhere, another bird joined them.

"So, here's the famous mixed flock," Funwind said with an arrogant tone. He looked at each bird. "I see that one-legged Mockingbird isn't with you. I knew he wouldn't be any help."

Everyone stared in shock at Funwind's words.

Suddenly, Thundercloud flew up and landed right beside Funwind. Funwind froze in a panic as the huge raptor stared sternly down at him with his hooked beak partly open. Thundercloud's eyes narrowed into slits and made the hapless song bird even more nervous.

Slowly, Thundercloud lowered his head until he was eye to eye with Funwind.

Funwind gulped nervously when

Thundercloud's beak rubbed against the tip of his own beak.

Finally, Thundercloud spoke in his deep, bass voice. "You know nothing about my friend Bluesky. He's the bravest bird I've ever met. What's more, he lies dying inside that house over there. And why? Because he was willing to risk his life to protect all of us -- including you, ungrateful and arrogant bird that you are."

"W-w-w-what ... ?" Funwind stammered.

"Why don't you just fly away," Windwhisper said while tears slid down her feathered cheeks.

Another bird flew up.

Ol' Gray Mama landed beside the diminutive Windwhisper.

"You're back already!" She looked around a moment and noticed the somber expressions on everyone's face.

"Where's my Bluesky?" she asked frantically.

Nightwind quickly told her all the details of their mission -- happy and sad. Funwind and Ol' Gray Mama gasped more than once as they heard of the terrible challenges that had befallen them that morning. They heard how all the birds faced the danger of the three dogs and how they braved the crazy man and his death-stick.

And they learned of the bravery of Bluesky.

"Did that one-legged Mockingbird really do all that?" Funwind asked with incredulity.

"Yes, he did!" Thundercloud replied firmly.

Funwind's beak fell open in awe.

When Nightwind continued the tale, everyone listened in silent respect -- especially Funwind.

As the Owl finished, they all turned at the sound of a closing door.

They watched as KC's dad stood and looked around the yard. He reached in his pocket and pulled out a white object. He carefully unfolded the handkerchief and inspected it.

"It's the food-nest with the poison!" Tootight sang out.

The man looked up at the bird's call, but they knew he wouldn't be able to see them because the leaves hid them from his view. He looked back down at the bag and its strange contents. Finally, he put the bag back in his pocket and headed toward the car.

"See, our plan is working! The man is taking the poison with him! He'll find a way to get rid of it!" Treeflower sang joyfully.

They watched the car drive off.

"What about Bluesky?" Ol' Gray Mama asked with great sadness. "Can't we do something for my poor Bluesky?"

"We can sing."

Dancingleaves smiled shyly, but the others stared at him in total shock.

"What?" they cried out together in surprise.

"We can sing for Bluesky -- and KC too, for that matter," Dancingleaves said simply.

"This isn't a time for --"

"Wait a minute!" Nightwind hopped up and down excitedly. "I think I know what he means!"

"What does he mean?" Tootight cried out. "I'm not really in a mood to sing any kind of song."

"No, not just sing!" Dancingleaves shouted. He

leapt off the branch and flew up into the sky.

"Then, what do you mean?" Blackfeather asked.

"We'll sing a Song-Tale! We'll sing about Bluesky! We'll sing about KC! We'll sing about their brave deeds!"

Nightwind soared up into the sky and flew in happy circles around the tree along with the Bluebird.

"And what's more, *we'll sing their Song-Tale clear around the world!*"

Thundercloud looked up at the sun. It was almost midday.

"But all the Song-Tales of the past were started with the rising of the morning sun. The Song-Tale traveled with the sun until it set and continued through the dark as birds sang it along. With the rising of the sun the next day, the Song-Tale returned to the original singers -- *that's how a Song-Tale is sung round the world!* It's too late to start one now," Thundercloud said in a matter-of-fact tone.

"We don't have much time," Dancingleaves said urgently. He quickly landed next to the great Hawk. "We have to start it now, right now! We'll sing it out, all of us, and with the rising of the sun tomorrow, it will come back, and Bluesky and KC will hear it! When they hear their song, perhaps it will make them feel better! That's why we have to start it today!"

"I don't know if they will hear it ... or can --" Tootight started.

"Hush!" Thundercloud said sharply.

"What do you mean?" Dancingleaves asked.

231

"Bluesky may not hear today or tomorrow or ever ..." Tootight hung his head sadly.

Dancingleaves turned away.

"I like the idea, and whether Bluesky and KC can hear the song or not, I think their courage deserves a Song-Tale -- especially Bluesky!" Thundercloud said with unexpected determination.

"I agree," Nightwind added. "Great deeds deserve to be sung, and all birds should hear about Bluesky and his wonderful tale."

The others shouted in agreement.

"Who is going to compose this song of praise?" Blackfeather asked, looking slowly from one bird to another.

"I will," Dancingleaves said decisively.

"You'd better get it done and quick," Blackfeather said. "I'll go tell all the Crows to get ready and that a new Song-Tale is about to be sung round the world. I'll meet you back here as quick as I can." The black Crow flew off to find his cronies.

"I will spread the word to all the Sparrows to get ready! I'll tell them that we're going to sing a new song clear round the world!" Treeflower flew off, singing as she went.

"We'll meet you here before the sun reaches its highest point," Nightwind said to Dancingleaves.

"I shall be right here -- and I'll have the song ready."

"I want to sing too," Funwind said.

"Will you sing a song about Bluesky?" Ol' Gray Mama asked him. "You've always made fun of him."

"I heard just now what he has done for all the

birds and animals, and I know he may even have given his life because of it. I-I have misjudged Bluesky." Funwind looked down with a shamed expression.

"Then, please add your voice when we sing of Bluesky. We need all the birds we can get," Ol' Gray Mama said with a smile.

"We'll need every bird. We're going to have to sing loudly! We're going to have to sing out like we've never done before in order to get this song going round the world!" Nightwind shouted with joy.

"I will sing!" Funwind exclaimed.

"We'll all sing!" Dancingleaves cried happily.

"And I will sing the loudest!" Funwind gazed at Dancingleaves with a determined look in his eyes. "I'll go tell all the Mockingbirds who live nearby to get ready. I'll have every Mockingbird ready to sing for Bluesky!"

They all left the dogwood tree singing with joy.

Dancingleaves flew to the upper branches and stared up at the clouds floating in the sky above. He closed his eyes and took a deep breath. He stood there silently while his mind and heart raced with emotion.

He thought of his friend Bluesky, about his kindness and bravery, about how he looked for the good in others. He thought about Bluesky's sadness and his joy, about his special journey, and all that the one-legged Mockingbird had done and experienced ...

And he began composing 'Bluesky's Song-Tale.'

Chapter Twenty-Eight

Daymoon groaned as he slowly stepped out of the nest. Bushhopper watched him with a concerned expression.

"You don't have to do this. We've got plenty of birds ..."

"I wouldn't miss this for the world." Daymoon bent over and grimaced. Lastly, he stretched his wings and looked around. "Where's the Bluebird?"

"He's over there." Bushhopper nodded to the other side of the dogwood tree.

"Let's go make history!"

Daymoon flew through the branches with Bushhopper right behind him.

They found all the familiar birds gathered around Dancingleaves.

Coolbreeze sat next to Treeflower. Tootight, Windwhisper, and Blackfeather sat on a limb just above. Dancingleaves and Nightwind were perched together while at the highest branch of the tree, Thundercloud stood straight and tall.

Across from them, Funwind flicked his long tail excitedly. In the trees all around them, hundreds of birds had gathered, birds of every feather, size, and family. Young and old, strong and weak, every bird who lived among the houses of Willow Hollow and beyond gathered in preparation of the new Song-Tale.

Nightwind smiled benevolently when Daymoon and Bushhopper landed among them.

"Our number is complete," Nightwind said. "Here is where the Song-Tale will begin." He spread his wings. "We will be the first birds to sing it forth from this starting point."

"And tomorrow, the song will come back to us here at the same tree with the rising of the sun!" Coolbreeze squeaked excitedly, finishing for the Owl.

"Can a song really be sung around the world in a single day?" Bushhopper asked with a tone of doubt.

"The few Song-Tales that have ever been successfully sung around the world were those songs that told a special story about a special bird." Nightwind's eyes grew far off. "The song's words must convey the passion and the wonder and the power of the tale. The song's melody must evoke the raw emotions of the story and stir the heart of the hearer so he fully understands and feels the song. The Song-Tale must itself become something special ... something that lives ..."

"The hearer must feel compelled to repeat the Song-Tale and thus help sing it round the world," Blackfeather added.

"And throughout time, the best Song-Tales will be repeated over and over again to each generation. Young birds in every generation will hear about the bravery, about the love, and about the lessons of life carried in them." Nightwind smiled and took a deep breath.

"The Song-Tale of Bluesky deserves to be sung," Dancingleaves said with a hint of sadness in his voice. "Every bird should know of his bravery and his great deed."

"They will! I just know they will!" Coolbreeze squeaked.

They all turned to Dancingleaves.

"Have you composed a song for Bluesky?" Nightwind asked.

"I have."

Nightwind looked around at the other birds. "We, the friends of Bluesky, must listen as Dancingleaves sings the Song-Tale for the first time. And after he has sung it, we must repeat it in all our different dialects and send it out to the world!"

Everyone nodded enthusiastically.

"Are you ready?" Nightwind asked Dancingleaves.

"Yes."

"Then, sing!"

Thundercloud hopped down to a lower branch and nodded toward the topmost branch he had just vacated.

Dancingleaves flew up to the highest point of the tree and sat just above Thundercloud. The great Hawk smiled at the small Bluebird, spread his wings, and soared into the sky. Everyone knew that Thundercloud would sing from on high in the dialect of his kind.

Dancingleaves looked around in every direction a moment. He saw the canopy of trees sprinkled like islands of green around the roofs of houses. He looked up. An army of small, white clouds marched across the blue sky.

His bright, blue feathers shimmered in the

236

sunshine while he raised his head, opened his beak wide, and sang forth in a strong, clear voice. The melody was deceptively simple, and yet each note pulsed with emotion.

Dancingleaves sang out with his heart and soul in every note and every word.

He sang of Bluesky's loneliness. He sang of his pain when all the Mockingbirds shunned him. He sang of how his father and siblings left him. And he sang about the day his mother died.

He sang of Bluesky's deep yearning for a friend -- a single friend in the entire world.

Finally, a ray of hope! He sang of how Bluesky met Ol' Gray Mama and Nightwind. He sang of Bluesky's journey to seek out the good in others.

Next, he sang of the birds Bluesky met and how a few -- a precious few -- became his friends. Then he sang of Bluesky's best friend, KC the kitty cat.

The song changed, filled with tension.

Dancingleaves sang about the *Death on the Wind* and how it threatened every living thing. He sang of the danger of the dogs and the man and his death-stick.

And he sang of how Bluesky volunteered to lead a mixed flock to save them all.

He sang of Bluesky's bravery in facing all these dreaded dangers. He sang about how Bluesky alone carried the poison, and how his friend KC then carried him when he could no longer fly.

And the Song-Tale ended with Bluesky and his best friend KC at death's door, both willing to give their lives so others would live ...

Chapter Twenty-Nine

Nightwind and the other birds repeated the Song-Tale, each in their own dialect.

Daymoon chirped in the crystalline voice of the Cardinal family. Bushhopper warbled with his powerful voice unique to his own kind. Coolbreeze squeaked enthusiastically while he zoomed all around the tree over and over again. Treeflower sang from a high branch with a gentle, flute-like twinkling of her beautiful voice. Tootight sang forth in the Robin's cackling chirps, and Blackfeather cawed with the Crow's bold and boisterous calls.

Thundercloud soared above them and flapped his great wings. He quickly rose higher and higher until he was high up in the air. His mighty cries echoed across the sky in every direction while he sang out to his brother Hawks.

Nightwind sang out although he knew most Owls would be sleeping this time of day. Still, he hooted and screeched with every ounce of energy he possessed, determined to wake every Owl with this special song.

Ol' Gray Mama cooed and warbled the stirring song with every fiber of her being.

True to his word, Funwind sang the loudest of them all, flying up in a circle from the high branch on which he'd perched, his wings and tail feathers spread wide. He burst forth, singing the Song-Tale about the one-legged Mockingbird and his courageous deed.

Dancingleaves smiled while the others repeated the song. From the topmost branch of that highest tree, his voice twinkled and trilled the Song-Tale again. He was determined to sing loudly enough so that every bird would hear!

As he sang with all his heart, tears began to stream from his eyes. His heart quivered with emotion each time he finished singing the last, stirring part and the notes drifted away on the wind.

He sang out a third time, no longer able to see because of the tears that now filled his eyes, but he sang louder, willing himself to do it although sadness filled his soul for his friend who lay at death's door.

All of the gathered birds sang out. They had heard the Song-Tale at least three times now, and they knew what to sing. An amazing and wondrous chorus lifted into the sky like a wall of sound, birds of every kind singing together for Bluesky.

In the yards that lined the adjoining roads around the street named Willow Hollow, all the birds in all the trees stopped what they were doing and listened with enraptured attention to the growing chorus.

Wrens and Chickadees, Titmice and Warblers, Mockingbirds, Cardinals, Bluebirds, Towhees, Catbirds, Thrashers and Sparrows, Crows and raptors of every kind -- every bird grew still and listened in hushed awe when they realized it was a brand new Song-Tale.

In an unexpected burst of birdsong, a second and even grander chorus sang out all at once and filled the air.

Every bird of every kind, young and old, male and female, sang out joyously in one voice.

They all sang Bluesky's Song-Tale.

They sang with relief in knowing that the poison had been found and their lives would no longer be in danger. They each felt an obligation to sing of the bird and the cat who were willing to sacrifice everything in order to accomplish it.

Every bird sang out in honor of the one-legged Mockingbird and his friend KC, the kitty cat.

The Song-Tale spread outward like a vast tidal wave of birdsong.

Coolbreeze zoomed higher into the sky. He squeaked back over his shoulder at the others.

"I'm going to go west as fast as I can fly and keep singing it on!"

"I shall too!" Thundercloud, still flying high in the sky, turned toward the west, and his powerful cries echoed toward the distant horizon.

"That's a great idea!" Bushhopper shouted.

"You go with them. I'll keep singing here until I can't sing anymore." Daymoon smiled a moment, and then he sang out again.

Bushhopper took off.

Coolbreeze squeaked even louder. He repeated the song in the dialect of the Ruby-throated Hummingbirds, and from every direction, hundreds of Hummingbirds rose above the trees and squeaked in unison, each one singing Bluesky's Song-Tale.

Blackfeather's raucous caws were soon repeated by dozens and dozens of other Crows. The old trickster flew into the air following the other song birds -- Coolbreeze, Thundercloud, Bushhopper,

Treeflower, and hundreds and hundreds of other birds -- and this growing cloud of singing birds all headed toward the west.

The chorus rose in volume until it was as powerful as the early morning chorus that birds sang each day to greet the sun. Thousands of birds now sang out together from every tree while more and more birds flew into the sky. The air reverberated with the song.

Amazingly, the chorus grew even more powerful.

As new birds listened for the first time when the Song-Tale reached them, it caused their hearts to beat faster and to burn with emotion for the one-legged Mockingbird on which the song was based.

As every kind of bird joined their voices and the song spread westward, the earnest voices of the Mockingbirds were always heard the loudest and leading the way.

The growing wave of the song spread west past the invisible border of Georgia and Alabama.

A huge, gnarled old oak tree stood in the middle of a field noisy with birds. A flock of over five hundred European Starlings cackled and twittered about in noisy confusion when the aural wave of the Song-Tale reached them, but they were so busy singing their own songs that not a single bird heard the Song-Tale.

Below the oak tree, an Eastern Meadowlark sat erect upon a wooden fence post with her head cocked to one side, listening intently. Her yellow breast feathers and black 'V' neck feathers contrasted with the waving green grass all around.

In spite of the raucous cries of the Starlings, she heard the words and music coming from the east.

When the last notes of the Song-Tale ended, the Meadowlark sat frozen a moment in awe while she contemplated the remarkable story. All at once, with her heart pounding with appreciation, she opened her long, tapered beak and burst forth in song, singing for the one-legged Mockingbird.

First one, and then a second Starling and then more heard the Meadowlark's sweet singing above their chaotic cries.

A hush swept through all the branches, and within seconds all five hundred plus Starlings were silent. In that aura of solemn surprise, they listened to the lone Meadowlark sing Bluesky's Song-Tale.

When the last notes echoed across the warm breeze, the Starlings looked from one to another in a rising tide of excitement.

Suddenly, the Starling on the topmost branch sang out.

Within seconds, every bird in the flock joined their voice as one. Over five hundred Starlings sang out the Song-Tale in a magnificent choir.

Other birds in nearby trees heard and quickly joined their voices in order to sing it along around the world.

The Song-Tale took on a life of its own.

The number of birds singing it along grew exponentially the farther the wave of sound traveled. Indeed, after each bird heard the words and felt the music, the song of Bluesky burned inside their soul, and then they immediately turned west and sang it on.

The sun passed its zenith and started its downward journey toward the western horizon.

The aural wave of the Song-Tale now reached its maximum speed as wave after wave of birds passed it along.

The Song-Tale reached the birds of the mighty Mississippi River and was sung across by Herons and Egrets and Ducks of many colors and breeds. Across the forests and fields, the Song-Tale spread westward, and a new phenomenon began to occur out in front edge of the aural wave.

Just before the wave reached a new area, all the local birds would go silent and sit perfectly still as if waiting. Somehow they realized something important was coming on the wind toward them. This strange, expectant hush among the birds now became the forerunner of the Song-Tale's wave as it approached.

As they waited with a feeling of electric suspense, they would finally hear the first bits of the chorus in the distance -- a wall of sound approaching them like a huge, invisible tidal wave.

Within seconds, the notes and words grew discernable, but they would remain transfixed, frozen in place, listening in awe to the story of the Song-Tale unfolding until the wave swiftly engulfed them.

Many birds cried out in ecstasy after the music engulfed them in its beautiful embrace. Others shouted in joy even before they heard the entire song when they realized what it was about -- *'a song about a one-legged Mockingbird and his best friend, KC the kitty cat!'*

Other birds would try to hush them with fussing cries so they could hear the rest of it ...

When the Song-Tale reached its end, every single bird within earshot would raise its voice and sing it along. No bird was unaffected by the power of this song. Every bird joined their voice to sing it round the world, singing it as passionately as if they had witnessed Bluesky's deeds with their own eyes.

Not a single heart of a single bird denied the power of the melody or its stirring message.

Across the vast western plains, the wave of song rolled inexorably onward.

A large number of Scissor-tailed Flycatchers rejoiced and sang while they balanced on their long, graceful tails -- tails twice the length of the bird itself. In the desert southwest, the beautiful red and brown Vermillion Flycatchers added their voices to the chorus. Now the Western Meadowlarks heard the dialect of their Eastern cousins and sang the song themselves.

The mighty wave of sound approached the immense forests of spruce and fir and redwood along the western coast. The Wrens and Sparrows and the Plovers and Hawks and the Ravens and Jays of the forest sang it on with joy. The beautiful Anna's Hummingbirds, with their gorgeous rose-red crowns and gorgets, urgently squeaked the song in their own dialect.

The largest birds in the world capable of flight, the California Condors, rose high above the rocky cliffs overlooking the Pacific Ocean and cried out, singing the Song-Tale out to sea.

Sandpipers and Grebes and countless varieties

of Terns and Herons and Gulls that lived on the beaches all raised their voices, soft and loud, melodic and raucous. The myriad cries of these countless shore birds sent the Song-Tale out over the wide Pacific Ocean.

The wave-tossed seascape stretched forth, seemingly endless in its watery vastness in every direction, but even here the sea birds who called this ocean home heard the Song-Tale too.

The Albatross and Frigatebird and all manner of Gulls and Terns each listened when the song reached them even far out at sea, and each bird of the sea turned west to sing it on with the slowly setting sun.

The sea birds that lived over the southern Pacific passed it on, as did their cousins to the north. On the hundreds of tropical islands that dot the vast Pacific, on isle after green jeweled isle, tropical birds listened with awe and respect and eagerly sang it along.

On the island of Taveuni, a small flock of Orange Fruit Doves cocked their heads to one side and froze in place. They were perched within the shade of the luxurious tropical trees while they listened with rapt attention. One at a time, each orange bird cooed enthusiastically to another with appreciation at what they had just heard. Then as one, they sang the moving lyrics.

The wave of the song gradually slowed -- not because birds did not sing it along as eagerly and as enthusiastically as before, but simply due to the fact that fewer birds flew over the vastness of the middle of the great Pacific Ocean.

And yet, the Song-Tale would gain impetus again when it reach another island and the indigenous population of birds raised their voices and flew up to sing it to their cousins out over the sea. From these many islands that dotted the Pacific, the Song-Tale surged forward again and again with renewed impetus when it reached each individual island.

The Song-Tale reached the shores of New Zealand and Australia far to the south just as the sun transformed into a dull, orange ball and sank toward the horizon. The Tui was the first family of birds to take it up with their eerie, metallic cries.

Soon the vibrant calls of the Brown Kiwi joined in.

Large flocks of stunning Rainbow Lorikeets added their raucous voices and sang it loudly and boldly. Flocks made up of hundreds and sometimes thousands of these rainbow-colored birds rose like a living cloud into the twilight air singing with such energy that animals and people alike stopped whatever they were doing to listen. While they listened in admiration, they wondered why these large flocks of birds were singing so vigorously in the early evening when everyone should be settling down ...

The birds of New Zealand quickly swept the song over its beautiful mountains and emerald forests.

On the island continent of Australia, more Lorikeets took up the song from their New Zealand cousins. The strident laughter of Kookaburras soon echoed within the sound wave and mixed with the chattering cacophony of the Lorikeets. After they heard the entire Song-Tale and felt its message, the Laughing Kookaburras sang it on with their powerful voices.

Across the island continent, Superb Fairywrens, Noisy Miners, Golden Whistlers, Bowerbirds, and native birds of all kinds raised their voices and urged the song onward across the immense plains and deserts of Australia.

The Song-Tale again slowed when it reached the heart of the great western desert where few birds lived, but although it slowed, the wave continued relentlessly.

Meanwhile, the Song-Tale reached the shores of Japan and China -- just as the lower circle of the sun touched the western horizon and dipped below it.

A distant cousin of the Mockingbirds, a family of Thrush native to Southeast Asia, took an especially keen interest in the Song-Tale. The Hwamei, or Melodious Laughingthrush, stirred themselves into action after they heard the story of their one-legged cousin who lived so far away. Their hearts went out to Bluesky because they felt his pain and his loneliness in the words and music of the song. Of course, every bird felt it too, but somehow they felt it a little more because Bluesky was part of their worldwide family.

At first individually, and then in greater numbers, these reddish-brown birds with a bold, white eye-ring and white stripe behind the eye sang forth energetically as if welcoming a new day.

Even those Hwamei kept in bamboo cages by their beloved owners suddenly sang out although their cages had already been covered for the night. In their houses, men and women paused and listened as if in a dream.

Across the darkening skies, the Hwamei sang the Song-Tale to support and honor their unknown cousin.

Although the Laughingthrush and other birds of the Thrush family could call Bluesky one of their own, every other bird who heard his Song-Tale and sang it onward began to feel a special closeness with the brave, one-legged Mockingbird who had come so far and done so much for others. Fairy Bluebirds, Red-Vented Bulbuls, Common Loras, Mynas, and countless others added their own unique voices to the wave of song rolling ever westward.

The first stars appeared in the darkening sky above, and now the birds of the night took up the song. Their voices took precedence and urged it onward.

Nightjars, Swifts, and Owls of every description sang out through the gathering twilight in the great lands of Asia. Other birds just settling down for the night suddenly awakened when they heard the first notes of the wave reach them, and these birds of the day sang the song several times before they settled down once again for sleep.

Of course, the Owls and other birds of the night cried out with their strongest voice just after the sun slipped below the horizon. Across the darkened landscape the Owls called and sang, piercing the growing shadows with their haunting cries. Yes, they sang the wondrous Song-Tale over and over throughout the night.

Another cousin of the Mockingbird now took a personal interest. The millions of Song Thrushes living across the vastness of Siberia, southward into the Middle East, and eastward throughout all Europe, roused themselves from their slumber and started singing. These brown birds with black-spotted cream breasts broke out in energetic song just like it was midday.

The wave of song grew more powerful still.

The night grew deeper across all the lands where the beloved Song Thrushes lived. When the wave of song reached a new part of the land, people inside their houses turned in awe to their windows at the sudden outburst of birdsong filling the night air outside. In house after house, doors opened almost simultaneously, and people walked outside. Men, women, and children stared into the darkness as if in a dream, listening in wonder to the chattering cacophony that permeated the night from every direction. People filled the streets and turned around and around while they pointed at the myriad of voices coming from every tree. The chorus of birds grew louder than even at the break of day.

Women pulled their robes close against the coolness of the night while they listened with appreciation. Children danced and laughed, and men simply stood in amazement while thousands of birds serenaded them with the Song-Tale of Bluesky.

As suddenly as the wave of sound arrived, it quickly faded away, but even then a special and almost sacred stillness filled the night air, almost as if every living thing were trying to hold onto the memory of that fleeting, extraordinary moment when song filled the world around them. Everyone and everything replayed that wonderful birdsong one more time in their hearts and minds, cherishing the memory amid the stillness, and then they walked slowly back inside their houses.

The night grew darker and deeper, but across Eurasia the birds sang it on as eagerly as the first birds that started it far, far away in the east.

After the night grew dark and very late, the wave of song reached the lands of Western Europe, but above the countless voices of every kind of bird who sang out in the night, the voice of the Song Thrush was always the loudest.

When the Song-Tale traveled through the heart of Europe another cousin of the Thrush, the Nightingale, joined their beautiful voices and took up Bluesky's song as their own.

These small brown birds normally sang throughout the night only during the spring, but even though it was past the middle of summer, they quickly awakened. The Song-Tale caused an intense empathy for Bluesky to burst forth inside their hearts. Soon thousands upon thousands of Nightingales sang out with a melodious chorus such as had never been heard before.

Countless people awakened when the beautiful song wafted through their partially opened windows. As they lay in bed listening intently, most quickly realized they had never heard the Nightingales sing so beautifully ever before.

When the wave of song reached the British Isles, even the tiny English Robins awoke from

250

sleep and eagerly joined the night chorus, mixing their well-known calls with the Nightingales, Song Thrush, Wrens, Titmice and Sparrows, and every other bird.

The night was alive with song for a few precious moments, and then the wave passed and left behind the darkness and silence once again.

On the countless shores of Great Britain, the Gull's raucous cries now echoed as they rose into the sky singing out as one. Along with the Gulls, shorebirds large and small joined their voices until the darkness reverberated with the Song-Tale at the place where sea and land met.

Finally, the wave of sound reached the stormy Atlantic.

Over these dark waters the Song-Tale would face its greatest challenge. Earlier in the spring, storms had been many and powerful, and few birds had dared fly through them. Even now, the Atlantic remained a stormy and forbidding ocean, and few birds ventured far out upon it. Unlike the Pacific, few island homes for birds existed in this ocean desert to urge the Song-Tale along when it slowed.

All throughout the history of birds, many Song-Tales had failed to cross the Atlantic's storm-tossed waves. Many Song-Tales faded away somewhere above the middle of the Atlantic Ocean when the night was farthest along and the darkness greatest, with few birds to hear them and sing them onward.

Sadly, those that faded away never reached the status of legend.

Chapter Thirty

In the southern latitudes, the wave of sound moved out of Australia and into the Indian Ocean. Once again, its impetus slowed in the middle of the ocean where few birds flew and sang.

The wave of sound carried across the hundreds of islands of Malaysia and Indonesia and on through Thailand and into the subcontinent of India.

The sleeping peoples across the nation of India were abruptly awakened when the wave of sound caused the birds to sing out like it was midday. From the east to the west, the great cities of India were awakened by an eruption of birdsong while the wave rolled westward -- Kolkata, Raipur, Bhopal, New Delhi, Bangalore, and even Mumbai.

Among the chorus of birds, the voices of the Red-vented Bulbul, the House Crow, the Singing Bush Lark, and the Common Myna were the loudest, but none sang as loudly as the Orange-headed Thrush, who trilled and warbled for their distant cousin and sang the Song-Tale like he was one of their own.

Urgently, they sang it on and caused the wave to surge on through the deserts of the Middle East and into the darkened jungles of Africa.

Under the starry sky, the wild birds of the tropical jungles added their voices as the wave of song continued westward through the night. The strident cries of the Green Wooded Hoopoe, the raucous calls of the Great Blue Turaco, and the braying of the Trumpeter Hornbill pierced above the chorus of general birdsong. The famous songbirds of Africa -- White-fronted Bee-eaters, Lilac-breasted Rollers, the various families of Sunbirds, and the six species of Mousebirds -- sang with skill the moving Song-Tale of Bluesky.

Among the exotic birds of Africa, the huge population of African Thrush took it up and sang the loudest in empathy for their distant one-legged cousin, the same way the Song Thrush, Hwamei, and other members of the Thrush family had sung it when it reached their home.

Through the jungle forests and across the grassy plains, the African night grew noisy with birdsong while they urged the Song-Tale onward.

When the night grew darkest, the Song-Tale entered the lands of westernmost Africa and finally reached the coastline of the southern Atlantic Ocean.

Like with the other oceans, the birds that dwelt above the vast waters were much fewer in number then those who lived near land, but unlike the Pacific Ocean, very few islands existed in the southern Atlantic Ocean. Gradually, the impetus of the great wave of song slowed as fewer and fewer birds sang it.

Somewhere over the waters in the deep darkness of the night, the Song-Tale slowed and slowed until finally a lone Albatross heard it. The solitary sea bird turned west and sang it onward ...

But no other bird was there to hear.

In the southern latitudes, the Song-Tale faltered and faded away on the harsh, whistling winds above

253

the crashing waves of the south Atlantic.

***

In the northern latitudes, the great flocks of Plovers and Sandpipers on the rugged coasts of Ireland and Portugal sang it out to sea. Sea birds flying over the vast North Atlantic picked it up one by one and sang it onward.

Shearwaters, Petrels, and Seagulls now heard the wonderful Song-Tale for the first time. They laughed and cried as the power of the song reached into their hearts, and like all the birds before them, they gladly turned toward the west and sang it on.

They knew the Song-Tale was now on the last leg of its round-the-world journey, but like the southern Atlantic, strong storms had scattered far and wide the birds that flew these open waters.

Like the southern Atlantic, few islands with bird populations existed here to give new impetus while the wave of song traveled over the dark waters. Seagulls grew fewer in number the farther over the sea the wave of song traveled. In the middle of the ocean, only the bravest birds dared to fly.

Once again, the Song-Tale gradually slowed as fewer and fewer birds heard it and fewer and fewer sang it onward.

Finally, somewhere far, far above the darkness of the North Atlantic, a small group of Terns heard the Song-Tale from a single Seagull.

He was so far away and his song was so faint that the Terns almost missed it on the wailing echoes of the wild, night wind.

The tiny white birds flew closer together and listened harder to make sure they picked up every detail of the stirring song. The whistling of the wind suddenly grew louder and drowned out the faint song, forcing the Terns to turn around and fly back toward the east to hear it better. Straining their ears and focusing all their senses, they listened to the Seagull while he sang the Song-Tale again.

Slowly, the distant voice of the Seagull faded away into nothingness.

Though they had barely heard the simple but beautiful melody, and the inspiring words had been distant and faint amid the lashing of the whistling winds, still the power of the song moved them. They determined in their hearts that the song would not die with them.

Somehow, they would send it onward, but they also realized that few birds would be within earshot to the west.

They decided that they would fly westward all night long and sing it together. They hoped that all their voices joined together as one would be loud enough for the next birds to hear it. They flew fast and sang boldly. Over and over again they sang Bluesky's Song-Tale.

High above them, the stars slowly began to fade and the eastern horizon changed from a deep, pure black to a lighter shade. The morning sun was coming, and so far the Terns had not heard any birds answer back that they had heard and would sing the song on to the coast of America.

With the night coming to an end, the twelve Terns sang out even more urgently. They hoped deep within their hearts that some bird, any bird, would hear it and pass it along so the precious

255

Song-Tale could finish its worldwide journey back to the original singers in time to become legend.

As the twelve Terns sang each note as loudly and as clearly as possible, the wind suddenly changed direction. In that vital moment, the wind blew strong and powerful from the east toward the west, and the notes and words of the Song-Tale were carried swiftly on its invisible folds.

But there were no birds to hear.

With each mile the wind carried it, the song sung by the twelve Terns grew fainter.

And fainter ...

Chapter Thirty-One

Two Magnificent Frigatebirds glided effortlessly on the currents of air far above the waves of the Atlantic Ocean.

Above them, the stars had almost all disappeared except for those that shone the brightest. On the eastern horizon, right at the point where the sky met the sea, a narrow band of sky glowed pale orange. The rising of the sun was coming apace.

Windrider glanced at it and smiled. He looked forward to welcoming a new day.

He held his long, slender wings straight out, the middle joint of each wing angled upward while he twisted his long, fork-tailed feathers to maximize his gliding ability. He pointed his thick beak straight down, which caused the loose flesh of his scarlet throat pouch to shake.

Windrider was an old and experienced Frigatebird. He had already flown several times parallel to the southeastern coast of the United States, at times flying far out over the Atlantic in the process.

Now he found himself flying much farther out than usual, and the only bird he had seen in days was the Frigatebird who accompanied him, his best friend, Fishcatcher.

"We shouldn't be flying way out here. Our kind don't normally fly out this far over the Atlantic. It ain't normal," Fishcatcher squawked in his raspy voice. "We don't belong way out here. It's tough enough catching fish as they swim just below water, but I hate it, because it's so lonely out here!"

"It's the strong winds and storms," Windrider said in a solemn tone. "It's scattered most of the birds."

The two birds glided on the currents of air a long while without saying another word. Both birds liked it that way. They spoke when they had something to say but otherwise were content to fly silently between the pale blue dome of the sky above and the dark blue ocean below.

Long minutes passed between them with only the sound of the wind breaking the silence.

"I feel so old." Windrider sighed, feeling the familiar throbbing ache in his shoulder joints flaring up again.

"It's better than the alternative." Fishcatcher chuckled.

"I feel so useless too." Windrider turned his head and began a wide circle far up in the sky. "I'm old and breaking down and just not good for anything anymore ..."

"You are good for something!" Fishcatcher retorted in a positive tone.

"What? Name me one thing I'm good for."

"You can still find fish from way up here! Your eyes are still good. Shoot, I can't do that. I've got to hunt closer down to the water." Fishcatcher smiled.

Windrider sighed again. He continued his large, lazy circling while his troubled thoughts continued. Finally, he spoke again. "I've always wanted to do something *special*. You know, something that ...

well, something *important*. That meant something, so people would remember me when I'm gone."

"Who says you won't?" Fishcatcher asked.

"I'm too old now. What can an old bird like me do?"

"I don't know, but I know you could do it!"

"I'm a *has-been*. I'm worn out and slowly falling apart. I'm ... I'm a nobody." Windrider shook his head sadly.

"Who in the world am I talking to then?" Fishcatcher asked sarcastically, his voice tinged with humor. "I must be going crazy then, if I'm flying around way up here in the sky talking to *nobody*!"

Windrider smiled, but the same tired and sad expression returned.

"Listen," Fishcatcher began. "Ain't no need of you feeling sorry for yourself. You're just going to make yourself miserable. You need to look on the bright side of things!"

"That's just it, old friend. There is no bright side."

"Of course there is! You just gotta open your eyes and see it!"

"Have you looked around and seen where we are right now?" Windrider asked with an angry edge to his voice.

Fishcatcher looked slowly around.

In every direction, he saw nothing but the wide, open waters of the Atlantic Ocean. The only movement was the rolling of the waves. For days now, they hadn't seen another Seagull or another Frigatebird, though a couple days back they had run into a small flock of Terns heading northeast.

Yes, they were truly alone over this saltwater desert.

"Yeah, well, we are pretty much alone way out here in the middle of nowhere," Fishcatcher conceded. "That's why *normal* Frigatebirds don't fly this far out!"

"I kind of like it out here all alone. There's no distractions, no noise except for the sound of the wind and waves below." Windrider looked over at Fishcatcher with a glow in his eyes. "A bird can really clear his mind out here and think about things."

"I don't know. I don't like to think too much, myself. It gives me a headache." Fishcatcher shrugged.

"It's good to clear your mind, my friend. It's good to think things out and see beyond the mundane routine of life. There's more to life than simply eating, sleeping, and mating." Windrider felt an especially strong current of wind pick him up. He adjusted his long, forked tail to catch the wind's power and rose higher into the sky.

Fishcatcher maneuvered the edge of his slender wings, caught the updraft, and rose quickly after his friend.

"Listen, all that's fine, but maybe we ought to go find the coast and find other ..." Fishcatcher began. Then he stopped and stared at Windrider, whose expression had changed to one of powerful concentration.

Windrider brought his head up and cocked his ear to one side. He listened intently.

Fishcatcher listened a moment too, but he couldn't hear anything except the wind and waves. He continued, " ... of course, some birds ain't fit company. Those kind, we don't need --"

"Hush -- did you hear that?" Windrider said urgently, holding his head still as he listened more.

Fishcatcher looked over at Windrider with a puzzled expression. "I don't hear anything. What are you talking about? I hope you're not hearing things now!"

"Listen hard! It's faint, and the wind has almost drowned it out, but ..." Windrider paused as he listened harder.

Fishcatcher focused. He forced the whistling sound of the wind into the background and strained his hears to hear.

"It's those Terns we ran into a couple days back. They're singing a Song-Tale," Windrider whispered.

"Oh, I love Song-Tales," Fishcatcher chattered. "I hope it's one of my favorites. You know, I love the one about --"

"Hush, you old bird!"

Fishcatcher shut his beak in surprise at the harshness of Windrider's tone.

"It's a new Song-Tale!" Windrider said with surprise. "And it's been sent around the world this very night."

Fishcatcher looked around at the lightening sky. On the far horizon to the east, an orange band of sky sitting over the ocean's edge glowed brighter.

The sun would rise very soon now.

"A new one?" Fishcatcher squawked. "There hasn't been a new Song-Tale sung round the world

261

in my lifetime. Where did it start?"

"It's just now coming back to its origination point."

"Well, there's not much time then. The sun will rise here soon. Can we sing it on fast enough to beat the sunrise?" Fishcatcher asked.

"Hang on ... what's this?" Windrider cocked his head to one side and listened.

"What? What?" Fishcatcher asked excitedly.

"It's about a one-legged Mockingbird ..."

"A what?" Fishcatcher shouted in disbelief.

"And his best friend is a cat! And other friends ... an Owl and a Hawk and --"

"What?" Fishcatcher squawked in complete disbelief. "What kind of nonsense is that? A cat is a bird's best friend? And a Hawk?"

"Wait ... wait." Windrider listened some more. "This Mockingbird led a mixed flock to save all the birds, animals, and humans from some kind of danger, and ... and he and the cat carried the poison. No, wait, the cat carried the bird that carried the poison and took it to the cat's owner, who is now going to get rid it. Now, all the birds there are singing how Bluesky and KC saved everyone ..."

"More? Is there more?" Fishcatcher prompted eagerly.

"It seems the cat and the Mockingbird breathed the poison and may die." Windrider sighed. "No one is sure if they will survive or not, but all the birds from that area have sung this song round the world to honor them both -- whether they live or die."

"Wow!" Fishcatcher squawked. "That's some song!"

262

Windrider looked around with a concerned expression. "No!" he exclaimed.

"What now?" Fishcatcher asked.

"The Terns who sang this on mentioned they only heard it from a single bird. The birds are so scattered because of these storms, and there are so few birds out here anyway, I'm afraid we may be the only two birds left to finish it around the world!"

Fishcatcher gasped.

An expression of firm determination grew on Windrider's face. "We shall sing this song onward. We'll make sure it is sung round the world!"

"But how? We haven't seen another bird in almost two days!" Fishcatcher shouted.

"We've got to fly west with all our might -- and quickly! The day is about to dawn here, and the song will fail!"

Both birds lowered their heads and dove downward in order to gain speed. They turned to the west with their wings spread wide, heading for the unseen coast. When they reached their top speed, they flapped their wings even harder and started to climb again.

Windrider felt sharp, fiery pain in the joints of his wings, the all too familiar aches of an old bird, but he ignored the pain and continued his torrid pace.

On and on they flew as they covered first one mile and then another. They flew west, their eyes peering ahead intently for any sign of other birds.

Windrider glanced quickly back and saw that the thin layer of red sky had now coalesced to a small, glowing spot -- the spot where the upper edge

263

of the sun would peek over the horizon at any moment.

Windrider knew that the time had come! It was now or never.

With all his might, Windrider sang the Song-Tale.

Again and again, he sang to the west and sang it on round the world.

Fishcatcher joined his voice, and the two old birds sang with all their might over and over again.

Windrider felt his strength waning, and the aches and pains burned white-hot across his shoulders and down his wings. His wings slowly grew numb, and his energy faded away.

Still, he sang with all his might and all his heart.

"Faster!" Fishcatcher squawked urgently. "We've got to fly faster and sing louder!"

Windrider groaned when he finished the Song-Tale each time, and each time he finished he had to twist his neck and waggle his head, trying to shake off the raging pain.

And then he would he sing it again.

He didn't realize it, but he was flying lower and lower. His tired body lost airspeed, and he flew dangerously closer to the waves.

He sang anyway, forcing all of his strength into the song and ignoring the dangers of the water getting closer with each passing minute. Finally, as he was about to sing it out one more time, a piercing light caught his attention from behind. He looked back and saw a sliver of glowing light rise above the horizon.

The top edge of the sun rose above the ocean.

Windrider groaned with agony.

He closed his eyes; the excruciating pain filling his entire being. Worse, with all his energy gone, his body simply gave out. Windrider's mind slipped into the gentle folds of unconsciousness...

Windrider closed his eyes and began a slow, gliding spiral down to the cold waters below.

Frigatebirds cannot float, nor can they swim.

"Hey, Windrider! Keep your altitude, old boy. You don't want to get too close to the water," Fishcatcher called out fearfully.

Windrider couldn't hear him.

He'd given everything to sing the song onward, and now he slowly glided toward certain death.

"Windrider! Wake up! You're going down! You're going down!" Fishcatcher shouted frantically.

The old Frigatebird flew up beside his best friend and stared, but Windrider was almost totally unconscious now; he only had enough energy to hold his wings and tail fixed and ride the wind.

Windrider glided inexorably to his death.

"Hey, Windrider! What's wrong with you?" Fishcatcher finally realized his friend was flying in a daze.

"Come on, buddy. I'm here. Just hang on, okay? I'll stay right here beside you and help guide you." Fishcatcher's tone became soft and comforting, but his expression was fearful.

The wind changed and blew stronger from a different direction.

"Hey, angle your wings and catch this breeze now. Come on, buddy. Move your head to the right and fly into this nice wind," Fishcatcher said with an encouraging tone.

He looked down and saw the wave tops right below.

"Windrider! Ride the wind!"

Windrider didn't really know if he was asleep and dreaming or if he was imagining he heard Fishcatcher, but through the fog that filled his mind and in spite of the terrible aching that consumed his body, he obeyed his friend's words.

Windrider felt the breeze against his face and adjusted his wings.

"That's it! Angle the edge of your wings now. Come on! Now, twist your tail."

The wind strengthened, and Windrider rose higher. The wind against his feathers refreshed him. He felt a tiny spark inside his mind, and he became conscious that he was still too close to the waters.

He adjusted his wings slightly and rose even higher, but the fog returned.

"That's a good bird. Now, straighten your wings and use the wind. We'll take it easy a bit -- we're higher now. Let's glide in a slow circle to our right to keep this altitude." Fishcatcher smiled.

For several, long minutes, the two old birds glided on the strong winds. Fishcatcher stayed right beside his friend, giving him encouragement and guiding him, but although Fishcatcher helped, Windrider's exhaustion returned and they glided lower and lower until they were only ten feet above the waves.

"Okay, Windrider. You're going to have to wake up now, or it's all over. We've got to fly upward now. You've got to flap your wings, old boy," Fishcatcher pleaded as tears streamed down his feathered face.

Windrider heard Fishcatcher's distant voice through the deep fog. He struggled against the pain and exhaustion. Somehow, his friend's encouragement reached him.

He finally opened his eyes and looked at the water right below him.

"Too ... close ..." Windrider grunted.

He flapped his long, slender wings and lifted. Windrider groaned against the pain, but he flapped his wings harder, and slowly, he rose.

Slowly, ever so slowly, Fishcatcher and Windrider rose back up into the safety of the sky. When they reached a safe altitude, Windrider began gliding again in order to rest. At this altitude, the constant power of the wind easily kept him aloft while he adjusted his wings and tail.

He groaned painfully, because he had almost spent all of his energy once again to get this high.

However, he glided under his own control now. He knew he'd have to take it easy for a few hours until his strength returned.

He looked over at Fishcatcher and smiled.

"Thanks, old friend. Without you, I don't know what would have happened to me."

"You probably would have had to learn how to swim. Or at least learn how to float." Fishcatcher chuckled good-naturedly.

Windrider winked at his friend and laughed a moment. Then, he spoke with genuine sincerity. "Good ol' Fishcatcher. I owe you my life."

"Ain't that what friends are for?" Fishcatcher shrugged nonchalantly a moment. Then he also smiled and winked back at his buddy.

Windrider peered intently to the west, but he didn't see a single bird within sight. He thought back to the Song-Tale and suddenly remembered that he had never heard any response that the song had been picked up and sung onward.

He sighed sadly and then spoke. "I wonder if any birds heard us before the sun rose ..."

Chapter Thirty-Two

"Do you hear anything yet?"

Dancingleaves looked up at Tootight with a frantic expectation after asking him the same question for what seemed like the hundredth time. He took a deep breath and waited while the Robin listened intently.

Tootight perched from the highest branch of a tall pine tree. He craned his neck and stared toward the eastern horizon. A single point of sky on the glowing horizon blazed golden, heralding the imminent rising of the sun.

The plump Robin listened with all his might. He strained his ears, almost as if he could somehow will the Song-Tale to return, but after a few moments he shook his head sadly and looked back down at the Bluebird.

"The only bird song I hear is the normal 'welcome the new day' and 'welcome the sun' chorus," Tootight chirped with disappointment.

From high in the sky, the distant 'kee-har' of a Hawk echoed. Far, far above, Thundercloud and Morningsun glided in lazy circles with their wings stretched wide and their tail feathers fanned out perfectly.

"Thundercloud doesn't hear it either." Daymoon sadly lowered his head.

Scattered on branches just below Tootight, all the other birds lowered their heads as well. Even Coolbreeze felt the hope inside his heart fading

269

away.

"It's got to make it," Treeflower said with a forlorn tone. "It's just got to make it before the sun rises."

"I want it to hear it so badly," Bushhopper said.

"If only for Bluesky," Daymoon added.

"Yes, for Bluesky," Funwind said.

The sky lightened above them even more.

"Has the sun risen?" Ol' Gray Mama asked the question fearfully, hoping against hope that she was wrong.

Daymoon, Bushhopper, Nightwind, Coolbreeze, Ol' Gray Mama, Treeflower, Windwhisper Blackfeather, Funwind, and Dancingleaves all turned toward the east.

The trees surrounding them seethed with birds. In every tree and on every branch, birds sat silently while they eagerly awaited the return of the Song-Tale. Hundreds of birds filled the trees in this yard alone.

But here in this one tree filled with Bluesky's closest friends, no one dared to hope any longer. Instead, each bird waited in resignation with their eyes focused to the east.

"Not quite yet," Blackfeather whispered emotionlessly.

"But the sun is going to rise any moment now," Nightwind said with great sadness.

"We've failed ... " Dancingleaves looked away as tears streamed from his eyes. "We've failed our friend."

"I wanted so much for our Song-Tale to make it round the world, just like the other great tales about those wonderful birds and their wonderful deeds," Treeflower said with her voice full of emotion.

"He deserved it," Daymoon said with resignation. "He's such a good bird ... he deserved a Song-Tale."

"He still has a song," Blackfeather said firmly. "We'll remember Bluesky in song. Dancingleaves composed it, and we've sung it already."

"But ... it didn't go round the world." Bushhopper turned around, no longer facing the eastern horizon. "Bluesky's Song-Tale will not stand on the same level as the other Song-Tales of legend."

"I can't believe it!" Coolbreeze squeaked with sudden urgency. "It is such a great story!"

"A tale of love and courage and persistence in the face of the greatest odds," Windwhisper said in a despondent whisper.

"It is a song of friendship," Ol' Gray Mama added.

"It's a beautiful Song-Tale," Nightwind said.

"And ... it touched our hearts." Funwind nodded silently.

The friends of Bluesky all lowered their heads in sadness while they waited for the sun to appear.

Suddenly, they all raised their heads erect simultaneously. They looked at each other with puzzled expressions.

High up in the sky, Thundercloud and Morningsun cried out together.

"What's that? What are the Hawks saying?" Blackfeather said with an urgent tone.

"It's coming!" Thundercloud cried out again in a

strong voice.

They all turned to the east. The sky glowed so brightly it seemed the sun would pop up any second.

"Do you hear it?" Dancingleaves shouted urgently up to Tootight.

Tootight stood completely erect and listened.

"Wait! I see something!"

"You see something?" Coolbreeze asked in disbelief. "Aren't you supposed to hear it?"

"There's something happening to the trees in the distance!" Tootight shouted back.

"The trees?"

"They're ... uh ... *they're moving!*"

"Moving? How can trees move?"

"No!" Tootight shouted even more urgently. "It's not the trees. It's ... birds leaping into the air from the trees! It's like a wave of birds suddenly leaping into the air at the same time! And ... *it's coming!*"

Everyone held their breath.

"It's here! It's here! It's heeeeeeeere!"

Everything went totally silent for the briefest second. It seemed even the wind stopped. The silence was complete, almost like the trees and the birds and everything waited ...

In the next second, they were engulfed with birdsong.

A solid wall of sound crashed upon them from the east. Birds leapt into the sky shouting and crying with pure joy exactly as the wave of sound arrived.

The singing was deafening.

Suddenly, every bird sitting in the tree with

Bluesky's friends and in every tree around them jumped into the air at the same time. The air filled with thousands of birds flying in every direction and singing at the top of their voices.

In that moment, everyone recognized the Song-Tale of Bluesky.

"It's here!" Tootight sang out.

"It's finally here!" they all shouted with joy.

The air was alive with birds.

Hundreds and hundreds of birds leapt into the air from every tree within sight until the sky seethed with flying birds.

"We did it!" Windwhisper shouted with glee.

"Hooray!" Coolbreeze squeaked joyfully.

"Hooray," they all cried together.

At that very moment, the golden orb of the sun rose above the distant horizon.

Chapter Thirty-Three

Mark opened his eyes wide and instantly became wide awake.

He lay in bed a second longer, wondering what had awakened him so abruptly. In the next moment, he heard the reason.

Mark turned toward the closed window and heard the wild, joyous singing of birds. While he listened, he realized he had never heard birds singing so loudly and happily in all his life.

Next to him, Jane stretched her arms a moment. She stopped and then looked at him with surprise. "Are those birds?"

"Yes, I've never heard them singing so loudly before."

"They're better than an alarm clock." She pulled the covers up to her chin and rolled over to sleep a few moments more.

Mark got up, put his blue jeans and slippers on, and went downstairs, but instead of getting a cup of coffee, he walked down to the basement to check on KC and the one-legged mockingbird.

He flicked on the light and walked over to both boxes. Mark glanced at the mockingbird first. The bird breathed regularly with his foot still clenched.

Mark reached down and gently stroked the bird's head. The bird didn't move; it didn't even flinch at his touch.

It was still unconscious.

Mark shook his head and looked over at the box

with KC.

"Who is that pretty kitty?" Mark asked with a soothing tone. He caressed the top of her head and then gently rubbed her ears.

KC's breathing seemed to change a moment. However, she didn't purr, and there was no obvious reaction. Mark petted her more, hoping she would purr again like she had yesterday at the vet's office, but she remained unnaturally still.

From upstairs, the joyous sounds of the birds continued unabated.

Mark listened a moment, watching the two unconscious animals lying in the boxes. He came to a decision.

"Why don't I take you guys and put you on the back porch? The fresh air might do you good." Mark placed the tiny box with the Mockingbird inside the box with KC. He carried them both upstairs and out onto the back porch.

He looked around a moment in amazement at the sheer number of birds flying around this early in the morning. The air was alive with birds of every description, all of them singing joyously. After he stepped outside, waves of birds flew off. Still, it seemed there were still over a hundred left in his backyard alone.

Mark placed the boxes on top of the picnic table. He took out the smaller box and put it on the other end of the table.

"There, maybe these happy birds will wake you guys up." Mark stood a moment, hoping against hope one of them would wake up.

In spite of the volume of song that filled the air,

neither animal stirred.

After a few moments, he sighed and walked back inside the house to start the coffee.

***

"Look! The man brought Bluesky and KC outside!" Daymoon shouted happily.

Treeflower and Windwhisper cheered exuberantly and flew down closer. The Song Sparrow and the tiny Mockingbird perched on the closest tree to the picnic table while they watched the man carefully place the boxes on it. A moment later, KC's dad walked back inside.

Coolbreeze zoomed to the edge of the box with Bluesky and peered inside. "Bluesky! It's me, Coolbreeze!" he squeaked happily.

Now the rest of his best friends flew over and stood on the edge of the box. They all peered inside, but the only motion was the steady rise and fall of Bluesky's breathing. The one-legged Mockingbird lay completely still except for his breathing.

"We've got to wake him up!" Bushhopper cried with hope. "That's what we've got to do!"

"Yes, let's get everyone to help us," Nightwind said. He motioned to the hundreds of birds staring at them from the trees.

"We've got to sing it loud, everyone!" Bushhopper shouted out in every direction. "Everybody! You've got to help us!"

They all leapt into the air and started flying over the table again and again. Each time they sang out the same refrain.

"Wake up, Bluesky!"

"Wake up!"

"Wake up, Bluesky!"

"Wake up, wake up, wake up!"

Blackfeather cawed furiously. He flew over the table and boxes and their unconscious inhabitants again and again. Soon, dozens and dozens of other Crows joined him and cawed louder and louder.

In seconds, the other birds realized what they were doing and flew toward the table. The air above the table filled with flying birds shouting out, "Wake up! Wake up!"

The air filled with birds. Hundreds more birds joined them in their new chant every minute. Very quickly, a thousand birds flew through the air over the table and hundreds more perched on all the branches above the yard shouting with them.

The chanting chorus changed; the birds began calling out for both KC and Bluesky to awaken.

The sound of the birds exploded outward in every direction. Birds suddenly realized that the subject of the now famous Song-Tale was actually lying outside. He was there among them.

Word spread quickly.

From miles around, birds flew to the backyard of the house located at 3477 Willow Hollow.

The ground seethed with movement -- birds filled every square inch while they sang out for Bluesky and KC to awaken. The air grew thick with clouds of birds that flew over the table and over the house, but the clouds of birds turned and came back again and melted into other clouds of birds that dove over the sleeping occupants. The clouds swelled and undulated and moved like they were living entities themselves. A seething murmuration of birds ebbed and flowed and swirled above.

The ecstatic gathering continued to swell in numbers.

Soon, every branch in every tree was lined with birds perched shoulder to shoulder singing at the top of their voices. Several thousand birds in the trees chirped and whistled and sang out to them. Birds lined the top of the fence from end to end while they sang and flapped their wings, knocking against their neighbors and causing them to repeat the action all the way down the line.

The world was alive with birds and song.

The ground literally disappeared because birds covered every inch. The tree branches swayed under the movement of the birds while they hopped and sang out.

The huge, undulating murmuration of birds now coalesced into one vast cloud and filled the air completely above every yard and house on the street named Willow Hollow.

The volume reached a fever pitch.

"Wake up, Bluesky! Wake up, KC!"

"Wake up!"

"Wake up!"

"Wake up!"

Suddenly, a single, bright shaft of sunlight shone through the tree branches like a powerful spotlight. Wherever the warm sunshine lit up an area of the back yard, everything glowed with a golden luminance.

Gradually, the powerful shaft of light moved toward the table. When the beam enveloped each box, something wonderful happened.

KC's eyes twitched a moment against the bright light. In the next instant, she turned her head away from it. Her ears twitched, and she became aware of the terrific sounds of birds all around her.

The tuxedo cat yawned, and then she opened her eyes.

A great shout up went up from the tens of thousands of birds gathered.

Bluesky jerked in response to the sudden outburst and the harsh light.

He lay still a moment longer while he tried to comprehend the sounds and light. After a few seconds of grogginess, he realized that birds were singing all around him.

The more he listened, the louder and more joyous the songs became.

He wriggled around, keeping his eyes closed against the bright light. He worked himself against the side of the box and gathered his leg under his body.

Finally, he stood up.

He saw the old towels and the box around him and realized the man must have placed him inside it.

He opened his eyes and looked around.

The singing of birds grew absolutely deafening.

Bluesky's eyes widened, and he stared around in shock.

Birds were everywhere!

The air and the trees and the ground were completely covered with birds, and they were all singing, every last one of them. He couldn't quite comprehend what they were singing about though.

He listened harder while the fog inside his mind

cleared.

And then he realized they were singing his name.

Chapter Thirty-Four

"Who are all these birds?"

Nightwind smiled down at Bluesky with a twinkle in his eyes. He spoke powerfully in order to heard above the signing, but he did not shout; his tone was one of complete conviction.

"*They're your friends.*"

Bluesky looked around in amazement.

Birds were everywhere -- birds of every shape, color, description, and family. Just on the ground, thousands of birds were chirping, hopping, singing, and from time to time flapping their wings with delight. Bluesky couldn't even see the grass because of the sheer numbers

A Zoomer zipped above, squeaking merrily while he circled above him again and again and again in sheer joy

Bluesky realized it was Coolbreeze.

Suddenly, twenty or thirty more Hummingbirds zoomed around the vast throng of birds that surrounded him.

The more he looked, the more birds he saw.

They filled the trees, they completely covered ground, and the air was a living cloud of birds. There were more than thousands; there were tens of thousands of birds.

In the distance, the voices of countless others sang out in unison, repeating his name. It was like a wall of sound that rose to the top of the sky. The songs, trills, warbles, twitters, and calls were louder than any 'Morning Chorus' Bluesky had ever experienced.

Bluesky looked through the mass of birds on the patio around him and saw KC yawning. All along the edge of her box, small birds stood and sang for her. Bushhopper and Coolbreeze stood near her head chirping with excitement.

More birds kept arriving, and the cheerful cacophony rose to a climax ...

"How can they all be my friends?" Bluesky asked, dumbfounded.

"A Song-Tale about you has been sung around the world, Bluesky." Nightwind's eyes gleamed with joy. "Every bird in the world has heard about your courage and your kindness and your love. And most important, they heard how you were willing to sacrifice your life so that others might live. And more ..."

"More?" Bluesky shook his head, trying to clear the fog out of his mind.

"They know about your best friend, KC, and her bravery and sacrifice. And she risked her life because she loves birds, just as you do."

"I do love all birds," Bluesky said sleepily. He yawned a moment and continued. "Mama said ... she said ... *there's good in every bird*."

Ol' Gray Mama flew down and landed next to Nightwind. She smiled at Bluesky with tears in her eyes.

"Bluesky, my sweet little bird. My, my, you have tried so hard to find a friend, and now look -- thousands of birds are singing for you. Best of all, *they're all your friends*!" Ol' Gray Mama kissed him gently on top of his head.

Treeflower smiled at him from where she stood between the two boxes.

Windwhisper stood next to her, smiling with an expression of deep joy. Bluesky noticed Windwhisper's eyes. Her beautiful eyes seemed to be filled with love and caring just for him.

He smiled back.

"Oh, he has more friends than that!" Tootight laughed merrily. "I believe we can rightly say that you have friends all around the world now."

"Really?" Bluesky gasped.

"Every bird in the entire world is your friend today!" Bushhopper shouted with joy.

Bluesky thought back to the time when he had fallen out of the tree, the day after his mother died. He remembered the wonderful dream he had dreamed. And now ...

"And we were your friends first!" Daymoon chirped proudly.

"Wow," Bluesky whispered in awe.

"Look how far you've come, little Mockingbird," Blackfeather said with a laugh. "All you wanted was a single friend like Treehopper, and now, now you have more friends than any bird I know!"

Coolbreeze zipped up and hovered right before Bluesky. "I'm so glad you're alive!" he squeaked enthusiastically.

"I'm glad too!" Bluesky chirped back.

"Do you know who composed your Song-Tale?" Ol' Gray Mama asked in a soft voice.

"No." Bluesky looked at each of his closest

283

friends, searching their expression for the answer. They all smiled proudly. "Who did it?"

"Dancingleaves," she replied.

"I don't know what to say," Bluesky said to the shy Bluebird.

"You don't have to say anything," Dancingleaves said. "And although I composed it, we all had a part in it -- in a way. It took all of us to sing it round the world, but it started with us, your best friends!"

Tears of joy fell from Bluesky's eyes.

"We love you, Bluesky," Treeflower said.

"Yes. We love you, good friend," Daymoon added.

All of his best friends who were closest to him repeated those same words -- 'we love you, good friend' -- while he stared at them with a whirlwind of emotions exploding inside his heart.

Bluesky's heart quivered with a happiness that filled his entire being-- and it was such a feeling of overwhelming joy and bliss that it exploded inside him like a volcano. It felt like he had never experienced true happiness until this very moment.

"I am so happy," Bluesky said while more tears rolled down his feathered face. "I never thought ... I never hoped ... *that I could ever be this happy!*"

***

Inside the house, Mark was watching the morning news on the television. He had already turned the volume up three times because of the noisy birds outside. The birds burst forth again in a new round of singing, completely drowning out the newscaster. He sat there a moment, frozen and

284

listening in shock with his cup of coffee halfway to his mouth.

"How can they be singing even louder than they were before?" He shook his head in wonder and brought the coffee cup to his mouth.

Suddenly, the volume of the bird chorus increased tenfold!

Mark stopped in mid-sip, the steaming vapors swirling around his nose and face. He stared toward the breakfast nook and the window, trying to imagine how many birds must be out there. His eyes grew wider and wider as the chorus seemed to grow in volume without end.

If he had been playing his stereo that loud, the neighbors would already have called the police to complain.

He stood up and bounded out of the room.

The bay window of the breakfast nook was filled with movement. He counted at least thirty birds flying around the feeder, but none of them were feeding.

He walked to the back door that led to the patio where he had laid KC and the little one-legged mockingbird about ten minutes ago.

He opened the door and looked out.

The cup fell out of Mark's hand and shattered on the entryway, coffee spilling over his bare feet, but he didn't even feel the hot liquid. He simply stood there, transfixed at the sight before him.

There were birds everywhere.

Mark stood for several long seconds, trying to comprehend what his eyes showed him.

"J-J-Jane!" Mark stuttered.

Suddenly, his eyes were drawn to the box with KC.

KC was awake and sitting up!

And there were birds standing all around her -- and singing to her!

He looked over to the shoe box with his heart pounding inside his chest.

Yes! The one-legged mockingbird was awake too, looking around with its beak wide open.

Mark realized his own mouth was hanging wide open just like the one-legged bird.

As he stared happily at the one-legged mockingbird, Bluesky looked back at Mark with a twinkle in his eyes. "Hello, KC's dad! I'm so glad you helped us! You saved our lives!"

Mark stared at the bird a moment. "Are you singing to me?" Mark asked Bluesky.

Bluesky whistled his happy greeting again.

Mark only heard the happy chirpings -- but that was enough. He stepped carefully forward, since the patio was literally covered with birds. They flapped their wings and scurried away while he slowly put one foot down and then another.

He made it to the picnic table, and there he stood dumbfounded, surrounded by birds that almost seemed to want to land on his head and shoulders.

A second later, two birds did just that. One bird landed on each shoulder. In the next moment, he felt a bird land on his head and just stand there, singing away.

"M-M-Mark, what's going on here?" Jane stood in the doorway staring at him in total disbelief. He turned to her.

Dressed in her bathrobe, she stood there staring in shock. Her mouth had also dropped open. She looked from Mark back to the birds and back at Mark again, and all the while her eyes grew wider and wider.

Finally, she spoke. "*Honey, what are you putting in that bird seed?*"

"I'm ... not sure."

Jane carefully stepped outside. She gently brushed birds aside while she crept next to Mark. She smiled happily while singing birds whirled around both of them.

Without thinking, Mark held out his right hand with his forefinger extended. In less than a second, a bright red cardinal landed on his finger.

Mark's mouth fell open with surprise. He held his forefinger closer and stared at the beautiful red cardinal. The cardinal lowered his tail, raised his red crest erect, and opened his orange beak wide.

Daymoon then sang with such lovely trills and crystal-clear chirps that it easily pierced through the cacophony around them. Daymoon sang a song -- *just for Mark.*

Mark's mouth dropped open even more.

He now held up his left hand, forefinger extended. A Towhee landed on that finger and sang his familiar song.

Bushhopper, too, sang out a happy tune -- just for Mark.

Seconds later, sparrows and robins and bluebirds landed across his shoulders and arms and sang out to him with joyous cries.

Mark gasped.

Jane held out her forefingers, and a song sparrow and a mourning dove landed on each and sang to her.

Treeflower and Ol' Gray Mama sang for Jane.

"What's going on?" Katie asked. She stepped outside rubbing her eyes with little Philip right beside her.

Katie saw the birds on her parents' fingers and many more on their shoulders and head. She quickly held out both of her pudgy little forefingers.

Windwhisper and Dancingleaves landed on each and sang for Katie.

Philip laughed with glee and held out his forefingers.

Two ruby-throated hummingbirds zoomed up, hovered a moment before the delighted boy, and then both landed on his tiny fingers. Coolbreeze and his friend squeaked excitedly for the laughing little boy.

***

Two Hawks suddenly swooped down and landed on either side of the box that held KC. The smaller songbirds flew away, though all of them sang out joyfully and not with fear. A second later, a young, strong Crow from Blackfeather's flock landed on the back side of the box.

"Well, KC. How are you feeling?" Thundercloud smiled mysteriously.

"I'm feeling better, thank you," she purred.

"Now, what was it Bluesky once told us about you?" Thundercloud asked with a twinkle in his eyes.

288

"Something you always wanted to do ..." Morningsun added slyly.

KC looked from one Hawk to the other. "I always wanted to fly with the birds."

"Well now, we can't give you wings and feathers," Morningsun said. "But we thought this might be the next best thing."

"What?" KC meowed questioningly.

"Hang on tight," Morningsun advised. "This might be a little rough at the start."

"Rough?" KC asked with a hint of fear.

"Ready?" Thundercloud asked the other birds perched around the box.

"Ready!" Morningsun and the crow replied.

All three birds leapt into the air at the same time while grasping the box with the small tuxedo cat inside.

KC looked down and meowed in surprise and with a little bit of trepidation. Then she promptly closed her eyes.

"It gets more fun," Morningsun panted. She flapped her wings harder along with the others.

KC's human family and all the other birds looked up at the unexpected sight.

Slowly, the three birds carried the cat in the box higher and higher into the air. When they reached the tops of the trees, they began a slow circle around the yard.

"I'm ... just ... glad ... KC ..." The Crow grunted each word, taking deep breaths in between.

"Is a small cat!" he gasped out all at once.

"Open your eyes, KC!" Thundercloud cried out. "You're missing the best part of flying!"

KC opened her eyes.

The birds didn't fly with such jerky motions now that they were flying at speed and more easily balancing the load between them.

KC looked down in amazement. She felt her heart flutter with joy while she watched the world passing by underneath.

"Meeeeoooooow!" she cried out in greeting when she saw her dad and mom and the two kids staring up at her while she passed overheard.

**

"Oh, Mark! Did you hear KC? Do you think she's scared?" Jane stared up at the flying cat.

"I'm not sure."

"I think she's having fun!" Philip laughed with glee.

"Me too!" Katie cried out and pointed to the sky. The birds on her fingers flew up but quickly landed back on her arms and continued singing along with all the other birds.

They all watched in amazement while KC the kitty cat flew.

**

"I've always wanted to fly," KC meowed gratefully to the three birds that carried her on their wings. "It always looked like so much fun!"

"It is fun," Thundercloud said. "I'm glad we could share it with you this one time."

"And help make your dream come true!" Morningsun cried out with joy.

They circled the yard and the house a second time. Thousands of the birds gathered on the ground and in the trees burst out in song, serenading the flying cat.

A group of around fifty birds now began to follow the three birds carrying the box with the cat. As they flew around a third time, more and more birds joined the flying entourage.

For the first time in the history of the world, a cat flew in the air with a flock of birds.

***

Mark, his wife, and the kids watched in silent amazement. The three birds holding the box came around one last time and then gently placed it back on the picnic table next to the one-legged mockingbird.

"I can't believe it!" Mark gasped.

"It's all so incredible," Jane said, looking around at all the singing birds.

"It's really fun!" Katie laughed.

"I like it!" Philip shouted with glee.

"What's going on out here?"

Mark and his family looked over at a gap in the bushes and saw Mrs. Williamson standing with her eyes open in surprise while she surveyed the fantastic scene. A few seconds later, birds of all kinds landed on her shoulders and her arms and sang to her. She laughed with delight, holding her arms up and dancing around slowly in a circle.

Even more surprising, Bounce stood completely still as birds landed on her head and back. The only movement she made was the high-speed wagging of her tail while she enjoyed the personal attention of the birds.

***

Bluesky looked at all the birds and at KC.

291

Buddy now walked up with his back covered with singing birds. The furry black cat meowed happily to the birds, who sang along with him.

Bluesky smiled at the joyous scene that immersed him. Inside his pounding heart, he felt so happy. He didn't want this moment ever to end, just like he had never wanted that wonderful dream to end.

After a few more moments, he felt an overpowering urge to join in the singing. He leapt up into the air. Hundreds of birds sitting on the ground nearby flew up and chased noisily after him.

He flew up toward the clouds high above, singing with every beat of his heart and every stroke of his wings.

***

In a whirlwind of movement, all the birds took flight. The air became a cloud of swirling birds singing and smiling and shouting aloud. The sky grew dark with birds above the house located at 3477 Willow Hollow.

The birds sitting on the fingers and shoulders of the people took flight last.

Mark felt a pang of sorrow when the birds first left, but he quickly closed his eyes and listened, living again the precious moment when the birds had sung just for him.

A few minutes later, the swirling cloud of birds disappeared over the tops of the trees and headed toward the west, chasing after the one-legged mockingbird.

The resulting silence was almost shocking.

Mark stared at his outstretched forefingers and

wished it had not ended so quickly.

Jane and the kids looked around in astonishment at how empty everything seemed now.

"It felt like ... it felt like we were in the 'Garden of Eden' again." Mark smiled at his wife and children.

"Daddy, I like it when the birds land on my finger and sing to me," Philip squealed with delight.

"Me too. My birds even kissed me on the cheek!" Katie laughed.

Jane brought her hand to her face and examined it a moment. "Yes, it was wonderful."

In the gap of bushes on the other side of the fence, Mrs. Williamson waved happily. She smiled widely at them and walked back to her house with Bounce right beside her.

"I think Mrs. Williamson liked the birds, too, don't you?" Philip asked.

"I do." Mark smiled. "I certainly do!"

Mark sighed and started for the door.

"Oh, Mark!" Jane exclaimed with a tone of obvious regret.

Mark felt his heart skip a beat. He knew what that tone meant. It meant something was wrong. "What is it, Jane?"

"Honey, you should have grabbed your video camera!"

Chapter Thirty-Five

Two hours later, Mark received a call from the police. The lab results had returned, and the substance was found to be highly toxic. They had obtained a warrant to go search Charles Marcion's land for more of it.

They invited Mark to come along and observe.

An hour later, he and his best friend Walter got out of the car near Marcion's trailer. About a dozen police and other government vehicles were already there.

Mark and Walter stared at the rusted hulks of the exposed fifty-gallon barrels through a pair of binoculars. Thirteen barrels had been found inside the small hill where Marcion had hidden them many years ago. Even now, the police were calling the EPA to have them properly disposed.

"I still can't believe it -- *toxic fertilizer*." Mark shook his head.

"I did some research on the Internet," Walter said. "The fertilizer industry wasn't well regulated back in the seventies and early eighties. There was a term coined back then -- 'Magic Silos.'"

"Magic Silos?"

"Yeah, industrial waste labeled as 'toxic' was sold as a component to help make fertilizer. When this toxic waste was trucked to these silos and mixed with legitimate compounds, it somehow 'magically' lost its toxic label. These companies saved money in two ways -- first, not having to pay

294

the high price to properly dispose of their toxic waste. And second, they found they could actually sell it for a small profit!"

"That's ludicrous!" Mark said angrily. "And totally unethical!"

"You would think so, but for many years fertilizer from these 'Magic Silos' was legitimately sold and used by farmers and homeowners until ..."

"Until?"

"Until some accidents occurred." Walter sighed.

"Until some people died, right?" Mark asked.

"Fortunately, only a few known deaths were attributed to this toxic mess. However, quite a few acres of land were ruined, and a fairly large number of domestic and wild animals died. There was a pretty big incident down in south Georgia that brought national attention to this thing."

"Yeah, Marcion mentioned that," Mark said. "Why do people do stupid things like that? Don't they know they're poisoning the air that we all breathe? And the water we drink? And the land our children play upon? Why do they do it?"

"Greed," Walter said matter-of-factly. "Greed -- pure and simple."

"Marcion lied to us about the entire thing, right from the start," Mark said with distaste.

"He probably pocketed some money by not sending every single barrel to the disposal site," Walter said.

"He endangered everyone! His actions caused so many women to lose their babies! And even my Katie got sick. She could have died too!" Mark said with bitter anger.

"How could anyone live with that on their conscience?" Walter asked.

They grew silent while two sheriff's deputies escorted Marcion out of his trailer with his hands handcuffed behind his back. Marcion walked with a noticeable limp, and his right foot was wrapped in gauze.

As soon as he caught sight of Mark, Marcion shouted angrily, "That's him over there! Yeah, he's the one that sent those birds!"

"Sure, sure," one of the deputies said in a condescending tone. "I'm sure he talked them into it."

"He did! He did! Those birds attacked me and my dogs. It was like ... it was like they had a plan. It was like one of those Hitchcock movies, you know!"

"Sure, sure. C'mon, old man, let's get in the back of the car."

"I'm telling you, he sent those birds to get me! That's why I shot my foot!"

Mark and Walter watched in total silence.

"Sounds like he's lost his mind," Walter said.

Mark rubbed his chin, deep in thought. "You know, it's kind of crazy, but when I found that French fry bag with the toxic fertilizer in it, my cat KC and a one-legged mockingbird were lying right next to it. Just like ..."

Walter's eyes opened wide. "Just like what?"

"Just like they had -- they had gotten a sample and were bringing it back to me."

Walter and Mark stared at each other a moment.

"Naw, I guess there has to be some other

explanation," Mark said with a shake of his head.

Chapter Thirty-Six

Later that same day, Bluesky flew over to talk with Nightwind.

"When did you become my friend?" Bluesky asked with a hint of puzzlement.

"I've considered you my friend from the first time we met." Nightwind's eyes twinkled.

"Birds were always asking me if we were friends."

"See, they knew."

"I guess I'm a little dumb."

"No, you just couldn't see past your sorrow at the time." Nightwind blinked his eyes with friendliness.

"Why did you want me to go out and meet all those birds? And then find out what was good and beautiful about them?"

"It's not good for a bird to isolate himself, and I could tell that your sadness was so great it might overwhelm you if you kept to yourself too long. I felt that if you met other birds, it would take your mind off your sorrow. I hoped when you talked with these other birds and discovered the good in them, that it would provide you a small measure of happiness in return."

"It did make me forget my sadness -- for a little while -- and it was fun meeting different birds and finding out what made each beautiful in their own way." Bluesky smiled brightly.

"I especially hoped that when you looked inside

each bird -- searched for the beautiful qualities of their heart -- that you would not only admire those qualities but would seek to imitate them. After all, imitation is the sincerest form of flattery." Nightwind chuckled.

"And a Mockingbird should know about that!" Bluesky laughed.

Nightwind laughed jovially.

Bluesky paused in thought a moment. "That sounded like something Tootight would say!"

"See, your friends have rubbed off on you already!" Nightwind laughed in reply. "And so the bird proverb is true -- *'fly with wise birds, and you will become wise.'*"

"Or if you -- *'fly with funny birds, you will become funny!'*" Bluesky laughed.

"And if you fly with kind birds, or happy birds, or fun-loving birds ..." Nightwind smiled, waiting for Bluesky to finish.

"You will become those too."

"A bird's closest friends are a powerful influence on him. One does well to choose his friends carefully. A bird will emulate his friends, knowingly or unknowingly, but if you choose friends with good character, with noble qualities, what better things to emulate? And those good qualities will make you a better bird -- and make you and your friends happier."

"You are wise, my friend."

Bluesky thought back to the beginning of his long journey. He remembered how fearful he had been -- fearful of rejection. He looked deeply into Nightwind's eyes. "Sometimes, I felt like they were all just ... just ... *putting up with me.*"

"No, the birds you met on your journey, the birds who embraced you and answered your questions and welcomed you to come back again, they are your real friends."

"I didn't know that at first. I thought they were just helping me with my journey of discovery and answering my questions."

"You became friends though."

"Yes, even after I discovered the good in them and their kind, we kept talking, and we started flying together and singing songs together."

"And playing," Nightwind added.

"Somewhere along the way, we all became friends -- even you and I." Bluesky smiled.

"And they proved their love and friendship to you. In your darkest hour, they joined your mission and supported you at every turn!"

Bluesky thought back to all the birds he had met on his journey. He remembered meeting each one for the first time -- Treeflower, Dancingleaves, Tootight, the Day flock, Daymoon and Bushhopper, Coolbreeze, Thundercloud, Blackfeather, and especially KC.

"Did you know that I would make friends when you sent me on that journey?"

"I didn't know it for certain, no, but I had hoped that some of the birds would look at you in return and see the good in you -- that they would see your fine qualities -- and that they would see beyond your missing leg and see the *real you*, just as you were seeking to do with them."

"You are a very wise bird."

"Most of the time." Nightwind chuckled.

"You are the wisest bird I know," Bluesky said with a laugh. "And also my good friend."

Nightwind blushed.

"I guess my journey is over now, right?" Bluesky asked.

"A journey never ends." Nightwind laughed. "I hope you will always look for the good in everyone you meet and always take time to appreciate the beauty in the world around you."

"I will."

"And remember, you can never have too many friends."

"Absolutely!"

Nightwind laughed out loud.

"I guess you have friends all around the world now. Friends you haven't even met yet!" Nightwind laughed heartily.

Bluesky laughed with him.

"You realize you've added your voice to the 'Song of Life' now." Nightwind blinked his eyes slowly. "Every time a mother bird sings 'Bluesky's Song-Tail' to her babies, they will learn about you and your love, your kindness and your compassion, and especially your courage. They will learn of your journey, your family, and your friends, and through the words of that song, they will become your friends too."

It was Bluesky's turn to blush. He even felt a little uncomfortable, thinking about mother birds singing about him to their babies. He hadn't really done anything special -- he had only done his best.

"Tell me, what are you going to do now?"

Nightwind asked.

"I'm going to find the tallest tree and sing all day and all night, I feel so happy!"

"And what will you do after that?" Nightwind watched him closely.

"I'm going to travel to the coast and see the ocean." Bluesky smiled, and his eyes twinkled. "And I want to meet a Pelican named Waveglider."

"Will you travel alone?"

"Daymoon and Bushhopper are going with me. Blackfeather and a couple other Crows are joining us too, and Coolbreeze is going." Bluesky paused, feeling a little embarrassed again, though he wasn't quite sure why. "And, well, Windwhisper wants to go too."

Nightwind chuckled in a knowing fashion.

"What are you laughing about?" Bluesky asked emphatically.

"That Windwhisper, she's a pretty little bird. I think she would make a nice mate for you, eh?"

Bluesky blushed. In fact, he felt his face and entire body grew hot with embarrassment. "Well, um, maybe... but I do think she's pretty, and she's a very nice bird."

"Not only is she pretty, but she's kind and caring." Nightwind patted Bluesky on the back with his wing. "Don't let her get away."

"I won't."

"What will you do after you go to the coast and meet Pelicans?"

"I've heard that far out to the west there are forests with trees so tall that they touch the sky, and they live for thousands of years. I'd like to see them

302

and meet the birds who live there."

"If you decide to go there, do me a favor," Nightwind said with a sudden intensity.

"Sure. What is it?"

"Let me know, because I'd like to tag along too ..."

Epilogue

Far away on the distant horizon, the sun's luminance dimmed. After a few minutes it became a glowing, orange ball and slowly sank toward the water's edge.

A narrow band of the sky began glowing reddish-orange just above the point where the sea and sky met under the sun. When the lower rim of the sun finally touched the water and disappeared underneath, the band of sky quickly changed hue. Now it became a vibrant electric orange, and the clouds hugging the horizon glowed pinkish-red as if on fire.

A spectacular sunset blazed forth in all its glory.

A purplish darkness gradually spread along the edges of the high clouds and soon engulfed them in deep shrouds of purple shadow while the sky gently darkened. The sun sank lower into the waters. In an instant, the formerly white clouds high in the sky were completely transformed. Now they floated dark and purple far above the dying ember of the sun while the narrow band of glowing sky grew fainter and fainter ...

Another day came to an end like every other day -- and yet as unique as an individual snowflake.

Windrider flew effortlessly on the fresh, ocean breeze underneath the darkening sky.

The first star of the evening sparkled to life in the violet darkness far above.

Fishcatcher soared up beside him, and the two

Magnificent Frigatebirds sailed silently and content side by side.

"I want to thank you for saving my life yesterday." Windrider smiled over at Fishcatcher.

"You would have done the same for me," Fishcatcher replied matter-of-factly.

Windrider closed his eyes and breathed deeply the salt-laden air. "I sang my heart out yesterday. I gave it my all ... hoping that the Song-Tale would complete its round-the-world journey." Windrider sighed. "I just hope some bird heard me and sang it on, but how will we know for sure?"

"I don't know," Fishcatcher said.

They watched the sun finally sink below the water.

Suddenly, the raucous cry of a Seagull came from behind.

"Well, I haven't heard that screechy, nerve-jangling cry in quite a while -- and I didn't miss it a bit." Fishcatcher chuckled.

Windrider didn't say a word. He craned his neck and listened a moment in silence. All at once, his beak dropped open in surprise.

"Did you hear that?" Windrider cried out.

"No. Actually, I was trying to ignore the old Gull."

"He's singing about that one-legged Mockingbird."

"Oh, yes, I thought I caught a bit of that part, but we've already heard that Song-Tale before," Fishcatcher said.

"No! There's more! There's a new bit that says Bluesky lived after all!" Windrider shouted with joy.

"How about that!" Fishcatcher exclaimed. "What about the kitty cat?"

"Yes, she lived too!"

"I like it when everyone lives in the end!" Fishcatcher whistled exuberantly.

"And ... you know what this means?" Windrider shouted even louder.

"That everyone lived happily ever after?"

"Well, I hope so, but more has been added from the birds that started the Song-Tale, by Bluesky's personal friends. This Song-Tale has achieved the status of legend! It means it did go round the world! That means a bird did hear me yesterday before the sun rose!" Windrider shouted with joy.

Fishcatcher cried out with laughter, and Windrider joined. They laughed for a few moments, realizing their efforts had been rewarded.

"I'm glad for you, Windrider. See, you did something special after all," Fishcatcher said.

"I feel so good inside. It's a nice feeling, and I feel like I did something important ..."

Fishcatcher and Windrider rode the currents of air a long time in a comfortable silence.

"Did you hear that? There's more!" Fishcatcher said. He turned back and flew to the east, but Windrider continued, intent on listening a few more moments.

"Did you hear that last bit too?" Windrider asked as the Gull's cries faded in the wind.

"That Bluesky is off with some of his friends and flying to the coast to meet Pelicans, and especially to meet one named Waveglider,"

Fishcatcher answered promptly.

"Yep, that's the part." Windrider smiled with gladness. "I know a Pelican named Waveglider. He's a good old bird, too." Windrider glided effortlessly a few moments, thinking deeply.

Fishcatcher looked at his friend.

"You know what I want to do?" Windrider finally asked.

"You want to meet that Pelican too?"

"No. I want to meet that one-legged Mockingbird," Windrider said.

"Yeah! Yeah, that's a good idea. I'd like to go back to the coast anyway -- that's where Frigatebirds belong!" Fishcatcher said excitedly. He paused a moment in thought.

"What are you going to do when you meet that one-legged Mockingbird?" Fishcatcher asked.

"Maybe we can be friends."

***

Our Feathered Friends of the Southeast
A. C. Wages

Message to Readers:

Birds are one of the few wild species that live side by side with humans on planet Earth.

Our feathered friends live in every region and over every ocean. Birds are found on mountain slopes and in deserts, deep in the darkest rainforests and across endless plains of waving grass. Throughout history, birds have existed on every continent, every country, and almost every island in the world. They have proven very adaptable.

But their greatest accomplishment has been adapting to the onslaught of civilization.

As civilization spread across Earth, the once vast stretches of meadow and forest, the natural home to birds and other wildlife, inexorably disappeared. These abodes of countless species of birds gave way to farms, towns, and cities. As these great changes transformed the planet, birds not only survived, but they thrived.

Birds are the only species to coexist in close proximity with humans. Birds dwelling within the very center of major metropolitan cities still retain their *wildness and natural freedom*. Cats, dogs, horses, and other animals had to be domesticated and trained to coexist within the confines of civilization and under the direct guidance of humans. Of course, rodents have also been adaptable and able to live close to civilization, but not in the open like birds.

Falcons, hawks, and owls hunt pigeons among the steel and glass skyscrapers of cities. Songbirds of every kind nest and live in the trees and bushes in these same cities and in their outlying suburbs. Wrens nest in flowerpots, sparrows nest under the eaves of roofs, bluebirds nest in the cavities of telephone poles. Cardinals, towhees, catbirds, mockingbirds, and many other birds live and breed in the trees and bushes all around our homes and the buildings where we work.

And yet, as successful and adaptable as they are, birds still need a measure of the natural world in order to live. If we cut down all the trees in our yards, if we remove every large bush, remove all the ground cover and allow only grass to cover our yards -- where will the birds live?

We must leave something for our feathered friends.

Trees provide our yards and houses shade in the summer and natural barriers against the cold winds of winter. More important, they are also homes for the birds.

Bushes not only enhance our property, they are a natural habitat for many kinds of birds. Remember that we share this planet with birds and other creatures -- lizards, butterflies, chipmunks, and squirrels. They have just as much of a right to live here as we do.

We must remember our role as caretakers of this world and of all its animal life. We must do our best to nurture and coexist with the flora and fauna around us. We can't continue to pollute the air and the water and the soil. Our factories, our cars -- *our way of life* -- must not destroy the cycles that support life; instead we must use our intelligence and design our machines and factories to be in harmony with these cycles!

Each of us individually must realize that we are accountable for our actions. If we throw trash out the windows of our car as we drive, it's the same as if we threw that same trash on the floor of our living room.

Planet Earth is our home.

And more, it is the home of all the living creatures around us.

Together, we can make things better. If we care enough to act, we can we provide a future home for our children and our children's children.

And a future home for the birds and animals and trees ...

But if we allow the asphalt and concrete and plastic to replace everything -- what then? What if one day there were no more forests? What if there were no more trees? Could the birds adapt? Or would they eventually become extinct?

What kind of world would it be if there were no more birds?

It would be a sad world indeed.

THE END

Author's note

This trilogy is dedicated to Karen Babcock, my editor and friend.

***

We are what we think. More precisely, the thoughts and meditations of our heart shape us and mold us as surely as the hands of a potter mold and shape a lump of clay.

So, think wonderful thoughts. Meditate on what is true and good. Fill your mind with goodness and kindness and love. Fill your eyes with beautiful sights and listen to melodies that are joyful and happy.

Every day, take time to contemplate and enjoy what is beautiful around you and always look for the good in others. You will find it.

Strive to learn something new every day.

And on your personal journey of life, always look for the good in others -- you will find it.

(Always remember, there is good in every bird, and every bird has a song to sing ...)

-- Tony Chandler

Other novels by Tony Chandler

The Last Dragon Of The North
Tony Chandler and Virginia Chandler

*"A hard hitting adventure. One rousing dragon-
fighting story,
with a thin slice of romance along the way." -- Piers
Anthony*

Owain Armstrong has been hired to hunt down a red
dragon that is killing livestock across Wiltshire .
The only evidence is a bloody patch on the ground
and the head of the dead animal. Owain begins to
track this nocturnal predator when news of another
dragon comes -- a much bigger dragon.

During his journey, Owain meets up with the
famous dragonslayers of the Northern Band: Katja,
a beautiful blonde deadly accurate with a crossbow;
Erik, a massive man short of temper and always
eager to fight; Lars, a man as cunning as he is
strong; and finally Edlund, their dynamic leader.

When meeting Owain, the band of weary slayers
long had been on a quest to kill the last dragon of
the north. But they soon hear strange tales -- tales of
the Green Dragon Inn and the monster that lives
inside the mountain.

And for a price, anything is possible...

Mothership
Tony Chandler

Winner 2002 EPIC Award -- Best in Science Fiction

In the midst of Galactic War a new life-form is born -- an AI starship. But with all its weapons and sophisticated programming, the sentient starship is not equipped for its greatest challenge -- that of becoming the mother to the last three children of humanity.

The deadly T'kaan soon begin the hunt again after they discover that the human race is not quite extinct. As Mother faces these impossible odds, she discovers that deep inside her massive memory systems she holds another treasure--a knowledgebase that contains all the science, lore, wisdom and art of the human race since the beginning of time. Now Mother must fight not only to save humanity from extinction, but also from being forgotten by the rest of the universe...

Borne on Wings of Steel
Tony Chandler

The sequel to Mothership

Mother, along with their newfound friends, continue their search for other survivors of the human race who may have escaped the T'kaan genocide. They travel to the farthest known worlds of the universe, but fail to discover the first solid clue that anyone else survived. After many long months of fruitless searching, their hopes again begin to fade.

But there is conflict even within Mother's family. The torment and loneliness among the final three survivors of the human race create division where there should be love.

Minstrel leads them to a planet famous for its vast collection of data gathered from every corner of the known universe. Perhaps here among the greatest single store of data ever gathered by any alien race, they might discover if other humans survived the T'kaan genocide

Lost in Time
Tony Chandler

Gordon Smith and Sarah Nightingale are lost in time ... And most disturbing, they have no memories of their lives prior to time traveling. As they journey through Earth's timeline, they search for clues to their previous life and to the most important question of all -- what happened to wipe out their memories?

The one thing they do know -- they are being chased throughout time by dangerous Shadows and the faceless Anon. But, they have a plan. They travel back to meet Jane Austen and set their strategy in motion. But events quickly spiral out of control.

Gordon and Sarah are forced to travel again in order to rescue William Shakespeare. A new and greater enemy threatens Earth's timeline with an evil act that could change history forever. As the battle reaches its climax, they discover that time and space is shifting in a state of flux all around them.

They now find themselves in a desperate race against time itself!

The Song of Life Trilogy

Vol. 1: Bluesky and Sunshine
Vol. 2: The Journey
Vol. 3: The Singer